The Paris Conspiracy

A Nathan Grant Thriller

Kenneth Rosenberg

www.kennethrosenberg.com
Front Cover by Damonza.com

Also by Kenneth Rosenberg

The American (Nathan Grant #1)
The Berlin Connection (Nathan Grant #3)
Russia Girl (Natalia Nicolaeva #1)
Vendetta Girl (Natalia Nicolaeva #2)
Spy Girl (Natalia Nicolaeva #3)
Mystery Girl (Natalia Nicolaeva #4)
Enemies: A War Story
No Cure for the Broken Hearted
Memoirs of a Starving Artist
The Extra: A Hollywood Romance
Bachelor Number Five
Bachelor Number Nine
The Art of Love

Chapter One

On overseas trips, the Secretary of State was protected by the Diplomatic Security Service. Those agents assigned to this mission were among the best of the best. Nearly all of them had military backgrounds, many including service in the special forces. They were good at what they did, no question about it. Not once in the history of the agency had they lost a Secretary of State. There was Benghazi, of course, in which the U.S. Ambassador to Libya lost his life, and the embassy bombings in Kenya and Tanzania. Nathan Grant didn't blame the DSS for any of those. This was a dangerous business. Sometimes things went wrong. That was why you always had to be on alert, especially in an unstable backwater like this one.

Officially, Nathan wasn't even here. He no longer showed up at all on the CIA payroll. He'd resigned that position more than a year earlier, when he'd run off to marry the love of his life, the beautiful and charming Jenna Taylor. After she was tragically taken from him, Nathan got his revenge, but he still thought of her every single day, replaying that instant when the bomb went off. Eventually, he came to the conclusion that the only way to move forward was to lose himself in work, and the only work he was really good at was this.

Even during his previous career as a CIA operative, however, Nathan always had his issues with the job. Long before he arrived at the agency he was trained as a U.S. Army Ranger, with multiple combat missions under his belt. He knew how to defend himself. In his role as an American spy, he wasn't sanctioned to carry a weapon. That would go against U.S. government policy, besides being a violation of international law. Contractors, on the other hand, well, they could be more easily disavowed. And so began the latest career move for Nathan Grant.

Never before in history had such a high-profile representative of the U.S. government visited this small country in the heart of Africa. The same could be said for Nathan. He'd been told it was all about combating the growing Chinese influence in the region, but the reasons for this diplomatic mission didn't matter so much to him. What mattered was that intel pointed to a potential plot on the secretary's life. They'd nearly scrubbed the trip entirely, but in the end, the administration was determined not to let an uncorroborated threat derail their efforts. Thus, here they were.

From Nathan's vantage point on the rooftop of a cargo storage facility just outside the perimeter fence, he saw the local airport spread out before him. There was the runway heading east to west, the hangars where corrupt officials kept their private planes, and the small terminal built in the 1970s of now-crumbling concrete. Parked on the tarmac was a U.S. Air Force Gulfstream 700, surrounded by eight members of the DSS in dark suits, despite the stifling heat.

When Nathan spotted two large, black SUVs and an armored Humvee moving toward the plane, he lifted a pair of binoculars to his eyes. He'd been in country for two weeks, on his own. The DSS didn't know he was here, nor did the Department of State. Nathan was working on behalf of Graham Masterson, Deputy Director of the CIA's National Clandestine Service. Masterson's boss was concerned about the activity of a terrorist organization operating in the country's hinterlands. This particular organization was seen to pose a direct threat to the United States and its interests. The few CIA operatives already working in the country were unable to gather much in the way of information. It was too dangerous for them to leave the capital. That's where Nathan came in. Operating outside official channels, he could go where he wanted when he wanted, fully armed, as long as he didn't get caught. If he somehow ended up in local custody, Nathan would be on his own. There would be no American government coming to bail him out. They would completely disavow him. The same would apply if any rebel groups found a way to nab him. Realistically, it was an assignment that only a fool would take on. When he'd married Jenna, Nathan was ready to give up the life entirely. His plan was to settle down in Northern Virginia and open a hand-crafted wood furniture business. They'd have a few kids and maybe he'd coach their sports teams in his spare time. Nathan's days of drama and intrigue were supposed to be behind him. Now, all he wanted to do was forget those visions, and this was the easiest way he knew how to accomplish that. No past, no future, only the immediacy of this present moment.

The vehicles he was watching pulled to a stop beside the plane and Nathan saw yet more agents emerge. They opened doors to the SUVs and out stepped Joshua Parsons, the Secretary of State himself, along with several members of his staff. During Nathan's weeks on the ground, he'd traveled the country on a Royal Enfield Himalayan motorcycle, posing as an adventurous traveler. He didn't seem to fool anyone, but he hadn't learned much either. There'd been a few dicey situations, but he got out of them with the help of his Glock 19, strapped now in a holster beneath his shirt. All he needed was for the secretary's plane to safely depart and he could return home himself. This was Nathan's first assignment as a contractor, and while it hadn't gone horribly, he wasn't sure if he wanted to continue after this. Part of the problem was that he knew Jenna would never have approved. From somewhere beyond the grave, she was watching him, and if she could speak Nathan knew what she would say. She'd tell him to stop with this craziness, to open that furniture store, meet another woman he could love and settle down after all. Unfortunately, Nathan couldn't bring himself to do that just yet. The pain was still too raw.

"Sorry, Jenna," Nathan said quietly as he scanned the perimeter with his binoculars. "Maybe after this one is over. Maybe then I'll hang it up. At least I got some frequent flier miles out of the deal." Nathan saw no signs of trouble along the entirety of the fence. On the tarmac, Parsons and his staff were escorted up a set of stairs and onto the plane. The door closed and shortly afterward, Nathan heard the whine of the jet engines. The plane began to move, taxing toward the near end of the runway. When it was aligned with the center stripes, the pilot waited a few moments for clearance from the tower. Nathan knew that Masterson had expected somewhat more from him. The CIA wanted intel about any potential plots, and Nathan hadn't been able to provide any, but at this point he didn't really care. He'd done his best, and the secretary was still alive and well. That would have to do.

The pitch of the engines rose as the pilot pressed forward on the throttle and then released the brakes, sending the Gulfstream hurtling down the runway. When the plane reached rotation speed, the nose came up, and then the rear wheels as the aircraft lifted into the sky. Nathan watched as it gained altitude over the suburbs of the capital city. That was it. Mission complete. Time to go home. He was about to head back down to his Enfield when a flash of light caught his eye. Nathan's heart seized as he saw a streak of smoke shoot upwards from a tight-knit warren of neighborhoods on the airport's edge. A surface-to-air missile tore across the sky on a collision course with the airplane and then, BOOM! Impact. The missile slammed into the twin engines at the Gulfstream's tail and exploded, sending the plane plummeting toward the ground. It all happened so fast, and yet it seemed like slow motion. One second, Nathan was watching the plane fall, knowing how helpless he was to do anything about it, picturing the occupants inside as they fell to their deaths. The next second, the plane hit the ground, slamming into the residential neighborhood and exploding in a massive fireball. The shock wave reverberated outward until it shook the building beneath Nathan's feet. It took his brain another split second to process what had just occurred before he snapped into action, racing across the rooftop toward the stairwell as the remaining DSS agents on the tarmac simultaneously jumped into their vehicles and sped toward the gate.

Into the stairwell Nathan flew, and then down, down, down, to the ground floor and out, past the pair of guards he'd paid off for entry, who now stood wide-eyed, unsure of what had just happened. Nathan hustled around a corner, jumped onto his waiting motorcycle and inserted the key. He hit the starter switch, popped the bike into gear and barreled off down the street. He wasn't sure quite what he was going to do, but he did know the general vicinity from which the missile was fired. The DSS could deal with recovery at the crash site. Nobody came out of that alive, Nathan was sure, but if he hurried he might be able to find out where the missile came from.

The streets were crowded with pedestrians in colorful robes, as well as beat-up old Toyota trucks, stray dogs and more than one mule. Nathan weaved through all of it like an obstacle course, laying on his horn and steering around a knot of congestion. The *why* of the attack wasn't a concern to him at this moment, but the *how* spun through his mind. The plane would have been equipped with the latest missile defense system, but at such close range there was no time for flares to deploy. Then again, he couldn't assume the missile used heat-seeking technology at all. It might have been laser guided. It might have been manually targeted. The real question for the moment was whether or not Nathan could locate whoever was behind it, and without being killed himself in the process.

Tearing through narrow alleys and corridors, Nathan neared the area from which the missile must have been fired and then slowed to scan for signs of activity. A local police vehicle with lights flashing screamed through an intersection just ahead of him, heading in the direction of the crash. Nathan kept on, up the block. Shopkeepers were pulling their doors closed and pedestrians scurried off the street and into their apartments as anxiety spread through the population. Only the curious youngsters loitered outdoors, adolescent boys mostly, gathered on the corners and eager for a little excitement. A foreigner on a motorcycle gave them something interesting to look at, as they gawked and pointed at Nathan, waving to get his attention.

"Hey, mister! Where you from, where you from?!" one shouted.

Nathan pulled to the side of the road and peered up at the apartment windows above him as curtains slid closed and the residents inside made themselves scarce.

"Fahid, you come in off the street!" one woman shouted down from her third-floor flat.

"No!" A boy of ten hollered back at her. "I no come up!"

"You come now, or I tell your father!"

The boy ignored her, turning instead to Nathan Grant and working his way to the front of a small pack. "You, what you do here?" he said.

"He come because..." Another boy used one hand to simulate the plane going down. "Kaboom!"

"What do you know about that?" said Nathan. In the distance, a column of smoke rose skyward from the crash site.

"Plane go boom, everybody dead," said Fahid.

"Did you see it?"

"No. Me no see."

"I did," said another boy, this one quiet and skinny, standing toward the back.

"What did you see?" Nathan asked him.

"It blew up. They shot it."

"Who?" Nathan pressed. "Who shot it?"

"They did. The fighting men."

"What fighting men, do you know where they are?"

All of the questions were making the young man anxious. His head went down, his shoulders slumped. Clearly, these boys knew more than they were letting on.

"You know where they are, don't you, Fahid? The fighting men. Can you show me?"

Fahid thought it over, considering what he might get out of the deal. He eyed the Enfield, from one end to the other. "You give me ride?"

"Sure. I'll give you a ride. Why don't you take me to the fighting men?"

Before Fahid said another word, he climbed up and onto the back seat of the motorcycle, wrapping his arms around Nathan's waist.

"Fahid, you come up here right now!" his mother shouted down again.

"Which way?" Nathan asked him.

Fahid pointed straight ahead. Nathan pulled away to the utter joy and astonishment of all the other boys in the pack, some of them chasing the bike halfway up the block. Fahid tapped Nathan on the right side and he turned right, three blocks up and a tap on the left. When Nathan turned this corner, Fahid called out. "You stop!" After Nathan pulled over to the side of the road, Fahid jumped off the bike. "Me go no more."

"Where are the fighting men, Fahid?"

The boy's eyes gave away his fear as he peered down the street. He raised a hand to point in the general direction of a four-story apartment building, then turned and began heading back the way they had come. Nathan watched him go before turning his attention to the apartments in front of him. This street was eerily silent. Nathan propped his bike on the kickstand and climbed off. He saw nobody in any of the windows above, but that didn't mean he wasn't being watched. Trying to approach from the front would be a bad idea. Instead, he walked around to the rear and then down an alley strewn with garbage. At the building beside the one in question, a dumpster was pushed against the wall just below a fire escape. Nathan scrambled on top and then pulled himself up onto a ladder. He climbed the fire escape, one floor after the next until he reached the rooftop. From here, he overlooked the building Fahid had pointed out. Nathan immediately spotted two men wearing brown robes on the opposite side, both holding AK-47 rifles as they scanned the street below and the smoke still rising in the distance. They hadn't noticed Nathan, yet anyway. Beside them on the roof was a hand-held surface-to-air missile launcher. Nathan kept low and slid across the roof on his belly, hidden from view by a three-foot-tall lip in between the two buildings. He moved right up against it and very carefully removed the Glock from his holster. He was outmanned and outgunned, but he had the element of surprise on his side. The question was, how many more of them were waiting in the building just below?

Nathan wished he had a silencer, but he'd have to make do. Graham Masterson sent him here to gather information, not engage the enemy, but these men had just murdered the Secretary of State and his entire delegation. Nathan couldn't just let them get away with that. This wasn't the type of spy mission he'd come to know, it was more of a flashback to his ranger days, except that this time he was all on his own. Even if he succeeded, he was in hostile territory in a foreign country with no extraction plan besides a commercial flight out scheduled for that evening. "Here goes nothing," he thought to himself before rising to the edge of the lip and peering over. The two men were gone.

Nathan's adrenaline surged as he scanned the roof. On the far side was a stairwell, with a door propped open by a large cement brick. It was the only way they could have gone. Nathan could just leave and notify Masterson about what he'd seen, along with the coordinates. Maybe the Air Force had a drone standing by. If so, they could level the place. But then again, maybe not. Nathan was a believer in the old wisdom that if you wanted something done right, you did it yourself. Besides, there would be less collateral damage that way. Who knew how many innocent civilians might live in the building? He rose to his feet and hopped over the lip onto the adjoining rooftop, moving forward past the missile launcher as he went. When he reached the door he paused, pointing his gun down the stairwell. From somewhere below he heard animated voices, speaking in a language he couldn't understand. Nathan made his way down one flight. The men's footsteps moved ahead of him, banging on the stairs as they went. Nathan hurried after. From the bottom came the echo of a door swinging open and then slamming shut. They'd left the building. He was in danger of losing them.

Reaching the ground floor, Nathan paused for a split second before bursting through the door and onto the street. The two men were halfway up the alley and climbing into a dusty pickup truck. It was only now that he was spotted. The man on the passenger side shouted to his partner and then raised his weapon. Nathan slipped back into the stairwell as a volley of bullets peppered the steel door. So much for the element of surprise. In a flash, he'd gone from being the hunter to the hunted. By any logical measure, these men would come after him. Instead, he heard the engine of the truck turn over and then the skid of tires as they tore out of the alley. Nathan emerged again to see them turning right at the corner. He chased after and around, stopping to holster his gun before jumping on the bike. He hit the starter switch again, popped the bike into gear, and raced after them.

"What are you doing, Nathan?" he said to himself as he flew up the street. He knew this was lunacy, but that didn't stop him. It was the principle of it as much as anything. Nathan didn't like to lose. These men were cold-blooded killers and he had to do what he could to make them pay. Up ahead, he saw the man in the passenger seat toss his gun into the truck bed through a window in the cab. Next, the man himself squeezed through as the truck lurched and weaved, turning right and then barreling toward the outskirts of the city. The man propped himself up in the truck bed and aimed his weapon, firing now as they went. Nathan eased back, allowing for some further distance between them as he skirted from one side of the road to another.

As they continued along, the character of the neighborhood changed, with residential buildings giving way to commercial until they were passing through a warehouse district. The longer this went on, the better the chance that the shooter would eventually hit his target. It was only the fact that the man was bouncing around so much in the back of the truck that kept him from taking better aim. If he'd had a more stable platform, Nathan would be a dead man. He was about to turn around and let them go when a semi-truck shot out from a cross street and nearly collided with the pickup. The smaller vehicle swerved to avoid impact, hitting a curb as it went. The shooter in back flew up into the air and out of the bed. It all happened so fast that Nathan hardly had a chance to react. One moment, the man was in the truck shooting at him and the next he was sprawled on the road. Nathan rose to his feet on the Enfield's foot pegs and revved the throttle as he lifted the front wheel into the air and then rode right over his assailant, bouncing across him like a log. When he landed on the other side, Nathan didn't stop. Instead, he kept after the pickup, which now swerved hard right and then hard left as the driver struggled to maintain control. As he arched in a broad right turn, the left wheels lifted off the ground. The pickup slowly went over, until it flipped completely and then rolled, once, twice, three times before slamming into the side of a warehouse and ejecting the driver through the front windshield.

Nathan pulled over beside the wreck to find the driver in a crumpled heap, still alive but only just. As Nathan approached, the man seemed unable to comprehend what was happening. His eyes showed fear, but more than that, confusion. He watched Nathan but was unable to speak. A small knot of spectators emerged from the warehouse to witness the commotion. Nathan didn't waste any time. He rifled through the man's pockets and pulled out a mobile phone. First, he wiped the screen clean on his pant leg and then took the man's right hand and pressed his fingertips onto the glass, one at a time. He put the phone in his own pocket and then grabbed the man's hair and yanked out as many strands as he could. These he slid into his pocket as well. Amongst the crowd around him on the sidewalk, he sensed a growing hostility. It was time to depart. Nathan jumped on his bike and headed back the way he had come. With some luck, he'd catch his flight before things got any more complicated than they already were.

Chapter Two

The meeting place was a secure, unmarked office in McLean, Virginia, a short drive away from CIA headquarters. Because Nathan didn't officially work for the agency anymore, his position was what outsiders sometimes referred to as "Black Ops." Graham Masterson didn't want him showing his face around headquarters, or risk being logged in at the entrance gate. It was best to limit any paper trail. This location was close enough for Masterson to zip over for a meeting without being missed for too long. On this occasion, he was joined by his assistant, Mirabelle Horton. She handled Nathan's payments, listed in the books as "technical services," and also coordinated the intelligence, taking in what Nathan provided and directing it to the proper analysts. Now she sat beside Masterson in a small conference room with Nathan across the table.

"Nice job with the DNA and prints. Unfortunately, they weren't enough for an ID." Masterson looked through a file on his laptop. The man was in his mid-40s with short brown hair and black-rimmed glasses. He was career CIA, having been with the agency ever since he was recruited straight out of college. Nathan had known the man for years, and trusted him generally. He wouldn't have taken on the job otherwise. "The phone was a burner, but we did learn a few interesting things."

"Such as?" Nathan had only been back in the country a little over twenty-four hours. He was still suffering from jet lag, but glad to have made it out at all under the circumstances.

"The man wasn't local, we know that. Genetics tell us he was North African. Algerian to be specific."

"What was his beef with Parsons? Or I suppose I should say, with the United States?"

"That's the question, isn't it? Either he was a soldier of fortune or a die-hard believer in some cause. We can't yet say which. We did get some clues from the phone. The man had one number in his contact list."

"Anyone we know?"

"Not before now." Masterson looked to Horton, who opened a file on her own laptop and spun it around for Nathan to see.

"His name is Gamil Babouche," Horton said.

On the screen, Nathan saw a photo of a bearded man in a tweed jacket. He was heavy-set and looked to be in his late 30s, or perhaps a few years older. "Who is he?"

"His father was a leader in the National Liberation Front, known to be particularly brutal in the war against France. Apparently, the son is a chip off the old block. From what we can tell, he's a mid-level member of the IAA."

"The Islamic Army of Algeria."

"That's right," said Horton. "The phone you provided had a series of texts from Babouche directing the operation. He seems to have been the one pulling the strings. We still don't know why."

"Of course, the President is under an enormous amount of pressure to respond," said Masterson. "We can't just let the execution of a senior cabinet member go unanswered."

"What sort of retaliation are we talking about?"

"They'll want some flash and bang for the official response, but the Pentagon will take care of that end."

"You want me to kill Babouche."

"As we said, we can't let this go unanswered," said Horton.

Nathan felt as though he was levitating in his chair. This was a moment of truth that would only occur once in his life. He was being asked to assassinate another human being. It wouldn't be the first time he'd killed a man, but the others were in combat, following predetermined rules of engagement. It was him against them. Sure, a few of his CIA adversaries had ended up dead along the way, but those were technically accidents. He'd never in his life set out ahead of time to kill a man, at least nobody who didn't personally deserve it. The moral implications weighed heavily on him here. If he crossed this line, he'd be opening himself up to the shadowy life of a hired killer. But then, Nathan had witnessed firsthand the moment that a missile blasted the secretary's plane from the sky. If this Babouche person was responsible, then he deserved to die, pure and simple. The next question was whether Nathan could fully commit himself to the job. He'd suspected that it would come to this eventually from the moment he signed on with Masterson. This is what black ops was all about. If all they'd wanted was intelligence, they'd have relied on existing operatives.

"You'll be doing a great service for your country," Masterson pressed him.

"How far up the chain does this go?"

"All the way to the top."

Nathan didn't have much time to mull it over. The time to make his decision was now, on the spot. Perhaps a dark job was what he needed. In his current state of mind, he didn't want to think too hard. He just wanted a greater cause to fight for, and perhaps this was it. "Do you have location information?"

Masterson was relieved by the question. He had Nathan now. "Babouche spends most of his time in Oran, in Algeria. We have a few addresses for him."

"Will there be any assistance from the local authorities?" Nathan knew the answer to this one already, but he felt he'd better ask just in case.

"You don't exist, Nathan. We'll facilitate your documents and transportation. You complete your assignment and get out. No local contacts."

"What if things go south?"

"Officially, the United States government has no knowledge of your activities. You're a private citizen, acting on your own volition."

"Do you really think anybody will believe that?"

"Just don't get caught."

"What about weapons?"

"We'll take care of all the logistics. We want to move fast on this one, Nathan. Are you in?"

Nathan pictured himself in his workshop, planing a custom-made oak table, the sweet smell of sawdust in the air. It wouldn't be a bad life, opening the custom furniture business he'd dreamed of. He knew from experience how such work transported him into a zen-like state. But then, that wouldn't help him to forget all of the pain. This might not either, but somehow he was drawn to it by forces he couldn't explain, even to himself. Maybe it was wrong, but he wanted to make somebody pay; anybody, as long as they deserved it. Nathan didn't have to be an assassin for life. Maybe it was just this one job. For now, he would focus on the task at hand. He would let this one mission consume him. "Just because Babouche directed the job doesn't mean it was his idea. There might be more layers to this thing."

"Whatever you can dig up, let us know, but your assignment is the same. Getting rid of Babouche will send a message."

Nathan took a deep breath. In the end, this wasn't a decision at all, really. He was working on instinct now, doing what he must to placate the swirling demons in his mind. "When do I leave?"

"Tonight. We've got a flight departing Andrews at 23:00 hours. We'll want you there three hours ahead to go over the operational planning."

"Yes, sir."

"Nathan, you're doing a great service for your country."

"Let's just see how it turns out before we make any sweeping statements."

"I have every confidence in you. I wouldn't have brought you on otherwise."

"I'll do my best."

"I'm sure that you will."

Nine hours later, Nathan sat in an officer's lounge at Joint Base Andrews, waiting for his flight to depart. On the bar in front of him was a glass of single malt Scotch, neat. He'd felt it might calm his nerves, or at least help him sleep on the long leg to Ramstein Air Base in Germany. Above and behind the bar was a television tuned to cable news. Two commentators discussed video footage, set on a loop, showing a small building in Central Africa being blown to smithereens in a drone attack. This was the official U.S. response to the Secretary of State's assassination. The building was said to have housed leaders of the local rebel group deemed responsible. Of course, Nathan knew that wasn't entirely true. They might have had a hand in it, assisting Babouche in smuggling the weapons and manpower into the country. But then, maybe not. It was a good excuse to go after them, anyway, it seemed. Nathan took a sip of his Scotch, then downed the whole thing and waved for another. Where one was good, two were better.

In the back of the room, Nathan spotted a group of officers drinking beers as they took turns shooting pool. They were clearly enjoying themselves, making fun of one another and putting money down with each attempted shot. It left Nathan feeling a hole in his core. He'd always been surrounded by social networks of his own, as a wide receiver on the high school football team, in a fraternity in college, and earning his commission in the Reserve Officer Training Corps. After that, there was the camaraderie of Army life, and his years in the Rangers. Those men were like brothers to him. They would die for each other, and sometimes did. When he moved on to the CIA, it was an adjustment. It was harder to make friends when you couldn't tell people on the outside what you actually did for a living. Posted at U.S. embassies abroad, Nathan was always the odd man out. Nearly everybody else working in these compounds was a diplomat. Officially, Nathan was as well, but that game didn't fool anybody else in the embassy. The foreign service officers knew he wasn't really one of them. They never quite trusted him, and why would they? He was lying to them daily.

Despite all of this, Nathan did enjoy his time as an operative. He got to live in interesting places all over the world and had his finger on the pulse of what was happening. He felt that he was an important cog in the machinery, but after meeting Jenna, he gave it all up for her. Now he had no wife, no real friends, and no camaraderie with his unit or anybody else. To fill the void, he would focus on the task at hand and with time, perhaps move on to better days.

Nathan took another drink and looked back to the television. On the screen now was a senator, with whom he was deeply familiar. Jed Brogan represented his home state of Texas. Nathan never cared much for the man, who'd always seemed entirely full of himself, though now and then he made a good point. The volume on the TV was turned down, but Nathan read the subtitles.

"We demand a full investigation of this entire incident!" said Senator Brogan. "I'm calling for a Senate inquiry into this blatant assassination. What did the administration know ahead of time, and why did they send a high-ranking cabinet official into what amounts to a war zone? We must and we will get to the bottom of this!"

"What comment do you have on today's retaliatory airstrikes, Senator?" A reporter asked.

"Too little, too late."

Reporters shouted further questions, but the senator moved on, climbing into a black limousine before it drove off up the street past the Capitol. Nathan finished his second Scotch, closed out his tab and then lifted the duffel bag that rested at his feet. He made his way out of the club and on toward the tarmac, showing his ID at a checkpoint before walking out across the asphalt to a waiting Boeing C-17 Globemaster. A ground crew was still in the process of loading the last few stacks of crates through the rear cargo door. Nathan entered through the forward passenger door and was shown to a sidewall jump seat where he placed his duffel underneath and settled in beside a uniformed Army lieutenant. More crates were strapped down in front of them. An M-1 Abrams battle tank took up the center of the hold.

"Lieutenant Audrey Billingsley," his neighbor offered a hand. "Might as well introduce ourselves, it's going to be a long flight."

"Good to know you, Lieutenant." Nathan shook her hand. "Bradley Nordlinger." He gave her the name on his fake passport, provided to him just one hour earlier during a briefing with two of Masterson's men. They'd also passed him an untraceable 9mm SIG Sauer P938 micro-compact handgun with a silencer, which he carried now in his bag. He would not be declaring that to customs.

"What takes you to Ramstein?" she asked.

"Logistics."

"Ah, logistics. Keeping the machinery moving. You people are the unsung heroes of the Army if you ask me."

"We do our best."

"No uniform? You have the bearing."

"Happily retired from that life."

"I see, and I suspect you got a pay bump, too, am I right?"

"I can't complain."

Billingsley nodded knowingly. "I just want to get my twenty years in."

"How many left?"

The lieutenant exhaled deeply. "Eight, but I've come this far, might as well stick it out. I'd hate to give up that pension."

Nathan eyed the row of seats stretching down along the fuselage, most of them empty. He thought about getting up to move. Not that the lieutenant wasn't pleasant enough, but he wanted some time to himself, to process the information Masterson's men had shared. He decided that it would be rude to abandon her like that, so he turned his attention to the tank, where the ground crew busied themselves chaining it into place. If the thing shifted in flight it could bring the whole plane down with it.

"What sort of logistics are you in?" said Billingsley.

"Toothpaste," Nathan answered, thinking back to a previous cover story, and thus the girl he'd used it on. Whatever happened to Natalia Nicolaeva, he wondered? If he got out of this mission alive, perhaps he'd look her up.

"Toothpaste?" Billingsley didn't seem to buy it.

"You know, everything really. We supply the exchange. Anything a Soldier needs. Or an Airman." Nathan motioned toward a row of pallets stacked with wooden crates that were loaded just forward of the tank.

"I see. Well, I could always use some toothpaste if you've got any extra tubes lying around."

"Not on me, unfortunately." Nathan gave her a smile.

"Too bad. I'm surprised you don't fly commercial. Hell, you might even get a bump up to business class if you played your cards right. I always find the uniform helps, but I guess you can't swing that one anymore."

"No, it's OK. This was all a bit last minute."

"Toothpaste can't wait."

"That's right."

It didn't take much longer before the rear door swung closed and the aircraft was ready to go. This crew was well-practiced. Time was money, or during wartime, life or death, and they knew how to turn a plane around. As the four jet engines fired up, the lieutenant reached into a bag under her seat and pulled out a pair of headphones.

"Not to be anti-social, but I find that these help," she said.

"No problem at all."

Billingsley plugged them into her mobile phone and then scrolled through her music selections. Nathan made do with a pair of silicone earplugs that he removed from a case in his pocket and then slid into his ears. He would have some time to himself after all. Nathan buckled his seat belt and felt the plane vibrate beneath him as it began taxiing toward the runway. His mission briefing beforehand hadn't gone particularly well. Nathan wasn't left with a whole lot of confidence. The problem was the lack of any type of well-considered plan. He would land in Germany and meet up with a contact who would drive him south, through France and then along the Mediterranean coast of Spain to Almeria. From there, a speedboat would transport him through cover of darkness across the sea to a small fishing village on the coast of Algeria. Aside from the weapon in his bag, Nathan was also provided with a stack of euros and another of Algerian dinars. With these, he would find his way into the city of Oran, check into a quiet hotel and await further orders. The general idea was that the CIA would use their drone and satellite network to track Babouche's movements, relaying the information to Nathan who would track the man down and make the kill. Nathan didn't like it for a whole host of reasons. First and foremost was that Babouche was bound to be highly protected by a small army of fanatics. Did Masterson really think Nathan would be able to get to the man, alone and with one compact firearm? The next problem was that even if he did somehow succeed, getting out in one piece was a whole different proposition. He'd have the local police, army and Islamic rebels all gunning for him. Nathan thought back to what he was doing when Masterson first contacted him about signing on as a contractor. He'd been on that tropical island in Thailand, teaching scuba diving to tourists. It wasn't such a bad life. What had made him think this job offer was a good idea? Regardless, he was stuck into it now. There was no backing out. Before long, he felt the aircraft accelerate down the runway and then lift off into the sky.

On arrival at Ramstein eight hours later, a German customs and immigration officer checked Nathan's passport and customs form. He had nothing to declare, though if the officer had bothered to check his bag, the mission would have been over before it began. Instead of heading south, Nathan would be spending time in a local jail. That almost sounded preferable, but then he pictured the image of the Secretary of State's plane going down in flames. Gamil Babouche was an immediate threat to the security of the United States. He did need to be taken out, and Nathan would do his best to accomplish this goal.

Once he'd made it through customs, the drive to Spain was mostly uneventful. Nathan and his escort took turns behind the wheel during an 18-hour journey. When they spoke, they kept it superficial, talking about their favorite sports teams back in the U.S., or movies they'd enjoyed. Nathan's travel partner was a young operative with the CIA who reminded Nathan a little of himself at that age and knew better than to ask any probing questions. When they arrived in Almeria, Nathan checked into a hotel, had an early dinner alone at a restaurant along a seaside promenade, and then returned to his room for a few solid hours of sleep. At 2 a.m., he was woken by his alarm. Nathan got out of bed fully dressed, slung his duffel over one shoulder and made his way down to the local harbor. An autumn chill hung in the air as he followed his directions to a slip that held a long, sleek cigarette boat with four 300 hp diesel outboard engines on the back. Waiting at the helm was a middle-aged man in a dark wool sweater that covered a bulging gut. On the dock beside the craft was a much younger deckhand.

"Good morning," the captain said to Nathan. "You're my charter for today?"

"To Oran?" said Nathan.

The man nodded and Nathan climbed aboard, dropping his duffel in the stern. The captain fired up the engines and motioned to his crewman, who untied the lines and then jumped aboard as they drifted from the dock.

"How long is the crossing?" Nathan asked.

"Two hundred kilometers," said the captain. "If the seas are calm, we can make it in two hours."

"And if the seas are rough?"

"The forecast is in our favor." The captain eased the boat forward and steered them through the harbor until they were outside the main breakwater. Ahead of them stretched the dark expanse of the sea, and above, the glittering stars of the universe, with the Milky Way Galaxy stretching from one horizon to the other. "You might want to sit down and hang on," said the captain. Nathan did as suggested.

The man pushed the throttles full forward and they took off across the water, flying like astronauts through the dark of night. Two hours later he was soaking wet from the ocean spray and shivering from the cold, his hair and skin caked with salt. The constant pounding of the hull against the waves left his gut twisted in knots. The captain eased the throttles back and the boat slowed. Ahead, Nathan saw electric lights lining the Algerian shoreline. He also made out the ghostly image of a small fishing vessel in the dark with all of its running lights switched off. The deckhand pulled out a flashlight and handed it to the captain, who pointed it toward the fishing boat and signaled, three bursts, then a pause, and then two more. From the other boat they saw two flashes in return, then a pause, and then three more. The captain continued forward slowly until he'd pulled up just alongside. "This is the end of the line for me, safe journey to you," said the captain. "Vaya con Dios."

"Gracias." Nathan lifted his duffel and tossed it to the crew on the fishing boat, then climbed up and over the gunnel.

"Welcome aboard." This crewman was young and skinny, with a thin mustache and quiet demeanor. "Follow me, please." The man led Nathan into the wheelhouse, past a sturdy captain who stood behind the helm and eyed the newcomer without saying a word. The crewman continued with Nathan in tow down a stairway, through the galley and into a cabin with two bunks on either side. "You stay here until we enter port," the man said. "Not on deck."

"How long will that be?"

"We must fish first. If we come without catch, no good."

"Fine."

"Food and water in the galley. Head next door."

"Thank you." When the door shut behind him, Nathan stripped off his wet clothes and hung them on a ladder, then took out a clean set from his duffel and put them on. However long they wanted to fish was fine with him. It would give Nathan a chance to catch up on the sleep that he still sorely needed. He climbed into a bottom bunk beneath a rough wool blanket and closed his eyes, feeling the pitch and sway of the sea beneath him as he drifted off once more.

By the time they entered port, Nathan was awake and having coffee in the galley. He heard shouts from above as the crew tied the boat to a dock and then all went quiet when the engines shut down. A few minutes later, the captain came down the stairs. "You go now," he said.

"Yes, sir." Nathan downed the last of his coffee before moving back to the cabin to retrieve his things, stuffing the damp clothes back into his duffel. The captain followed him back up the stairs and then watched as Nathan disembarked and moved along the dock while the rest of the crew busied themselves unloading the day's catch. It was still early in the morning as Nathan took in his surroundings, but the rising sun oriented him toward the east. The port backed up to an industrial zone, with warehouses, a mechanic's shop, and a marine supply business. He continued past and on up a quiet road until he came to the outskirts of a small town and then found his way to a two-lane highway. Checking the map on his phone, he saw that he was 70 kilometers from Oran, the last known residence of Gamil Babouche. Nathan stood on the northbound side of the highway and stuck out his thumb.

It took roughly thirty minutes before a rusted pickup pulled to the side of the road and the driver rolled down his passenger window. Nathan hurried to the vehicle. "Oran?" he said.

The driver was in his early 60s, with curly, salt-and-pepper hair and brown skin creased by years in the sun. The bed of the truck held crates of live chickens, piled high one on top of the other. "Where you from?" The man was skeptical of this foreigner.

"Canada," Nathan replied.

After a moment of thought, sizing Nathan up, the driver nodded. "OK."

Nathan opened the door and climbed in. When he'd swung the door shut, the man pulled back onto the road. "Why you here in my country?"

"I'm a tourist."

The driver looked him sideways. "Tourist? Here?"

"You have a beautiful country."

This comment appeased the man. "Yes. Very beautiful. It is true."

For the next hour, Nathan did his best to carry on a conversation without giving anything about himself away. He didn't like having this man as a witness to his presence here, though it was safer than taking a bus, with a driver and a whole slew of passengers. When they reached Oran, Nathan asked to be dropped off on the outskirts of the city and then continued on foot. Approaching the city center, he checked himself into a mid-range hotel. Masterson would know exactly where Nathan was, using his phone to track every movement. With some luck, he'd know where Gamil Babouche was, too. Nathan didn't have to wait long before he got a text from Mirabelle Horton over an in-house encrypted app.

I trust your journey has gone smoothly. Attached you will find a link that will provide real-time tracking for your target. We request that you engage and dispatch at soonest available opportunity.

Nathan walked to the window and threw open the curtain. Three stories below he saw a crowded city square where a farmer's market was in progress, with vendors selling produce from behind crowded tables. He took a deep breath, inhaling the salty aroma of the sea. It was an enormous responsibility he'd taken on, of course. If all went according to plan, somewhere in this city a man would be dead by the end of the day. Nathan took his phone and tapped a response. *Understood.*

Chapter Three

The map on Nathan's phone showed a pulsing red dot representing Gamil Babouche's location. It wasn't far from the hotel. The app estimated ten minutes walking. The possibility existed that Nathan could simply stroll on over, take care of the job, and flee the country before the sun even set. Not that he would be rash. Shooting a man in broad daylight would be tricky, especially if there were any witnesses around. It was also to be expected that a man like Babouche would have bodyguards. Nathan might be forced to take them out, too. At the very least, he would walk on over and scope out the situation. From his duffel bag, he pulled out a small knapsack and then placed his pistol inside, along with a pair of binoculars, his wallet, and half of his cash. He put the rest of the cash in a room safe, then filled a water bottle from the sink in the bathroom and put that in the backpack as well. Lastly, he donned a pair of sunglasses on the top of his head, slung the pack over his shoulders and headed out.

Down on the street level, he crossed a busy boulevard and entered the square, making his way past the stalls of fruits and vegetables, bread, nuts and candy, where ordinary citizens were busy shopping for the week. Vendors called out their prices while animated shoppers haggled for a better deal. On the opposite side of the square, Nathan continued down a narrow, cobblestone alley, shaded by tall buildings from the growing warmth of the North African autumn sun. He passed men sitting at an outdoor cafe smoking strawberry tobacco from the large water pipes known as hookah. Rechecking the map, Nathan saw that his target was moving, though only slowly. If he hurried, Nathan could still catch up. The man appeared to be heading across the sprawling November 1954 square. But then he turned around. Then he turned right, and then left, and went back the way he had only just come. What was going on here? Nathan picked up his pace. When he arrived at the square he saw a large obelisk with the statue of an angel perched on top. On the pavement below, a man was in the midst of a spirited football game with three young children, no bodyguards in sight. As the ball skipped across the ground, the man ran left, then right, dribbling around two boys who must have been eight and ten years old. The third child was a girl who couldn't have been more than five. On his phone, Nathan watched the pulsing dot move up and down the square. The man passed the ball to the girl, who kicked it between what was likely her two older siblings. When the ball bounced off the stone base of the pillar, Gamil Babouche raised his arms and gave a cheer before lifting his daughter in the air to celebrate, kissing her on the cheek. Nathan Grant felt an overwhelming despair wash over him. He found a seat on a nearby bench. What on earth was he going to do now?

As he watched Babouche playing happily with his kids, Nathan reminded himself that the Secretary of State had kids, too. So did several members of his staff that died with him that day. Just because Babouche was a father didn't lessen Nathan's obligation to fulfill his task. It only made it harder. He couldn't shoot the man in broad daylight, in front of his children. Maybe some operators would have no problem with that, but Nathan carried around his own set of morals. Babouche still had to die, but Nathan wasn't about to scar these kids for life with the memory. He'd have to follow the man and catch him alone, or at least without his children around. For now, Nathan simply observed, trying to take the measure of the man. He came across as a genial sort, with a broad smile as he dribbled the ball back and forth, finding joy in the moment. This surprised Nathan, and bothered him some as well. He'd expected the man to be a hardened terrorist with a brooding demeanor. Babouche was a reasonably handsome man, well dressed in brown slacks with a tweed jacket. Resting against the base of the pedestal was a brown leather briefcase that must have belonged to him. If Nathan could get his hands on that, the CIA would no doubt glean some useful information from the contents.

After some time, Babouche lifted his daughter into the air and placed her on his shoulders before reaching down to pick up the briefcase. His older son took the ball and the four of them headed off across the square. Nathan let them get a little ways ahead before standing to follow. After crossing a set of tram tracks, they continued past an ornate theater building and on up the block until they came to a small takeout restaurant. Why no bodyguards, Nathan wondered. It all seemed unusual. Babouche led the kids inside and then went to the counter where he looked over a menu board and then placed an order. Nathan took a seat at an outside table and watched the scene through the window. When Babouche had paid, he and the kids sat at a table inside. While they waited for their food, he took out his phone and made a call. When he hung up, Babouche went back to the counter and placed another order.

The entire process of stalking this man felt strangely intimate to Nathan. He didn't know much about Babouche, hardly anything, really, but the more he saw, the less confident he felt in his assignment. Did Masterson get it wrong? This man, this Gamil Babouche, did not seem like the extremist type, or a killer at all for that matter. Nathan considered himself a good judge of character. Those skills were honed by years as a proper CIA operative, recruiting foreign agents. Nathan understood what type of man he could count on to flip to their side, either for ideological reasons or financial. He knew what buttons to push, and when to give up trying. For all he could tell, based upon what he saw now, this was just an ordinary family man going about his business.

Nathan stood and entered the shop, moving to the counter himself where he looked over the menu board. The selections were written in Arabic and English, along with photos. He chose a half chicken with fries and a sparkling water, paid in Algerian dinars, and then took an empty table beside Babouche and his kids. A few minutes later, a woman entered a shop wearing a long flowing robe and a headscarf. Babouche stood and greeted her, kissing her on the cheek before she joined them. From the children's reactions, this was obviously their mother. Nathan was sent to kill a ruthless terrorist. Instead, what he found was a happy family. It was his first assignment as a hired assassin, and likely to be his last. It just felt all wrong, on multiple levels. At the core of it, Nathan was ashamed to be here in this position at all. He didn't like the prospect of what he'd become. He very nearly got up and walked out the door, never to look back. It was only his gnawing hunger, an actual physical hunger, that kept him planted in his seat. He hadn't eaten a proper meal since Spain, and so he settled in to wait for his chicken. In the meantime, Babouche's order came out first and they spread the plates across the table. The family was much like any other, with the kids diving into their food and arguing over whose meal was whose. Gamil played referee, dividing up the portions while their mother mostly stayed out of the fray. To Nathan, it was a view into what he'd thought his own future might look like, before his wife was taken from him. Watching Gamil Babouche in this role was like watching some alternate-universe version of himself. Nathan felt the strange sensation that he'd been sent on this mission to kill off that other Nathan once and for all. Maybe this was how he was meant to move on with his life. He would gun down that vision, putting an end to any paternal fantasies he might have had. He would launch himself forever into the dark side.

When Nathan's food came out, he picked up a fry, dipped it in some sauce and took a bite. Looking up again, he saw Babouche's younger son staring at him with wide eyes. Nathan froze momentarily, feeling like the grim reaper come to life. He forced a smile and the boy smiled back before turning away. Nathan swung his chair around so that he didn't have to look at them any longer and quickly ate the rest of his meal. On the way back to his hotel, he continued to ponder the situation. How possible was it that Masterson had it wrong? Nathan didn't want to kill an innocent man, but then again he hadn't yet entirely ruled out going through with it. He'd known from the start that taking on this role would lead to moral challenges. He just hadn't expected them to be so stark on his very first assignment.

Once back inside his room, Nathan called Masterson directly through his secure app, though he still had to be careful about what he said. There was no guarantee that local intelligence didn't have bugs planted in his room. Any conversation could end up as evidence against him. Ideally, he wouldn't be talking to Masterson at all, but under the circumstances, Nathan felt that he needed further direction.

"Tell me the job is done," Masterson answered right away.

"Not yet."

"Why not, is there a problem?"

"I would say so, yes."

"What is it?"

"You didn't tell me the man had kids." Already, Nathan had said more than he should have.

Masterson's pause reflected his frustration. When he spoke again, a hint of anger came through in his voice. "Nathan, it's not your job to make decisions. It's your job to follow orders. Do you understand?"

Now it was Nathan's turn to hesitate. "I want to make sure the intel is right on this one. That's all."

"This order comes from the top. You understand what that means? The top, Nathan. Are you going to be a good soldier?"

Nathan's left hand formed into a fist. He felt like slamming it into the wall. The President of the United States was giving him an order. Who was Nathan Grant to say no? "I just wanted to be sure, that's all."

"Don't call back until it's done. In fact, don't call back at all. Just get it done, Nathan." Masterson hung up the phone.

Nathan walked to the window and looked out onto the square below. The last of the vendors were packing up their stands and heading home after a long day. Nearby, a pack of teenagers rode skateboards, flipping them up in the air to do rail grinds on a concrete bench. Further on, a couple sat side-by-side holding hands. Tonight in this city, three young children were going to lose their father. A woman would become a widow. If all went well, Nathan Grant would board a ferry bound for Europe as a newly initiated merchant of death.

Chapter Four

He stood outside the apartment door wearing a black leather jacket, with his right hand tucked inside a pocket and grasping his SIG Sauer handgun, silencer attached. The pulsing red dot on his app had told him that Gamil Babouche was inside. As the man of the family, he was likely to answer the door himself. When he did, all Nathan needed to do was fire one shot between the eyes and flee down the stairs. The next ferry to Alicante departed in an hour and Nathan intended to be on it. The irony wasn't lost on him that Masterson would go to such lengths to smuggle Nathan into the country, but as far as getting back out, he was on his own. Part of that was down to timing. Masterson couldn't be sure when, exactly, Nathan would carry out his assignment. As it was, Nathan just wanted to get it over with at this point. The morality still haunted him, but after speaking to Masterson, he pushed those feelings deep down inside. Nathan was still a soldier at heart and this order came directly from the Commander-in-Chief, or so he'd been told. He didn't know the nitty-gritty details of the situation. It wasn't his job to. He only knew what he was sent here to do. That meant ringing the bell, and when Babouche answered, Nathan would put all qualms aside and carry out his task. He would kill this man, right in his doorway. He tried not to think too hard as he reached out with his left hand and pressed the button.

From inside the apartment, Nathan heard the commotion of a family not expecting visitors, with children hollering, dog barking, and parents trying to calm the situation. A dog complicated things, but Nathan would shoot that, too, if he had to. The sound of footsteps grew closer, and Nathan heard the deadbolt slide. This was it. In another few seconds, it would all be over. The door swung open. On the other side stood Gamil Babouche, holding his daughter in his arms. He eyed Nathan with a slightly perplexed expression, perhaps unsure which language to use with this foreigner standing on his threshold. "Can I help you?" he said.

Nathan stood where he was, frozen in place. Each second that ticked by seemed like an eternity, as though he were caught in some sort of tear in the space-time continuum. This man's entire life came down to this moment. Nathan was going to take it away from him. He would do as he was told, like a robot fulfilling a task. It didn't matter that the man's infant daughter was in his hands. Nathan had orders to follow. His hand tightened on the pistol grip, and yet he couldn't pull the weapon out. Instead, he looked to the child, who watched him with wide-eyed curiosity. A surge of emotion wrenched at Nathan's heart and he very nearly broke down and cried. Instead, he managed to maintain his composure, wiping away a single tear with his free hand. No man with a daughter as sweet as this could be a killer. It just wasn't possible. Babouche was a family man, not a terrorist. At this moment, Nathan was willing to bet his life on it. "I need to speak with you. It's very important."

"What is this about?" Anxiety showed in Babouche's expression.

"Please. Take a walk with me. No harm will come to you, I give you my word."

Babouche looked to his daughter, who pulled at his sweater and squirmed in his arms. From the kitchen, Nathan heard the sound of oil frying and smelled the aroma of garlic and onions. The mother called out and then the younger son peeked around a corner to see who was at the door. Babouche called back to his wife and then turned his attention to Nathan once more. "Give me a moment."

"Of course."

The door closed and Nathan took the opportunity to unscrew his silencer. He slid it into a pants pocket and then put the compact pistol back into the right pocket of his jacket. He hadn't decided what he was going to do at this point. Babouche might very well be calling the police, or retrieving a weapon of his own. Nathan realized that if he'd underestimated the man, he might end up being the one shot to death in this doorway, but then the door opened once more and Babouche was alone and unarmed. "Let's go."

Nathan followed his target down the stairs, through the lobby and out to the street. Neither said a word at first as Babouche led them away from the building. They headed toward the sea, with Babouche keeping his head down, deep in thought, as though he'd somehow expected this outcome. It was nighttime now and the street was lit by overhead lamps. The traffic was light as they continued for several blocks until they came to a promenade and turned west along the water. Nathan imagined it was a walk that Babouche took regularly, perhaps with his dog. Now he was leading on instinct, but clearly worried. "This is about my nephew, isn't it?" he said.

The question caught Nathan by surprise. "Who is your nephew?"

Babouche looked sidelong at Nathan. "If not him, then what?"

A scattering of pedestrians strolled along the walk, taking in the sea breeze beneath the stars. Far away, in an office in Virginia, Graham Masterson and his small team would be watching two pulsing dots on a screen, moving together in tandem. They might even have eyes on the pair from a drone or a satellite high above. What would Masterson do if Nathan disobeyed his order? First off, he'd send somebody else. Babouche wasn't likely to get off so easily. The next assassin would finish the job. But what would Masterson do with Nathan? This would certainly mean the end of his fledgling career in Black Ops, but Nathan didn't care about that. All he wanted right now was the truth, or as much as he could get of it out of Gamil Babouche. "What can you tell me about Joshua Parsons?"

Beads of sweat formed on Babouche's forehead. "The American diplomat, I read about him. What has this to do with me?"

"You'd better start talking. I don't have time for games."

Babouche stopped walking and stood beneath an overhead lamp to face his accuser. "If you believe that this is a game, you must think I have a peculiar sense of humor, sir. I assure you, I do not."

Nathan looked to his left up the promenade, and then to his right. They were alone now, mostly. An elderly couple was one hundred meters away but walking in the opposite direction. If he wanted to shoot the man when he was alone, now would be a good opportunity. If he wanted to. "All I'm looking for is the truth. If you can give me that, I will leave you be."

Babouche's anxiety was not assuaged. "I know nothing about what happened to this man, aside from what I read in the newspaper."

"Then why were the orders for his assassination sent from your phone?"

"My phone? That's impossible."

"Not according to my sources."

"Your sources are wrong."

"That's not good enough, Gamil. Perhaps it will help you to focus if I tell you that I was sent to kill you. If you can be entirely honest with me, I won't follow through with my assignment. You have to understand, right now I'm the best chance you have at survival. They'll send somebody else and the next time your assailant won't be so friendly. Why don't you start by telling me about your nephew? Who is he?"

Babouche's expression shifted from terror to despair and back again as he struggled to find a way out of his predicament. "He's my sister's kid. He's not a bad boy, honest, he's just... Sometimes he runs with the wrong crowd."

"Which crowd is that? Extremists? Is that it, Gamil?"

"No. No, not extremists." Babouche wanted to explain without giving up his kin, seeming to understand that one of them was likely to die.

"Did he have access to your phone? Does he live with you?"

"No, not any longer."

"But he was living with you, previously? How long ago?"

Babouche's head dropped further and his shoulders slumped. "Two days ago, he went away."

"Why? What was the reason?"

With the back of his right hand, Babouche wiped his brow, stalling for time as he tried to come up with an answer.

"The truth, Gamil, just tell me the truth," Nathan prodded him.

"He's a good boy, you must understand."

"Why did you send him away?"

"I didn't send him. He left on his own. I would never send him away."

"Why did he leave?"

"Because of the money."

"Gamil, spit it out! What money?"

"I don't know where it came from, but he was very happy. He said that he was rich, that he didn't need to stay with us anymore."

"Where did he go? Is he still in Oran?"

"I think he went to France, to Paris."

"I want to know his name, his phone number, and anything else you can tell me about how I can track him down. Understand? Tell me who his friends are. Where does his mother live?"

"I can't let you kill him. I can't betray my only nephew. You'll have to shoot me. I'm sorry. There is no other way."

"Think of your kids, Gamil. Think of your wife." Nathan realized as soon as he'd said the words that this was the wrong approach. He saw Babouche's entire frame heaving in sobs as the man buried his face in his hands, tears streaming out between his fingers. Just when Nathan had thought he couldn't feel any worse about himself, he was faced with the cold, hard truth that he'd taken on the role of a monster. Shame seeped into every pore of his being, but it wasn't too late to step back. "I'm not going to kill you, Babouche. And I won't kill your nephew either." It took some time before Babouche was able to take his hands away, wiping his eyes again with the back of his hand. Nathan took him by the elbow and led him to a nearby bench. "Here, let's sit down."

The two men took their places on the bench, looking out at the dark Mediterranean. Babouche was still silent, but shaking with fear. "You were supposed to be my first job," Nathan tried to calm his nerves. "I saw you there in the square, playing football with your kids, and then when your wife joined you for lunch... I knew I couldn't do it. I'm not a murderer, Gamil. I'm not a monster. I promise."

"My nephew, he's not a bad boy. Please, you must believe me."

"I'm not going to kill him, on my honor, but I need to know what happened. If he was involved in the Secretary's murder, he deserves a fair trial, but the perpetrators need to be held accountable." Babouche didn't answer. "Listen," Nathan continued, "your nephew was willing to make it look as though you were the guilty one. Why else did he use your phone and not his own? You may be eager to protect him, but he did not have the same concern for you. It very nearly cost you your life. If my people had sent anybody else on this assignment but me, it would have. If I were you, I would worry less about your nephew and more about yourself and your family. Until the full truth is revealed, you are in danger, my friend. Here is my small piece of advice: Get rid of your electronic devices, all of them, and take your family away for a while. Go as far as you can until this whole thing blows over. Use cash, no bank cards. Try not to show yourself in public."

These comments seemed to flip a switch in Babouche's brain as he realized that his nephew had indeed sold him out. A resignation descended on him and he nodded his head.

"What's your nephew's name?"

"Khalil," Babouche whispered.

"And his surname?"

"Haddad."

Before Nathan could say anymore, his phone began to ring. He pulled it out of his pocket and saw that the call was from Graham Masterson. What could Nathan possibly say to the man as he stood here having a conversation with his target? He might try to explain the situation, but Masterson wouldn't want to hear it. The only thing the deputy director wanted to hear was that the job was complete. Anything else was superfluous. Nathan powered down the phone and then stood, reaching his arm back before hurling the device as far as he could into the Mediterranean Sea, where it landed with a splash before sinking below the surface. "I suggest you do the same." Nathan looked up into the dark night sky.

Babouche pulled out his phone and tossed it in as well. "Please, all I ask is that you give him the same consideration that you gave to me."

"Of course."

As they walked back up the promenade, Nathan began to wonder for the first time if somewhere in that office in Virginia, Graham Masterson was writing Nathan Grant's name down on the hit list.

Chapter Five

The chance was better than average that at this moment a surveillance drone was still tracking Nathan's every move. He had no good reason to return to his hotel. Most likely, the CIA had already inserted a tracking chip in his luggage. There might be one planted into the soles of his shoes, or even the seams in his clothing. The gun as well would be suspect. Nathan dropped it into a garbage can and then walked into an open shopping mall where he quickly swapped his clothes for a new wardrobe of jeans, a blue t-shirt and another black leather jacket. He ditched his old clothing in another trash bin near the dressing room, along with his wallet and all of his credit cards. The only things he kept were his cash and driver's license, his actual American passport and another fake one that the CIA knew nothing about. This document was Lebanese, in the name of Elias Mansour. He'd picked it up from a Lebanese official during a previously sticky situation. It would come in handy now, if he could first evade these eyes in the sky on the way back out. With multiple entrances to the mall, that shouldn't be too difficult.

Passing a sporting goods store, Nathan saw a row of hats for sale. He purchased the one with the widest brim, pulled it on and then exited the mall from a different door than he'd come in. Now he just needed to find a way out of town. He walked two blocks until a bus pulled up to his left. Nathan climbed on without much concern for where it was headed. He paid the fare and found a seat toward the back. As the bus moved on up the street, he placed the hat on the seat beside him and inhaled. He was a fugitive now, in a sense. There was no telling what the CIA would do in this situation. It wasn't entirely implausible for them to come after him. Or maybe they'd release his name to the local authorities and have him arrested. One thing was certain, Nathan's career as an assassin was over before it had even begun. In truth, he was never cut out for the role. They might still catch up to Babouche in the end, but Nathan wanted nothing to do with it. Where, then, was Nathan going? What would he do? Traveling back to his Virginia apartment didn't seem particularly wise at the moment. Besides, now his curiosity was unleashed. He needed to understand the full details behind Joshua Parsons' killing, for his own sake. The first step was to follow the leads he had, and that meant tracking down Khalil Haddad. Perhaps if he figured out what was actually going on, that would square him with Masterson and the CIA in the process.

From the last stop on the line, Nathan exited the bus and stood on the edge of the road with his thumb out, hoping for a ride to Algiers. Masterson would probably expect him to leave from Oran, through the ferry or the local airport. It seemed to Nathan that it would be easier to get lost in the crowd at the larger Houari Boumediene Airport in the capital, but that meant a four-hour drive.

After twenty minutes without anybody pulling over, Nathan walked to a nearby fuel station and approached the diesel pumps, moving from one big rig to the next. He held out a single 100-euro note. "Algiers?" he said to each driver in turn. The third man he asked looked Nathan over with some curiosity and then reached for the money as he nodded. Nathan considered hurrying inside the small convenience store to purchase some snacks, but the driver was likely to leave him behind, and so instead he climbed in on the passenger side, pulled his seat belt across his chest and fastened the latch. When the driver was ready, they headed off to the east.

By the time Nathan arrived at the airport, it was after 2 a.m., following an uneventful journey. At this hour, the departure desks were closed. He did find a vending machine, but without small bills or a credit card, he was unable to use it. Instead, he settled in on a section of carpet near a waiting area to get a little shut-eye, setting his natural alarm clock to wake him in four hours' time. Shortly before 6:30 a.m., he opened his eyes to find a fair bit more activity going on around him than when he'd nodded off. Passengers were arriving for early-morning flights and a row of clerks stood behind the desks to check them in. Nathan went to an Air France counter and bought a ticket for the next available flight to Paris Charles de Gaulle, departing in just 90 minutes. When that was taken care of, he found a small shop where he was able to buy a new phone, then went through immigration control with his Lebanese passport. Settling in at a restaurant for breakfast, he ordered a cafe crème, along with a pain au chocolate, but that wasn't enough so he followed it with eggs Florentine and toast. As he waited, he eyed the crowd. Nobody set off any alarm bells, and so forty minutes before departure he finished off a second crème and boarded his flight. It had occurred to him, of course, that Kahlil Haddad was quite a common name. Luckily, Babouche feared for his life enough, or perhaps the lives of his wife and kids, that he'd acquiesced in the end and offered Nathan a few additional clues about his nephew. Was it enough to track him down? Perhaps. At the very least, Nathan would head up to Paris and see what there was to be seen.

The French capital at this time of year was often cool and damp. When Nathan landed, the plane pulled up to the gate through an early-season slush melting on the tarmac. Nathan exited up the jetway with the other passengers and then presented his passport to immigration control where it was stamped without question. He knew all arrivals were monitored by surveillance cameras, and he spotted several. The CIA had no reason to suspect he was in Paris, and even if they did, it probably wouldn't be worth calling in favors with French intelligence to track him down. Most likely, Masterson was extremely pissed off, but he'd probably leave it at that. Nathan would continue to cover his tracks as best he could, just in case. He knew he should probably just disappear back to Thailand for a while, or maybe South America. That would probably be the end of it, and he could simply get on with his life in whatever form it took. The problem was, he'd been sent to kill an innocent man under false pretenses. Until he had a better understanding of what was actually going on, Nathan just couldn't let this go.

It was only when he was through customs, with no baggage, that Nathan decided to take the civilized route and use some of his cash to get a nice hotel room and a decent meal. First, however, he had to make sure the intelligence services couldn't track the physical bills, for whatever that was worth. After so many years as an operative, being careful was second nature. He went to a foreign exchange booth in the terminal and first changed his dinars into euros. Then he changed his original euros into pounds. After that, he stuffed the cash in his pocket and caught a train for the city center, booking a room on the way with his new phone.

A quick search for Khalil Haddad confirmed Nathan's suspicions about the popularity of the name. He found more than a dozen in the Paris area alone and the Haddad he was searching for was probably not even on the list. He'd only just arrived, if he was even here already. In Oran, there were even more of them, though Nathan couldn't tell if any of these might be his man. Fortunately, under duress, Babouche had provided a few extra bits of information. First, Nathan knew that his Haddad was obsessed with a particular brand of motorcycle, a sleek French sportbike known as a Midual Type 1. In fact, he'd only just purchased one the week before. This thing was a rocket, with a 1036 cc 4-stroke flat twin engine and 107 brake horsepower. They were designed and manufactured in limited numbers, with a price tag of nearly $200,000 apiece. That left the obvious question, how did a kid like Haddad get his hands on one? Where did he come up with that kind of money? His uncle didn't seem to know.

Another thing that Babouche shared was that his nephew was also obsessed with a woman. They weren't romantically involved, as far as Babouche could tell, and he wasn't sure if they'd even met in person. This woman, whose real name he did not know, ran a motorcycle club in Paris specifically for Midual owners. Haddad was a member of the online group, with the username *Lion d'Afrique.* The woman in question went by the username *Olive.* If the young Khalil left Oran three days prior on the ferry and arrived in Spain the next morning, he should be in Paris by now even if he rode his motorcycle all the way. With a little bit of sleuthing, Nathan figured this pair shouldn't be too hard to find.

The hotel was in the city center, not far from the Tuileries Gardens and just a short walk from the U.S. Embassy. Nathan was hiding in plain sight, though he did plan to give that building a wide berth. After checking into his room, he headed out for a walk through the gardens to clear his head and then found a seat at a picturesque sidewalk cafe. It wouldn't be long before these outdoor tables were retired for the season, but for now, the autumn chill was still pleasant with his leather jacket on. From a bow-tied server, he ordered crepes with chicken and vegetables along with a cup of hot tea. While he waited, Nathan searched for the online Midual group. He found it easily enough, but the posts were set to private. He'd need to be a member to read them. Nathan thought of a username for himself. *Rocket Rider.* It wasn't particularly creative, but he supposed it would do. When he registered for the group, three questions popped up.

1) *How long have you been a motorcycle rider?*

Nathan's answer: *All my life.*

2) *Are you now in Paris?*

Nathan's answer: *Oui.*

3) *Do you own a Midual?*

Nathan's answer: *Oui, aussi.*

He wasn't sure if he would be accepted into the group at all, but by the time his tea arrived, he was already in. Now he could scroll through the threads and profiles at will. First, of course, he found Haddad's. The avatar was a roaring lion with a full mane. The profile itself didn't provide much more information. A photo showed a helmeted rider in full leathers taking a turn at speed. When he checked Olive's profile he saw just a Midual with an olive-colored fuel tank. These people didn't like to share much online, but Nathan did see a list of events. Most of them had already happened. These were Sunday rides all through the region, up to Dieppe on the northern coast, or down to Le Mans. The next gathering was in two days for a ride to Orleans and a tour through the Loire Valley. Olive was listed as the organizer and so far five participants were signed up, including the Lion of Africa. It sounded like a lovely outing. The question now was, where could Nathan get his hands on a Midual?

Chapter Six

Things would have been easier for Nathan if he'd had the resources of the agency backing him, but that didn't mean he couldn't manage things on his own with a little bit of determination. After several years spent undercover in this country he had plenty of well-placed French contacts. Considering which of them might be able to provide a Midual Type 1, only Philippe Legrand came to mind. Legrand was the consummate playboy, at least until his current wife managed to tame him for the most part. He had more money than an ordinary man would know how to spend. The family fortune went back several generations and involved real estate, vineyards and construction. Philippe expanded that portfolio to add an eCommerce platform popular throughout Europe. The result was that he had enough funds to live a spectacularly flamboyant life, and he made the most of it. The man also had a thing for fast cars, airplanes and motorcycles. If anybody on earth was likely to own a Midual, it had to be Philippe Legrand. The problem now was that if Nathan downloaded his contact list from the cloud, the CIA might pick up his trail. That didn't mean he needed to put it on his phone, though. Instead, he went down to the front desk of his hotel and asked for business services. The clerk directed him to a small office where he was able to use a desktop computer. First, he set up a Virtual Private Network to hide his tracks. Next, he downloaded a list of his contacts and then printed a paper copy. Finally, he used a hotel phone to dial Philippe's personal number directly.

"Bonjour, qui est-ce?" Legrand answered.

"Philippe, hello. This is your old friend Nathan Grant calling."

"Nathan Grant… To what do I owe the pleasure?"

"I need a favor."

"Of course. You Americans, at least you are direct. What favor is this?"

"Do you happen to own a Midual Type 1?"

"Now that is an interesting request. I thought information was your currency?"

"It was. I'm retired."

"Uh, huh." Legrand didn't seem to buy it. "At least you have good taste in motorcycles."

"Does that mean you'll lend me one?"

"Look, Nathan, I'm about to head to a meeting at Epernay. You are in Paris?"

"Yes. Place de la Concorde."

"You can arrive at my office in twenty minutes?"

"I'll be there."

"Wonderful. See you soon."

"See you." After hanging up, Nathan folded the contact list and slid it into an interior pocket in his jacket, then headed out to the street where the doorman put him in the back of a waiting taxi cab. "La Defense," he told the driver. Nathan's navigation app told him that it was nineteen minutes to Legrand's office. "Quickly."

By the time Nathan walked into the building, it was exactly twenty minutes since he'd hung up the phone. A security guard in the lobby escorted him into an elevator and pushed the top button. Twenty seconds later they emerged onto the rooftop, where a helicopter sat waiting on the pad. The guard called into his radio and was told to hold fast where they were. Another thirty seconds passed before the elevator door opened again and this time Philippe Legrand himself emerged, along with a second guard and an attractive young female assistant in a white leather jacket and Navy skirt.

"Hello, Nathan Grant!" Legrand beamed. He was tall and thin, with boyish good looks that belied his middle age, despite a touch of gray. Nathan always suspected it was the man's joy in life that kept him so youthful. He wore brown slacks with a white dress shirt, open at the collar, and a blue sport coat on top. On his face was a bemused expression. "It is a delight to see you, my friend. I would hope that it isn't merely a motorcycle that brings you to me."

"You know I'll take any excuse I can to share your company, Philippe."

"Then why has it been so long? No, don't answer! I know, you are a busy man."

"Not as busy as you."

"Come, let's catch up on the way." Legrand led Nathan to the helicopter, where a security guard sat up front beside the waiting pilot while the others took seats in the rear. Headsets were passed around and Nathan pulled his on and then adjusted the mic.

"You remember Claudette?" said Legrand.

"Of course, it's nice to see you again." Nathan nodded to the assistant as the rotor blades began to whirl.

"Likewise, Mr. Grant."

"By the way, I heard about your wife." Legrand reached out to place a hand on Nathan's arm. "Such a tragedy, I am truly sorry. I can't imagine how it is to endure."

"Thank you, Philippe. I appreciate that. How is Dominique?"

"Oh, you know, enjoying herself I suppose. She prefers the warmer climates this time of year. At the moment, she's enjoying our property on Martinique."

"The pair of you have it rough. Has anybody ever told you?"

"We make do the best we can."

The helicopter lifted off the roof and headed east, back toward the center of Paris. Nathan watched as the Eiffel Tower came into view, and the Notre Dame Cathedral. They flew right over the large open space of the Place de la Concorde. "There's my hotel," Nathan mused as he spotted it.

"If we'd had the proper permits, I could have stopped to pick you up," Legrand chuckled. "But tell me, Nathan, what brings you back to Paris? More than a motorcycle holiday, I imagine."

Of course, Nathan couldn't be entirely frank about it, but then Legrand wouldn't have expected full transparency anyway. "I'm doing some research."

"I see. On your own?"

"In a sense."

Legrand's curiosity was evident as he tried to decide how hard to push it. In the end, he avoided any direct questions, though he did poke around at the periphery. "I read about your Secretary of State. That was unfortunate."

Nathan looked from Legrand to Claudette, absorbed with her mobile device, and then back to his friend. "It was a tragedy, no doubt, I feel for the families."

"This world can be cruel and dark, but I don't need to tell you that. Enlighten me, though, why the Midual? That is quite a specific request."

"I've read that these bikes are a spectacular piece of engineering, crafted with the care of a precision watch. I just had to try one for myself."

"I see. Well, you are in luck because I happen to have not one Midual, but two. We can take them for a ride."

"I will enjoy that, though I was hoping to borrow one for more than a day."

Again, Legrand eyed Nathan with a deep curiosity that he knew would never be satisfied. "Perhaps we can come up with a challenge."

Nathan was not in the mood for games, but neither was he in a position to argue. "You name it."

"Excellent. First I need to discuss a few issues with Claudette before we arrive."

"Of course, go right ahead." Nathan turned his gaze out the window as they crossed the eastern suburbs of Paris and headed into the countryside. He only paid marginal attention as Legrand and his assistant discussed the details of a potential property acquisition. It seemed that Legrand was looking to expand his operations. After twenty minutes, his vineyards came into view. It wasn't the first time Nathan had been here. He was fortunate enough to have been invited to a few of the Legrand's renowned private parties, where the French elite mingled around the pool with gourmet food and the finest Legrand champagne. These were titans of industry, models, movie stars, and political figures up to and including the Prime Minister himself. When Nathan was with the CIA, associating with these people was part of his job, but with Legrand there was always more to it than that. The pair of them clicked from the start, and while Nathan understood that it was a mistake to take any of these relationships too personally, he did consider Legrand a friend. And why not? Philippe had a larger-than-life personality, and he was just plain fun to be around. He was a man who drank deeply from the cup of life, somebody who would reach his deathbed with no regrets. To use a sports metaphor, Philippe Legrand was leaving everything on the field. Nathan admired him for that. The man was an inspiration. It did help that he was born with a platinum spoon in his mouth, but Nathan didn't hold that against him.

The helicopter crossed over rolling hills as it approached the chateau, an enormous Gothic residence three-stories tall with manicured gardens laid out around a large, round fountain. Attached to the main building was a long garage where Legrand kept his vehicle collection. As Nathan already knew, this included both automobiles and motorcycles. On the far side of the garden was a helicopter pad with a round, white circle with a cross in the middle. The pilot lowered the craft to the ground dead center and began going through his checklist to shut down the engine. Two staff members hurried across the lawn from the chateau, ducking low to avoid the prop wash. The door was opened and Nathan removed his headset before following Claudette down the stairs with Philippe and the security guards right behind. When they reached the chateau, the group moved inside the cavernous foyer. Philippe took a quick look at his watch. "This shouldn't take me more than an hour," he said to Nathan. "Make yourself at home in the meantime. You know where to find the kitchen. Have Francoise make you something special."

"Thank you, Philippe."

Legrand put a hand on Nathan's shoulder. "Of course."

"Your guests are waiting in the blue room," said a man who appeared to be the butler.

Legrand turned next to Claudette. "Shall we?"

"Yes, sir." The pair of them moved off, leaving Nathan in the foyer with another member of the staff.

"Would you like some lunch while you wait?" said the woman.

"Absolutely."

Nathan ate alone in the main dining room at a long table beneath a sprawling chandelier, with a single server watching over him. The afternoon sunlight streamed in through a section of floor-to-ceiling windows. As he munched down on a meal of beef bourguignon over noodles, he gazed up at a ten-foot Medieval tapestry hanging on one wall, wondering how much more that rug was worth than the condo he owned in Virginia. He felt as though he were having lunch in the Palace of Versailles. Let them eat cake, indeed. He'd been offered his choice of wines, but opted for sparkling water instead. Whatever Philippe had in mind for this challenge he'd mentioned, Nathan wanted to remain sharp.

When the meal was finished Nathan still had some time to kill, so he let the server clear his dishes and excused himself. He was dying to check out those motorcycles and couldn't bring himself to wait any longer. He would go take a look. Nathan put his jacket back on and made his way through the foyer and out the front door, then walked toward the long garage. Parked in front of one bay was a black Bentley sedan. Beside the car was a chauffeur. standing with his sleeves rolled up and applying a coat of wax. "Bonjour," Nathan said as he walked past.

"Bonjour Monsieur," the man replied.

Nathan went through the open garage door and entered a large interior space. Spread out before him were multiple rows of classic automobiles, each and every one of them in immaculate condition. It was like Philippe Legrand's own personal auto museum. Nathan strolled down the first row, where he saw a red Ferrari beside a blue Lamborghini and a sleek, rust-colored McLaren F1. Continuing on was a selection of racing cars, still painted in their original livery. Nathan recognized what looked like the Porsche 917K from the Steve McQueen movie, *Le Mans*:

Powder blue with an orange stripe down the middle and the number 20 emblazoned on the hood.

In the far back corner of the garage, the motorcycles were gathered together in a clutch. Nathan counted twelve in all. Perhaps the showiest bike was a Harley Davidson Electra Glide, blue and white with a gleaming chrome engine, just begging to be taken for a ride. Beside it was a burly black Indian Chief. These bikes were all well and fine, but Nathan continued past a few Japanese supersports until he came to the prize that he sought. Side-by-side was the pair of Midual Type-1's, the first one with a blue fuel tank and the other in red. Each was a thing of beauty, almost enough to take Nathan's breath away. He approached the blue bike and did a full circuit, 360-degrees around it to take the whole thing in. This was as finely-crafted a machine as he had ever seen, with gleaming chrome fenders and wheels, and a solid, muscular engine. It was only now that Nathan realized what a big ask it was to borrow one. Putting a scratch on it was simply not an option. These bikes were built to be ridden, but an actual museum almost seemed like a better place for them. He threw one leg over the blue bike and sat on the seat, placing his hands on the handgrips, and feeling so comfortable that it seemed like this bike was custom made just for him. How did Khalil Haddad ever afford one? Whatever he was up to, the pay was awfully good. Now that Nathan was unemployed, the prospect of ever owning one himself seemed entirely out of the question, but a man could still dream.

"I see you found your way." Legrand's voice echoed through the garage as he appeared in the open doorway, now wearing a gray and black one-piece leather riding suit.

"All done with your meeting?"

"Finis. Time to ride." Legrand strode across the garage with purpose.

"What did you have in mind?"

"We can begin with a nice cruise through the countryside."

"I'm not going to argue with that."

From a cabinet along the back wall, Legrand took out a helmet and then found one for Nathan and handed it across. "Try this."

Nathan slid the helmet on, snug but not too tight. "Perfect."

Legrand passed across a pair of leather riding gloves and then put on his own, followed by his helmet. He cinched it tight, and then found two keys from a peg board on the wall, one with a red key chain and the other blue. He handed the blue one to Nathan.

When Nathan had his gloves on, he zipped up his leather jacket, inserted the key and pressed the electric starter. The bike rumbled to life. "After you."

Legrand started the red bike and led Nathan down the row and out of the garage, where they stopped side-by-side on the driveway. It was a cool, clear autumn in the late afternoon. Perfect riding weather. "There is a track nearby. We could see what these beasts can do."

"Something tells me you already know."

"Perhaps we can make a wager."

"I wouldn't expect anything less."

"Follow me." Legrand lowered his visor, popped his bike into first gear and raced off down the lane. Nathan roared after him, through a front gate and off the property. Together, they wound up and around the rural roads, through the village of Epernay and out the other side. After half an hour, Legrand pulled off the road and followed a private drive until they came to another gate manned by a single guard in a booth.

"Bonsoir, Monsieur Legrand," said the man.

"Anybody on the track?"

"No, Monsieur, it is all yours."

Legrand gave him a salute and then led Nathan through. Inside was an asphalt race track, presently deserted. The two men pulled onto the center and stopped with front wheels lined up against a starting line. They lifted their visors. "I love coming here in the evenings, it helps me unwind," said Legrand.

"I guess that means you have home-field advantage."

Legrand smiled in response. "We need to determine the stakes."

"What did you have in mind?"

Legrand gave it a moment's thought. "If you win, you borrow the bike as long as you want, no strings attached."

"And if you beat me?"

"I take home full bragging rights."

"Of course, that goes without saying, but I don't get the bike?"

"You prove to me that you're worthy." Legrand smiled again. "And you get the bike."

This, of course, was more than fair. It was really their egos on the line. "All right."

"Perhaps, if you feel inclined, you could even tell me what it is all about."

"Perhaps," Nathan replied. He didn't mind the prospect of telling Legrand some of it, anyway. If he'd still been working for the CIA that would be impossible but now he was on his own. "One condition. Whatever I say stays between us."

"Mais oui, of course. Shall we say, three laps?" Legrand revved his engine and then lowered his visor. Nathan swung down his own in response. As soon as his right hand was back on the throttle, Legrand took off like a rocket. Nathan raced after, playing catch-up from the start. This machine had a seemingly endless reserve of raw power, and they drew neck and-neck down the opening straightaway, reaching speeds of 225 kilometers per hour before braking into the first turn, a wide arc to the left. Never having ridden this course, not even once in practice, put Nathan at a distinct disadvantage. He had no way to know what was up ahead. If he held too much velocity through one turn, he might not be able to handle the next. If he played it too cautiously, Legrand would beat him. Nathan decided it was best to hang close behind his adversary for the first few go-arounds, to get a sense of the terrain, then go all-out through the final lap. Hanging on to Legrand's tail was even more difficult than Nathan might have expected. The Frenchman had talent. Nathan himself had some history of racing in his background, first dirt bikes through the wilds of his native Texas, and then sport bikes for a short period in his late teens. He'd won a few races, but this was something else. Each time they came to a turn, Nathan fell a little farther behind. He made up some of that distance in the straightaways, but as they came into the very final turn, he was a good sixty meters back with two laps to go.

At the apex of the turn, Nathan spotted a gravel patch extending out onto the track. He felt his rear wheel lose traction just a little as he clipped the side of it, but he recovered and bent low into the stretch as he gained incrementally on Legrand. On the second lap he felt better, anticipating the course. By the time he came around that last turn again, he knew to avoid the gravel and was now only forty meters back. He still needed to pick up the pace.

Legrand weaved through to turns on the final lap, eyeing Nathan as he closed the gap. When they approached that very last turn, Nathan was only three meters back this time. It was coming down to the wire. If only he'd had one more lap, he thought, he might pull out the win. Legrand looked back for the flash of an instant in the turn. Nathan ran slightly wide to avoid the gravel, but Legrand hit it dead on. Nathan saw the back wheel wobble. They were doing 145 kilometers an hour as Legrand struggled for control, but it all happened too fast. His bike went down and as it slid across the asphalt on one side, Legrand ended up on top, like a wild sleigh ride from hell with sparks flying up into the air as he went. Nathan quickly braked and then watched in horror, unable to stop the wreck or do anything at all. Legrand slid off the bike and skidded across the pavement while the Midual erupted in flames, slammed into a hay bale and exploded in a thunderous burst of light and sound.

When Nathan slowed enough, he swung back around and raced to his friend, motionless on the track. "Philippe!" Nathan popped his bike on the kickstand and jumped off before leaning down, afraid to move the man.

Legrand sat up and took off his helmet. "Merde! You beat me!"

"Are you all right?! Are you hurt?"

After climbing to his feet, Legrand dusted himself off. "It seems I survived." He looked to his motorcycle, consumed by flames. "The same can't be said for her, I'm afraid."

"I hope you have insurance."

"I suppose we'll need to ride home together." Legrand pulled out his phone and made a call, directing one of his people to come out and retrieve the wreckage. When he hung up, he shook his head and managed a laugh. "I think we both could use a drink."

"Shouldn't you be going to the hospital?"

"It's nothing a good Scotch can't cure. Let's go."

They climbed onto the blue bike, with Nathan up front, and headed back toward the estate. It seemed Nathan would be able to borrow his Midual after all.

Chapter Seven

The meeting place was in the Bois de Boulogne, the expansive public park on the west side of Paris. It was a crisp day, with puffy white clouds in a deep blue sky. A tranquil pond was ringed by trees whose vibrant orange, red and yellow leaves reflected off the water. When Nathan pulled into the parking lot, he saw two Miduals parked in an empty section on the far side. He eased his across and pulled to a stop beside them. Two men stood next to their bikes, with helmets hanging from their handlebars. They eyed Nathan and his motorcycle as he shut off his ignition, propped the bike on its kickstand, and took off his helmet. "I'm guessing this is the Midual group?" he said.

One of the men was slightly overweight with a round, bald head and a drooping mustache. He wore a black leather jacket and matching riding pants. He reached out. "I'm Claude."

Nathan shook his hand. "Elias."

The other man was small and skinny with a gray jacket and blue jeans. "Vincent," the man said and they shook hands as well. "Welcome to the group."

"Thank you." Nathan climbed off his bike and joined them in waiting for the others. It didn't take long. Next to arrive was Gaston, a handsome man in his early 20s, in a flashy, multi-colored riding suit. His smile gave away a bright, optimistic personality. A few minutes later came one more. This arrival kept his eyes on Nathan when he pulled up. He wore a scuffed black and yellow jacket with black jeans and riding boots. He took off his helmet to reveal a scowl of distrust. This man was also in his early 20s and of what appeared to be North African descent, with curly dark hair and a carefully trimmed beard. It had to be Khalil Haddad. Nathan reached a hand forward. "Elias Mansour."

"Lebanese," Haddad said.

"Yes."

"My name is Hakim." He shook the outstretched hand.

"The Lion of Africa?" said Nathan. *Hakim* didn't respond, but he wasn't denying it.

"It's just Olive now. She likes to make us wait," said Gaston. "It reminds us who is in charge."

"Olive is definitely in charge," said Claude.

They stood around their bikes, a few of them smoking cigarettes as they waited for their leader to arrive. Gaston admired Nathan's machine. "I like the blue. How long have you had it?"

"Not long, but I thought I should connect with some other aficionados."

"You found the right group," said Claude.

"Have you ridden yours long?"

"Two years so far. Best bike I've ever owned. Precision craftsmanship from a true Frenchman."

Nathan tried not to focus undue attention on Haddad, but it was all he could do to keep his cool. Here was a kid directly involved in the secretary's assassination, and Haddad really did appear to be just that, as though he'd only just barely managed to grow his scraggly beard. He was the one Masterson should have targeted, but now Nathan was bound by his word. He'd told Babouche that he wouldn't kill his nephew, and Nathan intended to honor that promise. He was still intent on getting to the bottom of the whole affair, and making sure that everybody responsible paid a price one way or another. Haddad was not the man at the top of the pyramid. Maybe he passed along orders, but he didn't come up with them. Khalil Haddad did not conceive of this operation, Nathan was sure of that.

"You look like an American," Haddad said to him. "Sound like one, too."

"I was born in Beirut. And you?"

At this question, Haddad appeared annoyed. All eyes were on him. As Nathan was well aware, France was built on multi-ethnic layers of social status. Dating back to the colonial days, Algerians made up a sizable proportion of the French population but were often treated as second-class citizens. The keepers of traditional French culture never quite accepted them. It meant that a man of Haddad's descent was always made to carry around a simmering insecurity, as though he didn't quite belong. Now that spotlight was on him. "I was born in Algiers," he stated.

"Have you been here long?" Nathan knew already that it was three days at most.

Haddad's face turned red. "Plenty long." He turned away just as the sixth and final rider appeared, heading toward them across the parking lot in a sleek, skin-tight green and white leather suit with a matching green helmet, on an olive-colored bike. Olive herself. When she reached the men, she rode around them in a circle, as though staking her territory before pulling to a stop without getting off. Olive removed her helmet, set it on her fuel tank, and then swung her head to flip her long, dark hair onto her back. She was gorgeous and sexy, with dark red lipstick and deep, black eyes, exuding an aura of danger. This was a woman who pushed limits, both her own and everyone's around her. Nathan had no doubt that underneath that sheer outfit was a body covered in ink. When she looked the men over, a smirk crossed her lips. "You boys ready to go?"

"Hello Olive!" Haddad had the enthusiasm of a boy with a deep and painful crush.

"Welcome to Paris, kid." Olive turned her attention to Nathan, looking him up and down before putting her helmet back on. "Let's go." She swung down her visor.

The others mounted their bikes and a roar took over the otherwise quiet morning in the Bois de Boulogne as they started them up and then followed Olive's lead heading south. They continued in a pack, weaving around traffic through the outskirts of the city. After twenty minutes they joined quieter country roads where they could let the throttles rip. Speeding tickets apparently didn't concern them. Slower vehicles provided a game of chicken to see who had the courage, or the stupidity, to pass in the closest of quarters. Olive egged them on, whipping around cars and trucks into oncoming traffic before dipping back to the right lane at the last possible moment. Anybody who failed at these tests of bravery was left behind. Olive waited for no man.

By the time they were halfway to the Loire Valley, it was down to four of them, and as they drew nearer, just three. Olive slowed and then pulled into the long, stately drive of a fairytale castle, with tall stone towers topped by blue tiles. Rapunzel herself could have lived in this place. They continued across a square out front, over a draw bridge, and entered an interior courtyard, where Olive pulled to a stop and parked. Nathan and Gaston pulled up beside her. Olive took her helmet off and gave them both a sly smirk. "Nicely done."

"We seem to have lost a few." Nathan shut off his engine.

"They know where to find us. I like to keep it interesting. Let's go find our table, shall we?"

"After you."

Leaving gloves and helmets outside, the first arrivals followed Olive through a massive front door, across the entryway and out to a restaurant in back, where they were shown to a table surrounded by an autumn garden with clear, plastic overhead tents to keep the chill at bay. It certainly beat the dingy, beat-up biker bars that most American motorcycle gangs hung out at.

"How did you find this place?" said Gaston.

"I've lived in Paris half my life."

"I've lived here all my life, I've never been here."

Olive seemed pleased by the remark. "It sounds like you need to get out more." When the stragglers began to trickle in some minutes later, it was evidently a walk of shame, though a few seemed more accustomed to the ignominy than others. Khalil Haddad did not take it particularly well. Not only did his arrival second from the last mean that he couldn't sit beside his beloved Olive, but he'd also been handily beaten by a girl. His surly attitude only deepened. Nathan knew that to play on it, all he had to do was be as charming as possible to their host. That would drive the boy to distraction. And so they ordered their lunch, and Nathan flirted, and Olive soaked up the attention of five manly bikers hanging on her every word. Now Nathan just needed to figure out where he was headed with this. What was his next step? If he'd still been working with Graham Masterson, he'd have been able to pass this information along and let them take the lead, but after the way things went down in Oran he still didn't trust them, and was certain that the feeling was mutual. Nathan was a logical, thinking human being. Taking orders in the Army was one thing, but it didn't work as well in this game. He watched Haddad stewing on the other side of the table. Before dessert arrived, Nathan excused himself to use the facilities. Vincent helpfully pointed the way. "Though the main foyer on the right," he directed.

"Merci." Nathan walked off across the terrace. As a matter of course, he did use the men's room, but when he came back out, instead of immediately rejoining the others, he took a detour into the courtyard. He'd come prepared. From one of his pockets, he pulled out two small, round tracking disks. These were not agency-issued, they were standard, off-the-shelf electronics. He'd picked them up at a small shop just a few blocks from his hotel that very morning. They'd work as well as anything the agency might have given him, plus they were connected to a free, downloadable app. Easy. The only problem was that he'd only brought two of them with him. He'd liked to have placed one on each bike, but as it was he'd have to choose. Of course, the first would be Haddad. That was without question, but the second? It had to be Olive. He doubted she had any involvement in the Parsons assassination, but it was best to keep an eye on her whereabouts just in case. From his other pocket, he took out a small vial of super glue and approached Haddad's motorcycle. He had to place them somewhere out of sight that wouldn't interfere with the mechanics of the bike. Nathan got down on one knee and looked up under the seat. This would do perfectly. He dabbed some glue on the first disk and then pressed it against a clean metal surface, holding it in place until it stuck. Next, he moved to Olive's bike and repeated the process. When he was finished, he hurried back in to join the others before he was missed.

After taking his place once more, Nathan considered how this whole thing might play out. If he was able to somehow get on Haddad's good side, they might become friends. Then he could work him a bit at a time to find out who his other contacts were. Was that even possible? More likely was that he'd follow the tracking disk to locate Haddad's address and then search the apartment when he wasn't home. Nathan would gather what intelligence he could and try to work his way up the ladder. When he was ready, he could pass it along to French intelligence and let them take care of it their own way. Nathan still had plenty of contacts over at the Directorate General. Of course, he'd still try to butter up Haddad as best he could, in case anything useful slipped out. "So, tell me, Hakim, what made you fall in love with the Midual?" Nathan used the name Haddad had given, though he knew it was fake, just like his own.

The entire table was sharing in this conversation when an even later arrival joined the group. Nobody seemed to expect him besides Olive, who looked up at the newcomer with a sensual smile.

"Hey baby," the man walked across the terrace and leaned down to kiss her on the lips. He was a burly dude, with biceps bulging beneath a tight blue sweater. His head was round and shaved smooth. Nathan was the only one who noticed Haddad squirm uncomfortably in his seat.

Olive turned to the chair beside her, currently occupied by Gaston. "Do you mind making some room?" she asked.

All eyes were on Gaston as it dawned on him that he was expected to move. "Oh! But of course." He scrambled to lift his cake and coffee as he relocated to a chair at the far end of the table. The newcomer didn't thank him, just took the now vacant spot beside his prize and then finally looked around to at least acknowledge the existence of the others, satisfied with his show of dominance.

"Meet Girard," Olive announced.

"No Midual?" Claude shook his head, pursing his lips in faux disapproval.

"The motorcycles, that is not for me," said Girard. "I am here for the cake."

"No motorcycle?!" Vincent seemed shocked that Olive could associate with such a person.

"I hope you do not mind that I join your little party."

"Not at all," Nathan replied. Something about the guy was ringing his alarm bells. More than that, he sensed an uncomfortable familiarity about the man, though Nathan couldn't quite place it. He might have come across him at some point in the past, but not knowing for sure put him in dangerous territory, He certainly couldn't ask. Instead, Nathan did his best to play it off. "My name is Elias," he offered a hand.

Girard shook the hand, but a flash of unspoken recognition showed in his eyes as well. "A pleasure."

"This is Vincent, Claude, Gaston and Hakim," Nathan made the introductions. Apparently, Olive couldn't be bothered.

Girard gave a wave and then turned his attention to the cafe. "Who do we speak to for some service?"

A waiter sidled up to their table with notepad in hand and after a brief chat, Girard ordered a coffee and a chocolate cake. Olive caressed his back and purred as Girard looked at Nathan with a quizzical expression. He raised one finger in the air. "Have we met?"

"I don't believe so."

This answer didn't satisfy Girard. "What did you say your name was?"

"Elias."

"Where are you from, Elias?"

"I was born in Beirut."

"I have many friends in Beirut, maybe you know them."

"I doubt it. I left that city as a boy. I've been wandering ever since. First with my parents and now on my own."

"Pity. What's your surname?"

"Mansour. And yours?"

From his furrowed brow it was clear Girard didn't like the tables being turned. He didn't want to be the one facing questions.

"Boucher," Olive answered for him.

Nathan shook his head. "I can't say that rings a bell."

"I have a cousin named Henri Boucher," said Claude. "Any relation?"

"No."

"Boucher is a very common name," said Vincent.

Something about Nathan seemed to have set Girard off, and the feeling was mutual. Nathan continued to scan his memory banks, and then finally it hit him. Three years earlier in Marseille, he'd managed to flip a member of the notorious Bou Zadjar drug cartel. It was an unusual arrangement. Hardened criminals didn't usually cooperate with the CIA, but Nathan had enough on the man to threaten many years behind bars. The cartel was known to be ruthless, their methods particularly brutal. To run afoul of them was to end up dead in the most painful of ways. Torture came as second nature, but that meant defections were exceedingly rare. The Zadjar cartel trafficked illicit narcotics from North Africa into Europe, but what interested the CIA was the flow of weapons that went the other way. Guns, ammunition and explosives were smuggled from Eastern Europe and Asia to the South of France. Bou Zadjar provided transportation for the last leg of the journey, across the Mediterranean Sea and into Algeria.

In his mind, Nathan flashed back to a seedy, port-side bar where he'd met one night with his contact. It was merely a brief update, to verify a few bits of information about a pending shipment, but then three men entered the bar and the contact went white as a ghost. Nathan remembered it clearly now. An unusual hush descended over the place as soon as these men stepped across the threshold. They were well-known, but nobody wanted to admit it. Instead, the other patrons pretended to go about their business quietly, not wanting to draw any undue attention to themselves. Nathan's contact slid his chair so that he faced the opposite direction.

"Friends of yours?" Nathan had said, but the contact didn't respond. He seemed unable to speak at all. As the men wandered through the bar, Nathan looked them over, trying to commit their faces to memory. One man was small and wiry, with creases in his well-worn cheeks. Another was fat and round, with an enormous baggy sport coat and pants that clung tightly to his prodigious belly. A third man had bulging biceps, and a round, smooth head. When their eyes met, Nathan detected a calm yet calculated malice. Though he'd only seen the man for a few brief moments at that time, he should have made the connection immediately. Now he had a name to put with that face. Girard Boucher.

That night in the bar, he'd had no conversation with the men at all. Instead, the threesome was escorted to a private room in the back, but that was the last time Nathan ever saw his contact. The very next night the man was found floating dead in the harbor with all of his fingernails ripped out and gunshot wounds to the thighs, abdomen, and ultimately the head. If Boucher made the same connection now, Nathan risked ending up with a similar fate. The Frenchman gave it another moment's thought before seeming to give up. He turned his attention back to his girl, flashing Olive a smile and feeding her a bit of chocolate cake.

Nathan was beginning to connect some of the various dots in this drama, though there were still many unanswered questions. He understood where the anti-aircraft missiles likely came from. Bou Zadjar provided the weapons, and Khalil Haddad directed their use. That still didn't explain who was behind it all. Why would a drug cartel want to assassinate the American Secretary of State? Of course, why did a drug cartel do anything? Money was always the answer to that, but who was paying them?

The rest of the lunch was relatively uneventful, with Haddad continuing to seethe at Girard's presence but saying very little. Claude and Vincent chatted mostly amongst themselves. Eventually, the little party broke up. The bill was divided and they headed out for their journey back to Paris. In the courtyard, parked beside their motorcycles was a Bugatti Veyron sports car. Nathan knew already that this machine had a top speed of over 250 mph, making it the fastest production sports car in the world when it was introduced. Maybe Boucher wasn't a motorcycle guy, but he certainly had a thing for speed, as well as very expensive tastes and the resources to satisfy them. He gave Olive another ostentatious kiss on the lips and then squeezed his way into the car and fired it up. The rest of the group donned their helmets and climbed onto their bikes. The roar of so much horsepower in one enclosed space reverberated off the ancient stone walls and shook the foundations as the parade moved out the gate and across the draw bridge. They reached the road and turned toward Paris, staying together in a pack this time as they went. Having beaten the men once, Olive's ego was satisfied for the day.

Nathan rode behind Gaston, with the other bikes staggered ahead and the Bugatti following behind. As they drew closer to the city, Boucher grew impatient, hitting the accelerator as he flew past, leaving Olive and the others in his dust. The man was in a hurry. As for the rest of them, they peeled off one by one, heading toward their individual homes. Passing inside the ring road, it was only Nathan and Olive left. He gave a nod before losing her in traffic. Only then did he head toward his hotel. Nathan pulled into the underground parking garage and found a space before taking the elevator up to his room. Closing the door behind him, he placed his gloves and helmet on the desk and then took out his phone. He opened the location finding app for his two tracking disks. A map of Paris showed two pulsing blue dots, one for each disk. The first one was moving north, entering the Barbes neighborhood in the 18th arrondissement near Montmarte. This was a well-known Algerian quarter, a little bit rough. This dot came to a stop just off the Boulevard Barbes. Khalil Haddad was home? Or was it Olive? It was the other dot that surprised Nathan. This one was stationary, just outside his hotel on the Rue de Rivoli. Nathan stepped out onto his balcony. From his view on the third floor, he saw cars passing up and back in both directions, and pedestrians scurrying along the sidewalk. Half a block away, on the other side of the street, he saw a woman in a green and white leather riding suit, straddling an olive-colored Midual motorcycle. Her visor was up as she scanned his hotel's facade. "Oh, you're good, Olive," Nathan said to himself. "Very, very good."

Chapter Eight

Sophie Journet was an officer with the GIGN, the National Gendarmerie Intervention Group. This was an elite counter-terrorism strike force, responsible for hostage rescues, terrorist surveillance and arrest, and various special operations. Nathan knew Journet well. During his posting in France, the CIA and GIGN cooperated on a number of issues and Journet was Nathan's point person for sharing information. They'd always had a good working relationship. Now Nathan needed some help. The question was, would she notify Langley, or could Nathan trust her to keep the whole thing confidential? In this business, trust was very hard to come by, but he'd decided to take the chance. Now he sat waiting in a cafe facing the courtyard at the Louvre. In the center of the square, he saw tourists wandering in and out of the modern glass pyramid that functioned as the entrance to the famed museum. Right on time, he spotted Sophie strolling briskly toward him through the crowd. She wore a navy-blue skirt and a matching blazer that showed off her biceps underneath. Her long brown hair was tied back in a ponytail. He'd always considered her to be attractive, though she had an edge about her. Sophie was perfectly pleasant when the situation called for it, but she was also tough as nails. She entered the cafe and made her way to Nathan's table. He stood and kissed her on each cheek.

"Bonjour, Nathan! What a pleasant surprise," she said.

"Bonjour, Sophie. Thank you for meeting me."

"I was under the impression that you had retired, yet somehow I don't believe this is a personal visit. Am I correct?"

"As always."

Sophie eyed him with curiosity as they took their seats. Nathan waved over a server and they each ordered a cafe crème and some pastries. When the server had gone, Sophie took a quick look around to make sure no other patrons were within earshot. Of course, they both knew that electronically, anybody could be listening at any time. One always had to be careful. "So, tell me, Nathan, what is this about?"

"I'm in a bit of a bind, Sophie, but I'd like some assurances that what I share with you today doesn't get back to my former employer."

This request seemed to catch her off guard. "You know I can't make that kind of blanket promise. What sort of trouble are you in?"

"It's not that I'm in trouble. Not exactly. It's more that I just need some space to figure a few things out."

"What sorts of things?"

"This is going to sound a little crazy, I know."

"If you want my help, you will need to be forthright with me. I don't have the time or inclination for anything less."

"Yes, I understand." Nathan knew exactly how unusual this was. "I'm tracking the network that blew up Joshua Parsons' plane in Africa."

"For who?"

"Myself."

This answer caught Sophie completely by surprise. "What do you mean, yourself? You must be working for somebody. A contractor, perhaps?"

"No, I mean myself. I want to know what happened, that's all, to satisfy my own curiosity and maybe pass along the information to somebody who can make use of it."

"You're tracking an international terrorist organization as a hobby? That is what you do in your retirement? Please, Nathan."

"Full disclosure, I was briefly working as a contractor myself, for my former bosses. I didn't approve of their methods."

"Which methods?"

"Assassinating an innocent man."

"Here, in Paris?! You can't mean it."

"No, no, not in France. I was to have fulfilled my contract in North Africa. Suffice to say, I didn't carry it out. Instead, my target led me here."

Sophie eyed Nathan with a look of disappointment. "I would never have pegged you as an assassin. I thought you had higher standards than that, more respect for the rule of law. I hope you are not asking me to help you murder someone, even if he is a terrorist. Frankly, I am beginning to regret taking this meeting with you, Nathan. I must inform you that if you break the law in France, I will commit the full resources of my position to come after you. Our friendship offers no protection."

"Nor would I expect it to. My goal is not to break the law."

"What is your goal, Nathan, you have already said that the man was innocent, have you not?"

"My original target, yes, but now I am on the trail of those who were actually responsible. I want to trace everyone involved, at every level. The GIGN can take all of the credit, but these people must be held accountable. I'm talking arrests, Sophie."

At this, Sophie's demeanor shifted slightly. "Are your former employers aware that you are in Paris?"

"I would never underestimate them."

"Of course not." Sophie cocked her head to one side and paused as the server returned with two cafe crèmes, a pain au chocolate and a croissant. He placed them on the table. "Anything else?" he said.

"Non, merci," Nathan replied and then waited until the server walked away before taking a sip of his coffee.

"Tell us everything you know and we will take it from there. That is the best I can offer, I am afraid," said Sophie.

"I want to be involved, to see this through to the end."

Sophie was still highly skeptical. "I will need to discuss this with my superiors. If they agree, we will take you in to a secure facility for a full debriefing."

"I'd prefer if we avoided your headquarters. Our people tend to monitor the comings and goings around there."

"Why the concern? You only just told me you were not in any kind of trouble."

"I'd prefer to keep a low profile, that's all."

Sophie thought it over. The entire thing put her on edge. "I can arrange to debrief you in one of our safe houses, someplace your people know nothing about. I would hope, after all of our history working together, that you would maintain discretion regarding the location."

"They won't find out anything about it from me, I can promise you that." Nathan broke off a piece of pain au chocolate and took a bite. It was all buttery, flaky goodness with a rich chocolate center. The French certainly knew how to live. While he finished his coffee, Sophie went outside to make some calls in private. When she returned, he paid the bill and they headed out together. "How far is it?" he asked.

"Not far. We can walk."

"I'm glad to be working with you again, Sophie."

"Just don't make me regret it."

The meeting went well enough, though of course, Nathan provided more information than he got in return. He shared some photos he'd managed to snap at his lunch in the Loire Valley, gave Sophie and two of her colleagues the names of everybody involved, plus the full background story as he knew it. He also shared the data from the two tracking disks that he'd fixed to the motorcycles. Before Nathan had turned off his phone that morning, Haddad's bike was still parked in the Barbes neighborhood. Olive was on the outskirts of the city but heading back toward the center. Nathan did learn more about the group's suspected drug running. They'd been under the watchful surveillance of the French state for some time, but while the occasional shipment was intercepted, the cartel's leadership always managed to escape arrest. In fact, nobody outside the cartel itself seemed to know the leader's identity, and those inside were far more terrified of giving up the name than they were of spending the rest of their lives in prison. To betray their leader meant certain death, they all understood. The authorities had a fair amount of detail on some of the lower-level members of the gang, all of whom had extensive criminal records and some of whom were currently behind bars. As for the head of the organization, there were only rumors. Some said it was a man of North African descent, raised in a poor family yet determined to make the whole world pay for the struggles he'd endured. Others claimed it was a woman of high society from the south of France, keeping her dark secret as she blended in with the wealthy elite. To law enforcement, this person was merely a shadow. Various nicknames emerged from time to time, but the one that stuck was The Fox. That could have meant either a man or a woman, but bringing this person to justice was already one of Sophie's highest priorities.

As for Olive, she was known to be an up and comer. Born Olivia Alami in Morocco, she'd moved with her family to a housing block in the Saint-Denis neighborhood at a young age, where she'd gained a reputation for ruthlessness. One didn't mess with Olivia, the rest of the children in the neighborhood learned quickly. Girard was equally vicious. He was the muscle, not the philosophical type. These days, Olivia was suspected of handling the occasional special project, but this was the first anybody at GIGN had heard of a possible cartel connection with the Parsons assassination. If Olivia Alami was indeed involved, the first question was why? What could possibly be worth generating that much scrutiny? At least now Nathan had some highly competent analysts on his side. These were people who'd spent their entire careers trying to track this Fox down. Though they hadn't had much luck so far, Nathan was glad to have their help.

After leaving the safe house, Nathan opted to take a stroll along the Seine to clear his head. He joined the river near the Pont Marie and crossed over to the Ile Saint-Louis. From there, he continued onto the Ile de la Cite and wandered past the facade of the Notre Dame Cathedral, still under repair after the tragic fire some years earlier. As he walked, Nathan did his best to unravel this mystery in which he found himself enmeshed. He had a list of players now, but no good explanation for how or why they were connected. Perhaps they weren't connected at all. What did Nathan *really* know? He knew that Khalil Haddad sent texts directing the assassins, through his uncle's phone. Afterward, he fled Algeria on his motorcycle and headed to Paris where he was obsessed with a career criminal who had a boyfriend known to be an enforcer in the same drug cartel. Nathan had no proof that Olive and Girard were involved with the Parsons affair directly. That would open them up to an awful lot of heat themselves, but then again, for the right price they were capable of just about anything. If somebody was offering enough to carry out the assignment, an enterprising woman like Olive might be interested.

Nathan crossed back across the Pont Neuf, stopping in the center of the cobblestone bridge to take in the view. Eyeing the Seine below and the classic French architecture of the buildings along the river, it was almost ridiculously romantic. Tall, stately trees lined the banks, and their bright autumn leaves reflected off the water. Jenna would have been entirely in her element here. He could almost picture her standing beside him with a bright smile on her face. "I'm sorry, babe," he said quietly. "I'm in it. I just can't let it go." Nathan continued across the bridge and then followed a path along the river, heading in the general direction of his hotel. Graham Masterson flashed through his mind, triggering a mixture of anxiety and guilt. Nathan still had some degree of loyalty to the organization. He'd spent nearly a decade of his life working for them. They deserved to know everything that he did, but then again, the way things had played out in Oran shook Nathan's confidence in both Masterson and the agency. They'd definitely be looking for him now, but what would they do if they found him? They weren't going to bump him off just because he failed to complete an assignment. He couldn't imagine that a man like Masterson was quite that callous. Eventually, they would undoubtedly track him down, to talk, but he'd deal with that when it came to pass. For now, it just seemed like a better option to try and stay one step ahead of them.

When Nathan reached the Tuileries, he left the river and strolled through the gardens, past a large, round pond with a towering fountain in the center. Mothers pushed babies in strollers, and toddlers played on the lawn. Lovers sat on benches holding hands. Nathan exited the garden onto the Rue de Rivoli and spotted Olive immediately. She was on her motorcycle not far away, parked along the side of the road with her helmet on and her visor down, yet looking straight at him. Nathan stood where he was, scanning the rest of the area. Fifty meters further up the road was Khalil, with two burly thugs in black leather jackets. Nathan turned back toward the park, but as he took a step, he ran nearly headlong into Girard Boucher. The man had somehow managed to sneak up on him from behind.

"Look who we have here." Boucher stood tall, puffing out his chest as he blocked Nathan's way.

"Move aside, Girard."

"No, no, I'm afraid not. You'll have to come with us, you see. We have some questions for you."

Nathan turned back to see the others all headed toward him across the gravel at a rapid clip. The time to make a break for it was now, before they got any closer. He was about to bolt when Boucher pulled a gun from his jacket pocket.

"You're not going to make this difficult, are you Elias?"

"You must want to talk to me awfully bad."

"Let's go." He nodded toward the street.

Nathan made a quick calculation. He could still run, and take the chance that Boucher wouldn't shoot him in such a public place, or he could go with them and take the chance that talking was all they really had in mind. Neither one of these seemed like a good option, but he decided to take his chances with the questions. Boucher walked behind him as they headed toward the boulevard. A black van pulled up and the side door slid open. Nathan was shoved inside. An armed thug joined him, sitting one row behind. The door swung shut. Outside the window, he watched Olive, Girard, and Khalil have a brief conversation. Girard climbed into the passenger seat of the van and the two others followed behind on their motorcycles as they pulled off down the street.

"You thought I wouldn't remember you," Boucher twisted around to look backward. "But I never forget a face."

"That's very handy."

Boucher scowled as he eyed Nathan with distaste. The van continued on through the city traffic. Nathan was beginning to wish he'd simply run when he had the chance.

Chapter Nine

They taped him to a chair in the back office of a shuttered auto repair shop, fastening him tightly around the ankles and wrists. Four of Nathan's adversaries crowded into the room; Olive, Girard, Khalil, and another of the armed thugs who brought him here. Olive was clearly in command, though she was disturbed. Whatever Girard Boucher said about Nathan had triggered her. She paced up and down in front of him, arms crossed as she considered how to proceed, then stopped in front of Nathan to peer at him head-on. "Girard says you are American, that you work for your Central Intelligence Agency."

"That's not true."

Olive furrowed her brow and gave a quick look to Girard, who shook his head.

"You know, my boyfriend, he loves to administer pain. Sometimes a little bit too much, even for me," she gave Girard a sly smile before continuing. "So tell me, American. Let's start with an easy one. What is your name?"

"My name is Elias Mansour."

"Liar!" shouted Haddad, who sat sulking on a nearby desk.

"It seems you've upset our friend, here," Olive said to Nathan. "We wouldn't want that, now would we? Let's try again, what is your name?"

This time, Girard stepped close, flexing his muscles and clenching his fists while he waited for the answer.

"Elias Mansour," said Nathan.

Girard pulled back one arm and punched Nathan hard in the stomach, knocking the wind out of him. As he struggled to breathe, Girard hit him again, this time across the jaw, leaving the taste of blood in Nathan's mouth. Girard wrapped his fingers in Nathan's hair and pulled his head up, leaning close so that their faces were inches apart. "Would you like to try again?"

"Nathan," he said this time. It went against his instincts to give up any information, but he couldn't quite see the point in concealing it. "Nathan Grant."

"That's better. And why are you following us, Nathan Grant?"

"Because I love the Midual motorcycle. It's a beautiful blend of style and power."

Again, Girard hit him hard in the face. It wasn't the first time that Nathan had been made to endure such a beating, but they never got any easier. The pain shot through him like an electric current. Girard knew how to inflict some damage, and this was going to show if Nathan made it out of here alive, though that was looking increasingly dicey. "Would you care to amend your answer?" The Frenchman lifted a large crescent wrench from a nearby table and held it in the air for Nathan to see. "Or would you prefer that we got down to business? You don't need those teeth of yours, do you? Because I could take care of that, free of charge."

"I prefer my teeth the way they are, if you'd like to know the truth."

Olive moved closer. "Then start talking, or I might let him knock your brains out next."

Nathan rubbed his tongue across his front teeth as he thought it over. What could he even say that might get him out of this predicament? He wracked his brains while he still had them. These people wouldn't hesitate to kill him in the most painful way possible, but he had to find a way to be worth more to them alive than dead.

"Why is it so hard to tell us what we want to know?" Olive continued.

"I'm not working for the CIA, I'm running from them."

"You will have to do better than that."

"It's true. We had a falling out. They asked me to do some things I wasn't comfortable with."

"What things?" said Girard.

"They wanted me to kill this one." Nathan nodded his head toward Haddad.

"Me?!" Haddad's face went pale.

"Not exactly. They wanted me to kill your uncle, to be precise."

"No!" Haddad jumped to his feet, seemingly unsure whether to work Nathan over with the wrench himself or merely flee the room. Nathan knew that he was taking a gamble here. If Olive and Girard were involved in the Parsons plot, they would kill him right away, end of story. But if they were not, and Khalil Haddad brought this pressure on them all by himself, then Nathan might potentially turn the others on the kid, switching the happy couple from adversaries to unlikely partners. At the very least, he might inject some hostility and distrust amongst them. That could buy him some time.

"What does his uncle have to do with this?" Olive eyed Haddad.

"He's lying!" said Haddad. "My uncle is a good man."

"I never said he wasn't, Khalil," Nathan replied. "And yes, I know your name is Khalil. Khalil Haddad."

Haddad came closer to Nathan, the veins in his forehead bulging with anger. "You know nothing."

"I followed you here, though, didn't I? From Oran? I knew just where to find you."

"Why did you follow him?" said Olive.

"To find out the truth."

"The truth about what?"

Nathan was giving too much away and getting nothing in return. If he was to sow doubt, he needed a better tactic. "More than just drugs, you deal in weapons," he said. "I know that much, but what about surface-to-air missiles? Is that something you've added to your catalog?"

Girard reached forward with the wrench until the cold steel came to rest on Nathan's forehead. "We're asking the questions here. Understand?"

"I'm just trying further the conversation."

"This is not a conversation," said Olive. "Why did they send you?"

"Look, I'm just spit-balling here..."

"What is this, spitting?" said Girard.

"Guessing. It means I'm guessing."

"You don't know why they sent you?" Olive watched Khalil as she tried to piece things together herself.

"I'll try to connect the dots. You brought young Khalil here into your organization as a representative in Northern Africa. Maybe you needed logistical assistance across the Mediterranean and Khalil was the man. He helped arrange the shipments, drugs north, weapons south. Or perhaps he organized the real estate end of it, lining up the warehouse space. "How am I doing so far?"

Girard peered at Khalil with the same doubt in his eyes.

"Kill him already!" Khalil cried out. "Bash his brains in!"

"I'd like to hear the rest of this." Olive looked to Nathan.

"All right," Nathan continued. "Well, young Khalil was responsible for storing the shipments in Algeria while they awaited a future home, but somehow a sideline venture came along. He'd always had his eye on this Midual, you see, but you weren't paying him enough to afford one. That's an expensive motorcycle. He needed it, though, for two reasons. Number one, I'll admit, it is a sweet ride. Who in their right mind wouldn't want a bike like that? But number two, that motorcycle was his ticket to get closer to you, Olive. Young Khalil has quite a crush on you. Just ask his uncle. If you can find him, that is. Unfortunately, his uncle had to go into hiding, because the CIA sent a contract assassin to bump him off."

"An assassin named Nathan Grant."

"I'd prefer not to come out and say that part directly, but yes, but you get the idea."

Khalil made his hands into tight fists as his face burned in humiliation. His eyes made a quick search of the room until they came to rest on a car jack sitting in the corner. Khalil lunged for the jack and pulled out the handle, a three-foot metal bar. In a flash, he came after Nathan, raising the bar in the air above his head and then bringing it down with force. Nathan was able to twist himself sideways, sending the chair crashing to the floor as the bar crashed down on the wooden armrest and glanced his forearm.

"Hey, hey!" Girard lunged after Khalil to restrain him, grasping the smaller man in a bear hug with his larger biceps. "Let's calm down now."

Khalil struggled to free himself, desperation washing over his face. The third man lifted his gun and pointed it at Khalil's head. "Easy, young one," he said.

"I think I touched a nerve," said Nathan, now on his side on the floor. "It seems our friend here doesn't appreciate the truth."

"We'll see about that." Olive turned to the gunman. "Lift him up."

The man handed his gun to Olive long enough to lift Nathan's chair upright, before taking the weapon back.

"Why the contract on his uncle?" Olive continued.

"Because young Khalil here set the man up to take the fall."

"For what?"

"The assassination of Joshua Parsons, the American Secretary of State. I'm sure you heard about that."

"Be careful before you begin to make accusations." Girard held tight to a squirming Khalil.

"Here's the way it went down, as far as I can tell," Nathan explained. "Your organization got your hands on some surface-to-air missiles and sent them south in search of a buyer. Khalil arranged to store them in a warehouse, but he didn't stop there. No, he is an enterprising young man. Not only did he find a buyer, but he also took on a project management position, directing the use of these missiles to murder the Secretary of State and everybody else aboard his plane."

"Is this true?" Olive asked Khalil. In response, he spat at Nathan but didn't say a word.

"Of course, he didn't want to be caught," Nathan continued. "Instead of using his own device to send the messages, he used his uncle's phone. He was right to worry, of course, because the CIA was monitoring the communications. They determined that Gamil Babouche was responsible, and they sent me in response." Nathan eyed Khalil again. "How am I doing so far?"

"I would die before I betrayed you," Khalil said to Olive.

"That much I believe," she replied.

"Whoever ordered the job paid him enough to buy a sweet new motorcycle that he rode to Paris to impress you with," said Nathan.

Girard squeezed Khalil Haddad tighter, like a serpent trying to choke the life out of his prey.

"Why don't you have one of your people in Oran do a little inventory check? See if any missiles and launchers are missing," Nathan added.

"Where did you get the money for the Midual, my friend?" Olive demanded of Khalil.

"You can't believe him!" he replied.

"Where did you get the money?"

"It is not my place to say," he growled.

"After all your uncle did for you..." said Nathan.

"You made a big mistake, young one," Girard hissed in Khalil's ear.

"What should we do with them?" said the man with the gun.

"I've had enough of this. Take this one out back and shoot him," she gestured toward Nathan. "Put the body in the work truck and dump him, the usual place."

"Hey, hey, wait a minute!" Nathan protested. "After all I've just given you? Come on!"

"Sorry, Mr. CIA. Your usefulness is over."

"Let me do it," Khalil smirked with pleasure. "I want to pull the trigger."

"No," said Olive before focusing on Girard once more. "Let's get rid of our Algerian friend as well. He's overstepped his bounds."

"Me?!" Khalil's joy turned to panic in an instant as he desperately squirmed to free himself, but Girard's strength was too much for him. "You can't! No! You don't understand!"

"Goodbye, young one." Olive gave him one last pitying look before she turned and left the room.

"I say we just shoot them right here," suggested the man with the gun.

"We do as she says," Girard countered. "The young one first. Get a tarp."

"No, not like this, you must listen to me!" Khalil begged for his life.

"What about him?" The man gestured to Nathan.

"He's not going anywhere." Girard dragged a kicking and struggling Khalil out of the room with the gunman right behind them. Nathan heard more commotion, with tearful cries for mercy. Alone in the office now, he quickly searched for any sharp objects he might use on the tape that bound him. He wouldn't have long, a minute or two at most before they came back for him. He saw the wrench on the table, and the metal bar from the jack on the floor.

"No, please, no!" Khalil shouted from somewhere out back, and then *bang*! A single gunshot rang out. The next sound was like a sack of potatoes dropping to the ground. Graham Masterson would have been happy to know that the man he was after, the real one and not his innocent uncle, had just paid the ultimate price for his crimes. How would he feel about Nathan Grant being next? Nathan wasn't so sure Masterson would care much, one way or another. To Nathan, it was the larger question that still nagged him, and that might go forever unanswered. Who paid Khalil to carry out this plot, and why? It seemed as though Nathan might not live long enough to find out.

"It looks like I'm coming, baby. You won't have to wait too long," Nathan said to the spirit of his wife, but he couldn't just sit back and let the bad guys win. Nathan would fight it out to the end, however he could. Backward and forward he rocked the chair until it crashed over to the floor once again, cracking the right armrest as it landed on the hard tile. Nathan pushed and twisted until his arm was mobile, still strapped to the shattered wood but with some range of motion. He used this hand to grasp the metal bar from the jack and managed to slide it underneath the tape on his opposite wrist. Using leverage, he wrenched at it, one, two, three twists until he was able to slide this hand out from the tape. Now only his ankles were bound. Did he have enough time? At any moment, Girard Boucher and his partner would burst back into the room. Nathan bent forward, using the bar on his right ankle. He'd made slight progress with the tape when the two men reappeared.

"Hey, hey, hey!" Girard hurried forward to grab the bar from Nathan's hands and yank it free.

"You can't blame me for trying."

Girard tossed the bar aside and then went through the desk drawers until he found a box cutter. He slid open the blade.

"Perhaps we should bleed him to death," said the gunman.

"How about you just let me go and we forget all about it?" said Nathan.

Girard use the box cutter to slice the tape from Nathan's ankles, then pulled him to his feet while the gunman kept him covered with the pistol. "We wouldn't want to disappoint Olive, now would we?"

"You could get her some flowers, you know, to make it up to her."

Girard pushed Nathan toward the door. As he stumbled forward, Nathan's eyes landed on the crescent wrench, still resting on the table. He took one more step before his right arm flew out and he lifted the heavy tool, swinging it around in one quick motion to crack the gunman on the wrist and send the pistol flying across the room. In the same motion, Nathan followed through and smashed the wrench against Girard's head, connecting with the right side of his skull. The man dropped to the ground, out cold. Next, he hit the head of the stunned gunman, who toppled onto Boucher. Two down.

Nathan dropped the wrench and picked up the box cutter. He removed the rest of the tape and then picked up the pistol and moved out of the office. In the garage, a few cars were parked in various states of disrepair. Nobody was in sight, unless you counted Khalil Haddad, whose corpse was spread out on a blue tarp just outside one of the open bays that led to a courtyard in back. Nathan would have preferred to wrest more information out of the kid, but it was too late for that. He was headed for the front door when it burst open with a bang and a blur of motion. Multiple figures appeared and almost before Nathan realized what was happening, he was surrounded by special forces troops in full body armor with automatic rifles. "Drop the weapon, down on the ground!" they shouted. "Hands on the back of your head!" Nathan did as commanded. His wrists were pulled behind his back and this time bound in handcuffs.

"You'll find two wounded in the office," he said to them. "I think the one out back is dead."

Nathan was dragged to his feet and taken out to the street, then thrown into the back of an armored truck. After what seemed like an interminable wait, the door opened and Sophie Journet ducked in. "Hello, Nathan."

"Sophie. Any chance you can take the cuffs off?"

"I'm afraid not. You left quite a mess in there."

"I didn't kill Haddad. That was the other two."

"You've put me in a very difficult position."

"You could have shown up sooner. Things would have been quite a bit less complicated that way."

"We got here as fast as we could."

"What about Olive?"

"We picked her up two blocks away."

Nathan looked upwards, toward the heavens. "Sorry, babe, I guess I won't be joining you yet."

"What?"

"Nothing. Just talking to myself."

Sophie looked Nathan over with concern. "First off, I think you need a doctor."

"As long as you're not taking me to jail."

She didn't seem entirely convinced. "I'll see what I can do."

Chapter Ten

After a brief examination at the hospital emergency room, Nathan was bandaged up, given prescription pain killers and cleared to go, by the doctor anyway. That didn't mean he was free to simply walk out. Instead, still handcuffed, he was taken by two uniformed members of the GIGN and placed in the back of a police vehicle, then driven to their headquarters. At least he wouldn't be spotted by any lurking CIA operatives, as he was brought in through a subterranean parking garage and then escorted straight into an elevator. Up five flights, he was made to sit in a small interrogation room.

"Can I get you anything while you wait?" said one of the officers.

"Coffee would be nice. Maybe a croissant." Nathan's voice came out slurred. Despite the painkillers, his face throbbed with pain. Where Girard had hit Nathan in the gut, the aching soreness reminded him of high school football and the day after a big game. That man certainly knew how to throw a punch. "I don't suppose you might take the handcuffs off now?"

With no response, Nathan was locked in, alone. A few minutes later, the officer returned with an espresso, an apple Danish, and the keys. "Merci," Nathan replied as the cuffs finally came off. The officer nodded before locking Nathan in the room once more. He didn't seem to be under arrest, officially. They hadn't processed him, or even taken his phone away. Apparently, all they wanted were some answers. Nathan could say the same. He lifted one hand to tenderly touch his swollen jaw.

After half an hour, the door opened again and Sophie Journet walked in along with a thin, distinguished-looking man with short gray hair. He was introduced as Inspector Nicolas Fontaine. Together, they had some questions for Nathan. Lots of questions. They asked exactly what had happened at the garage, of course, and what he could tell them about the others involved. Much of it was a repeat of what he'd told Sophie already. The fact that Nathan wasn't working with the CIA any longer complicated things, though of course they were going to contact the Americans, and Sophie couldn't do anything about that at this point. Graham Masterson would find out where Nathan was, and exactly what had gone down. What concerned Nathan more acutely at the moment was whether he might be facing murder charges. "What is the condition of the two men, Girard Boucher and the other one?"

"Ahmed Fadel is awake and stable. Boucher, he is in a coma. The doctors are not sure if he will survive," said Fontaine. "For your sake, let us hope so."

"It was self-defense," Nathan protested. "You saw what they did to Haddad. I was next."

"Yes, so you say."

"What have you learned from Ms. Alami?"

"Nothing yet," said Journet. "We thought we would speak with you first."

"Let me participate in her interrogation."

"No!" said Fontaine. "Out of the question. You're a private citizen, Mr. Grant, nothing more. You're not authorized to take part in any way."

"I can help you. I know what to ask."

"Tell us then. What do you think we should ask?"

"I want to be in the room."

Journet and Fontaine looked at each other. "He does have nearly ten years with the CIA," said Journet.

"We cannot risk compromising the investigation. Not a chance."

"Put me in an observation room, then. Let me watch. If I think you're missing anything, I'll send you a text."

The two agents considered this one and eventually Fontaine nodded his assent. "Perhaps we can make that accommodation."

"Excellent. When do we start?"

"You wait here, I have not made any promises." Fontaine stood and Journet followed him out of the room, leaving Nathan behind. This time he was offered water and a sandwich. After half an hour, he was collected and taken two floors further up where he joined three other agents in a small room with a large window. On the other side, behind a one-way mirror, sat Olive Alami, looking bitter and angry in a blue jumpsuit. Journet and Fontaine entered the interrogation room, introduced themselves, and sat across a small table from their suspect.

"You can forget it. I'm not talking. Leave me alone," Olive growled, her voice piped through a speaker into the adjoining observation room.

"You're in a lot of trouble, Ms. Alami," said Journet. "It might help your case if you explain things."

"I've nothing to explain. I was not there. What happened in that garage had nothing to do with me."

"We have an eyewitness who is willing to claim otherwise."

"Eyewitness… It's his word against mine!" Olive had a ferocity burning within her, but Nathan wondered if there might be a soft spot somewhere in there, too. Perhaps if they tapped into it, something useful might come out. Nathan wrote a message to Sophie.

Ask about Girard. They were involved, romantically. He hit send.

On the other side of the glass, Journet checked her phone. "What about Girard Boucher?"

"What about him?"

"Don't you want to know how he is?"

Nathan saw a desperation flash through Olive's eyes. She was a tough girl who couldn't show weakness, and yet this one question tripped an emotional response that she couldn't control. "What do I care?" she said, though it was clear that she cared quite a bit.

"We could let you see him," Journet continued. "If you're willing to talk."

"You can go to hell."

"He's in a coma. The doctors aren't sure if he'll survive. This might be your last chance to say farewell."

More visible cracks appeared in Olive's armor. Where previously she'd projected only fury, now fear and sadness were on display, and yet still, she wouldn't speak.

"Who paid Khalil Haddad?" said Journet. "Who was behind the assassination? Somebody wanted the American secretary dead. Give us a name."

"How the fuck do I know? I had nothing to do with it! Ask Haddad."

"We would, but you had him killed," said Fontaine.

"You can't prove that. I wasn't even there. I want to see a lawyer!"

"Cooperate and we'll let you see Boucher before it's too late. Just give us a name. Who paid Haddad?"

Nathan saw a single tear run down Olive's cheek. Was it stress or despair? Her head tilted forward as she stared at her hands. "I don't know."

"Who does?"

"Why are you asking me this?"

"Somebody in your organization knows exactly what was going on."

"What organization?"

"The Bou Zadjar cartel," said Fontiane.

At the mention of the name, a look of terror crossed Olive's face.

"Who is The Fox? Give us a name, Ms. Alami. You give us the name, we will take you to Boucher."

At this, Olive managed a laugh. "You want to sign my death warrant? Nobody speaks that name. Never."

"A clue, then," said Journet. "Anything. Nobody has to know it was you."

"He'll know. He knows everything."

Nathan realized that at the very least, she'd revealed The Fox's gender. That was progress.

"That's why we'd like to speak with him," Sophie added.

Olive's wry smile masked her predicament.

"Boucher might not have much time. It is now or never, Ms. Alami," said Fontaine.

The smile receded from Olive's face. The pressure was building.

"Have you met him, this Fox?"

"No Never."

"Is there anything you can tell us? Anything at all?"

Olive took a deep breath as she considered her options, pulled in two directions at once. One direction was loyalty to the organization. The other was to her man. In the end, she made her choice. "They say he was an orphan. Somewhere in the south. That's all I know."

"The south of France?" Fontaine asked.

Olive nodded and then dropped her head once more, a defeated woman. Journet looked to the mirror in the direction of

Nathan. In the small room on the other side, he sat entirely stumped. He tapped out a quick note to Journet. *Sorry, I have nothing.* Send.

Journet read the message and then looked up to Olive. "We will make arrangements for you to see Girard." Journet and Fontaine stood and left. A few seconds later, they entered the observation room. "It is not much, but it is something."

"We will need you to testify, at the murder trials," Fontaine said to Nathan. "You were the only witness."

"Sure, I'll testify," said Nathan. "If I'm guaranteed immunity."

"We can't promise you that."

"What about Boucher? What if he doesn't make it? I'm not going to take a murder rap over this."

"We will do our best to protect you," said Sophie.

"Does that mean I'm free to go?"

"For now," said Fontaine. "But you can expect us to come calling."

Nathan stood and nodded to them in turn. "Inspector. Officer Journet. Good day to you both." He walked out of the room with an enormous sense of relief and continued down the hall, then took an elevator to the ground floor. When he left the building, the first proper snow of the season was drifting from the sky and coating the city of Paris in a soft, white blanket. Nathan walked back toward his hotel through the quiet streets, wondering where this mystery might lead him now. Khalil Haddad was dead, but Nathan had a new target, a former orphan from the South of France, known in the underworld as The Fox…

Chapter Eleven

In a small cafe on Avenue Victor Hugo, just a few blocks from the Arc de Triomphe, Nathan peered out the window at Parisians trudging through snow that was piling up on the sidewalks. A young mother pushed a stroller through a small drift. A group of children darted up and down the block throwing snowballs. A fashion-conscious man in a tailored suit held a wool scarf tightly around his neck. Nathan picked at a Caesar salad as he considered his next move. A part of him, the more reasonable part, thought once more that he should quit already and go home. After all, this wasn't his battle. He was an outsider with no real skin in the game. He didn't work for the U.S. government. He had nothing to do with some European drug cartel. He wasn't a member of any law enforcement agency, in France or America, or anywhere else. Nathan Grant was merely a private citizen, nothing more, just as Fontaine had said. He'd only just barely escaped death at the hands of Girard Boucher, and the man responsible for directing the Parsons job, Khalil Haddad, was eliminated. Logic dictated that it was a good time for Nathan to walk away. Why, then, was it so hard to let it all go? Nathan had no interest at this point in ever working for the CIA again. That was his past, not his future. Throughout his career, both with the agency and the Army Rangers before that, Nathan had always understood that he was on the front lines in the fight for freedom. He was protecting the American way of life, and he was proud of that fact, but what he realized now was that in the process, he'd been forced to largely give up his *own* freedom. He had gone where he was ordered to go, fought who he was ordered to fight, and done everything else he was ordered to do. It made him part of something larger than himself, and gave him an identity, but it also obliterated any speck of individualism. Isn't that what the American way of life was supposed to be about? Rugged individualism? It was only this latest mission that really drove the point home. Finally, he'd been ordered to do something that he just couldn't abide. Once he'd refused that order, it meant he was entirely on the outs. There was no going back. From now on, Nathan was his own man, taking orders from nobody but himself. That meant he should just get on with his life. He should leave this episode to the professionals. And yet… curiosity was a powerful lure. More than just curiosity, Nathan felt compelled to see this through. Maybe it was his competitive streak, but deep inside, he knew that he had to find out who was behind the assassination and see justice delivered. After what he'd been through these past days, it all felt very personal. Nathan was angry, and frustrated, and despite knowing better, he just couldn't drop it. He lifted his phone from the table and dialed Philippe Legrand.

"Nathan!" Philippe answered. "How is my motorcycle? You haven't crashed it, have you?"

"No, Philippe, I haven't crashed it. I'll leave that part to you."

"Oh, you are a cruel man, but I suppose I deserve that. You're not looking for something else from me?" Legrand was suspicious. "Not one of the cars, I hope."

"No, I'm not looking to borrow a car."

"Of course, you know you'd be welcome..."

"I have a question for you. Have you ever heard of a man who goes by the name of The Fox?"

"Fox? What kind of a name is that? I would never associate with a man who would use such a silly name."

"I wouldn't expect you to be friends. I was only hoping you might have heard of him."

"Never. Who is he?"

"We suspect he directs a smuggling operation. Drugs and weapons."

"Those aren't my circles. The only criminals I associate with are purely white-collar."

"Do you have any contacts who might know something more?"

"If you want me to be honest, I'd rather not go poking around in something like this. Even asking the questions could be detrimental to my reputation."

"I understand. One last thing, though. I've heard that as a child he was an orphan. Does that ring a bell?"

"Orphan, you say?"

"That's right, somewhere in the South of France."

"It is funny that you mention this. I have an event to attend on Saturday night. It is a fundraiser, for orphans."

"You don't say. Who is organizing it?"

"The Dubois Foundation. Do you know it?"

"No."

"It is the charity run by Laurent Dubois."

"Who is he?"

"Who is *he*? You don't know Dubois?"

"I wouldn't have asked if I did."

"Laurent Dubois is one of the wealthiest men in France, Nathan. He has ties to shipping, telecommunications, construction..."

"And I suppose the two of you are fast friends."

"Well, you could say so, yes. The man is tres sympathique, as we say. Very friendly. You ought to come. If nothing else, the food should be excellent."

"I'm not looking so presentable at the moment, Philippe. Unfortunately, some of the cartel boys did a number on my face. Besides, I don't think I can afford the ticket price."

"Don't worry about that, I'll cover you. After all, it is a worthy cause, yes? As for your appearance, you've got a few days to recover. I'm sure it will be fine."

Nathan gave it a quick thought. Maybe he'd learn a thing or two about well-connected former orphans. It couldn't hurt to poke around a little. "Black tie?"

"Bien Sur."

"Should I bring a companion?"

"If you can manage it at such late notice. Otherwise, I could arrange one for you."

"No, no, I'll see what I can do. Where is it?"

"Chateau de Fontainebleau. I'll send a car to collect you at your hotel. Shall we say, seven p.m. on Saturday?"

"You're too good to me, Philippe. One more thing, though, and I hate to even ask, but you see I've tossed out all of my credit cards and I'm running a little low on cash."

"Which hotel are you in?"

"The Mandarin on Rue de Rivoli."

"I will take care of everything."

"Thank you, Philippe. It's only a loan. See you Saturday." Nathan hung up the phone and ate a bit more of his salad, chewing carefully before washing it down with a sip of mineral water. He hated asking for money, even as a loan from a billionaire, but sometimes these things were unavoidable. At least Girard Boucher hadn't knocked out any of his teeth. Nathan came out of that altercation in a whole lot better shape than the Frenchman. He checked his watch. If he was going to line up a tuxedo, and a date, he might as well get started.

The limousine dropped them at the chateau's main entrance shortly before 8 p.m. The palace itself was stunning. Nathan had visited it as a tourist once before, years earlier, and he was just as impressed the second time around. This was one of the largest such palaces in France, dating back to the 12th century and home to monarchs for roughly 800 years. These royals certainly knew how to live. A footman opened the door to the car and stood to one side as Nathan let his date out first, then emerged to join her. His face had healed some since the beating, but he still had a butterfly bandage on his left cheek and a fading black eye. If anything, it gave the impression that he was a tough guy. That wasn't necessarily such a bad thing. He wasn't sure if he should take Sophie's hand. They were role-playing here, right? The happy couple? But then, he didn't want to make her feel uneasy. In the end, she solved the dilemma, taking his hand in hers. Nathan gave her a smile and they walked across a gravel path toward the front stairs, following behind another couple. Whether this was role-playing or not, accompanying Sophie was still a heady experience. She was an attractive woman, smart and competent. He struggled to process his emotions. He was here on a mission, nothing more. This was not a date. With some luck, they might come away with a small kernel of intelligence that could help lead them to the identity of The Fox. But then, as they ascended the steps, he caught a whiff of Sophie's perfume and his heart melted just a little. He was lonely, he decided, that was all, and it was to be expected after his great loss. At some point, perhaps he would be ready to start thinking about having another woman in his life. This was not that point.

"These wealthy people, they certainly like to enjoy themselves when they're giving away their money," Sophie said.

"Just handing over a check is a lot less fun," Nathan replied, though he couldn't afford to be too smug. In his wallet was a portion of the 5,000-euro loan that Philippe had left for him at the hotel's front desk.

At the top of the stairs was a landing, where a tuxedoed doorman checked Nathan's name off a list. Lurking behind the man were two armed police officers, each carrying an automatic weapon slung over one shoulder. If Sophie recognized the men, she pretended not to.

"Welcome, Monsieur Grant." The doorman handed him a card embossed in gold letters with his name on it. "Please enjoy yourselves at the bar. When you are ready to find your table, you can hand this card to the maitre d'."

"Thank you very much."

"But of course. Have a lovely evening."

Continuing inside, Nathan and Sophie stopped at a coat check in the foyer to drop off their winter outer garments. Beneath a full-length suede coat, Sophie wore a classic blue gown, stylish yet conservative. Nathan's tux was a rental, but he still felt that he was making a good impression, aside from his battered face. It was always easier for the men when it came to the clothing considerations. A tux was a tux, in general. From the coat check, they were led into an enormous ballroom, where the rich and powerful of Paris gathered drinking wine and snacking on hors d'oeuvres while a string quartet serenaded them from one corner. Nathan paused to take a look around. He recognized a few familiar faces. There was the American ambassador, Nancy Cartwright, and her husband near the bar, chatting with a well-known French film director. Closer to the musicians he spotted Howard Collins, wealthy British media magnate. Nowhere in the crowd did he see Philippe Legrand, but Nathan knew that his friend preferred to make a late entrance.

"How about we start with a glass of wine, shall we?" said Nathan.

"Technically, I'm on duty," said Sophie.

"Oh, come on, you're French. I thought you people drank wine in your baby bottles? Surely a glass or two won't slow you down."

Sophie glared at him in response as the two of them moved on into the room. "If you'd like my opinion, I think an apéritif would be more appropriate. Perhaps a Pernod."

"That sounds like an excellent idea. I'm already happy that I brought you along."

"I'm not sure how happy I am that I came."

"Oh, come on. Free food and drinks, rub some elbows, and maybe we'll even learn something."

"I'm not convinced that there is anything here to learn."

They reached the bar and Nathan flagged down a bartender. "Deux Pernod, s'il vous plaît."

"Oui, bien sûr. With water and ice, I presume?"

"Yes, thank you," said Sophie.

While the bartender made their drinks, Sophie waved to a few people she seemed to know. "What makes you think this Fox person would have anything to do with a charity ball?" she asked Nathan.

"Why do you think most of these people are here?"

"To raise money for orphans."

"Wrong. They don't give a damn about orphans. They're only in it for themselves. It's human nature. Everything we do, we're looking to gain. Some of the people here gain by feeling better about themselves, perhaps as a way to assuage their guilt. I would say that is a small minority."

"So what are the others looking for? A tax deduction?"

"Some of them. Or perhaps they just want to mingle with the monied crowd. They want to associate with other wealthy people."

"You have a poor opinion of your fellow man."

"So says a member of the National Gendarmerie. I'd think you'd have it worse than me."

"You make a good point."

The bartender placed two drinks on the bar. "Voila."

"Merci." Nathan lifted his glass. When Sophie raised hers, they tapped the rims. "Salud."

"Salud." They each took a sip.

"None of these reasons for attending that you mention sound like one that would apply to a man named Fox. I highly doubt he pays taxes. I don't think he feels any guilt about his money, or pity for the orphans. I think this is all a waste of time."

"Perhaps, but then there is the reason that I suspect eight out of ten of these guests are here."

"Which is?"

"Public relations."

Sophie shook her head. "I think this is an American concept."

"They want to rehabilitate their image, in the eyes of society. Let's say you own an energy conglomerate, polluting the planet. Or you're Howard Collins, whose television stations spew toxic falsehoods. People might dislike you a little bit less if they knew you gave money to orphans. Right?"

"What about your ambassador? Why is she here?"

"She just wants to be where the action is, to remind people that America has an interest."

"Even if you are right about all of this, what does it have to do with The Fox? Just because he was an orphan? Even that is merely a rumor, told by a desperate woman."

"You're right, Sophie, tonight will probably come to naught," Nathan admitted, "but at least we can enjoy a nice evening out of it. Right?" Back at the entrance, he saw Philippe Legrand and his wife Dominique arrive. They were flagged down near the door by another couple and said their hellos before making their way further into the room. It was Dominique who first spotted Nathan, giving him a wave and tugging at her husband's arm. "Our patrons have arrived. Have you ever met the Legrands?"

"Not yet," said Sophie. "But I am aware of their reputation."

"What reputation is that?"

"They are known to be pillars of the community."

"See, that's what some good PR can do."

"You disagree with this assessment?"

"Not at all. Philippe is an upstanding gentleman and Dominique, well he was very fortunate the day they met."

As the Legrands approached, Philippe broke into a grin. "Well hello, Nathan, you look like you got run over by a truck."

"I told you. In this case, the truck's name was Girard."

"Don't listen to my husband," said Dominique. "He can be so rude. No filter. Is this what you say?"

"It's wonderful to see you, Domi." Nathan kissed her on each cheek.

Dominique was a woman of sophistication who carried herself with quiet confidence. She was tall and thin, with shoulder-length, wavy gray hair and a designer dress in deep red. Gold jewelry finished the look, with diamond studs in her ears and a matching ring. "Oh, yes, it has been far too long." She stepped back and smiled at Sophie. "And who have we here?"

"Sophie Journet, meet the Legrands, Philippe and Dominique," Nathan made the introduction.

"You can call me Domi. Everybody does."

"It is a pleasure," said Sophie. "I have heard so much about you."

"If it comes from Nathan, I'm afraid to know what," said Philippe.

"Oh, come on, Philippe," Nathan complained. "I was just telling her what a great couple you are!"

"Ah, ha," Philippe cleared his throat. "Then I do apologize. As long as you're not relaying my misadventures on the race track."

"I'll leave that incident between us."

"I am so very sorry to hear about your wife, Nathan," said Domi. "Such a tragedy, I can only imagine what you've endured."

"Thank you." Nathan never knew how to respond to such comments. Eighteen months had passed since that horrible day, yet he hadn't seen Dominique in that time. She was expressing heartfelt condolences, and for that he was grateful. It was when people ignored it, or tried to pretend it hadn't happened, that was more upsetting. Sophie Journet, for her part, appeared to be taken by surprise.

"I am sorry," Dominique said to her. "You did not know?"

"It's not my business," Sophie said.

"No, that's OK," said Nathan. "I should have told you."

"No need." Sophie put a hand on Nathan's forearm as she eyed him.

"I think that Domi and I could use a drink," Philippe patted Nathan on the back. "Do you two need a refill?"

"Not yet," said Nathan. "But soon."

A server with a tray of full champagne flutes happened past and Philippe flagged him down. "Ah, what have we here?"

"Veuve Clicquot, monsieur."

"Well, it's not Chateau Legrand, but it will do." He lifted two glasses and offered one to his wife. "Dear?"

Domi took a glass and held it in the air. "What are we drinking to?"

"Why, to the orphans, of course!" said Philippe.

"To the orphans," said the others before tapping their glasses and taking a sip. Nathan noticed Domi perk up as she looked across the room.

"Oh, there's Dubois!" she said.

The rest of them followed her gaze. Nathan saw a man who appeared to be in his mid-60s wearing the requisite black tuxedo. He was medium-sized with a sturdy frame, round face and short, gray hair. The man was built like a bulldog. Beside him was a glamorous younger woman, with long blond hair and a red dress that was perhaps a little too revealing for this occasion. She didn't seem to mind. The couple were standing near the entrance, with Dubois speaking to a dour-looking older gentleman.

"Perhaps we should say hello," said Philippe.

"He seems to be occupied," said Dominique.

"Nonsense! There's always time to speak with the Legrands."

"Yes, I suppose you have a point." Dominique turned toward Nathan and Sophie. "If you don't mind."

"Of course not," Nathan replied.

"We can catch up with you during dinner," said Philippe. "I believe we are seated at the same table."

"The entire meal should be fabulous," Domi added.

"I can't wait." Nathan gave a nod before the Legrands headed off to pay respects to their host. "What else do you know about this Laurent Dubois?" he asked Sophie.

"Only what I read in the papers."

"Which is?"

"Not much of value. He is wealthy, he gives to charity, he enjoys the company of young women."

"That much I already knew."

"The man is very well connected."

"Of course. Was he an orphan, by chance?"

"You can't believe that he is The Fox? Impossible."

"Why?"

"Because we have been looking for this person, this Fox, for two decades. You can't tell me he's been hiding under our noses that whole time. Laurent Dubois is involved with legitimate business ventures. He doesn't need to be smuggling heroin across international borders."

"All right. What do you say we mingle a little bit?"

"Mingle? What is this, mingle? I do not know this word."

"It means, let's go make some friends. Shall we?"

"Mais oui, whatever you'd like. I still do not understand why we are here."

For the next half hour, they worked the room, chatting with those they knew and trying to gather information on those they did not. Nathan had never met the current American ambassador before, but he knew her back story. She had a history in politics, starting as a representative to Congress at the age of thirty-five and then moving to the Senate before being bounced out of office in a "change" election. Since then, she'd served on the boards of several major corporations and founded a non-profit. When a former colleague won the presidency, Cartwright accepted this plum assignment in France. The word in political circles was that she might be a contender for the presidency herself when the current occupant's term expired. Was there a chance that Nancy Cartwright had any useful information? Not likely, though there were so many unknowns in this whole thing, he wasn't about to take anything for granted. A French drug cartel was involved in the assassination of the American Secretary of State. Of that much, he was fairly sure. Perhaps this Fox person wasn't French at all? Maybe he was actually American himself? Nathan eyed the ambassador's husband. He didn't know as much about him, but the man came across as mostly subservient to his wife and her position. Allen Cartwright was a nice guy, not a tough guy, and definitely no criminal mastermind.

Nathan scanned the room again. He was caught by surprise when he saw another familiar face. This was another U.S. Senator, but unlike Cartwright, he was a current officeholder. Jed Brogan represented Nathan's home state of Texas. What on earth was he doing here, so far away from either Washington, DC, or his home district? Apparently, he had some interest in supporting French orphans. Brogan was a handsome man, tall and thin with a square jaw. There was talk about him running for President as well, but from the opposite political spectrum as Cartwright. That made it even more peculiar to see him make an appearance here. Brogan stood near a food table with a woman who appeared to be his wife, along with two younger men, both also wearing tuxedos but looking ill-at-ease in them. Nathan had to satisfy his curiosity, if nothing else. "What do you say we go take a look at the appetizers?" he said to Sophie. "There's somebody I'd like to meet." Nathan took her arm and led her across the room. When they reached the table, he handed a small plate to Sophie and took one for himself. They each filled them up with meats and cheeses and slices of baguette, as well as a few other assorted hors d'oeuvres. Nathan was only feet away from Brogan, and when he turned around, he looked the man straight in the eye. "Senator Brogan, it's nice to see you here," he said.

The senator seemed caught by surprise. He eyed Nathan and then nodded. "Good evening."

"And to you. I'm one of your constituents, from the Lone Star State."

"Is that so? What part, may I ask?"

"Hill country. Born and raised on a cattle ranch."

"Ah, a true Texan. Not one of these transplants, or the city boys." The senator held out a hand and Nathan shook it.

"May I introduce Sophie Journet? This is Senator Jed Brogan."

"Nice to meet you, Sophie. What are you two doing here at this fancy shindig?"

"I was about to ask you the same thing," said Nathan.

"Me? I'm just here on what might be called a junket, but don't quote me on that, ya hear? You don't work for the press, now, do you?"

"No, sir. In fact, you could say I'm retired."

"That's my man. Let me guess, you got tired of chasing around after cattle all day, that it?"

"Something like that."

"I hope you didn't sell out. These ranches, you've got to keep 'em in the family, you know what I mean?"

"Absolutely. I'd never sell. Not on your life."

"That's my man. Let me introduce my wife, the lovely Meredith Brogan."

"Very nice to meet you, ma'am."

"Oh, don't ma'am me! I'm strictly Meredith." She shook Nathan's hand and then Sophie's.

"These two boys are members of my staff, Myles and Stuart." The Senator motioned toward his other companions. "They're the ones who finagled the invite to this do."

"Nice to meet you," said Nathan.

"We were coming to the continent anyway, for the conference at Elba next week," said Myles. "It's not as though we just flew over for this event."

"We need to fill the senator's schedule while we're over here, otherwise it doesn't look so good to the folks back home," said Stuart.

"Sure, I get it," said Nathan. "What's going on at Elba?"

"The climate conference?" Brogan said, as though Nathan were a bit of an idiot for not knowing. "All of the major heads of state will be there, from our President on down. It's important to have a seat at the table. I'm a member of the environment committee you see, I need to represent the United States Senate."

"That committee seems like an odd assignment for you, if you don't mind my saying."

"What do you mean, just because I'm from an oil-producing state? Somebody has to look out for our interests, ain't I right?"

"Or course." All of this small talk was fine, but it wasn't getting him anywhere. "Tell me, Senator, if you don't mind my asking, what do you think about the Parson's assassination? Has it impacted any of your travel plans?"

Senator Brogan scowled. "You sure you ain't a reporter? 'Cause you sure sound like one."

"Pardon my companion," said Sophie. "Sometimes he doesn't know how to stick to polite conversation."

The senator looked to Sophie. "He's a Texan that's for sure. We always speak our minds." He turned back to Nathan. "You want to know my opinion? I'd say the blame goes straight to the President's desk, that's what I'd say. If he wasn't so busy alienating the whole damned world, maybe we wouldn't have so many people out to get us."

"Well, when you are the richest country in the world, there will always be those who are envious," said Sophie.

"Spoken like a true diplomat," said Meredith.

"I tend to think it's our freedom they envy, more than just our money. They just can't stand it," said the senator.

Across the room, Nathan spotted yet another familiar face, this one speaking with the ambassador. It was a former colleague by the name of Ari Hoffman. When Nathan was assigned to the consulate in Marseille some years earlier, Hoffman was in Lyon. Now their eyes met from a distance and Nathan saw instant recognition cross Hoffman's face, followed by concern. One thing was clear, Masterson would be finding out exactly where Nathan was, if he hadn't already. At some point, Nathan was going to have to face the music and submit to a full debriefing. He hadn't broken any laws, though on some level that was the problem. His assignment was to murder somebody. Still, it wasn't like Masterson had anything on him. They couldn't lock him up for refusing to kill a man.

"Tell me, Grant," the senator continued. "How does a cattle rancher from the Texas hill country end up at a charity ball at the Chateau de Fontainebleau? Something tells me your career involved more than just raising beef."

"I spent some time in the diplomatic corps, made some friends over here. Now I'm just enjoying the quiet life."

The senator eyed Sophie once again. "With friends like these, I can't say I blame you."

Sophie bristled, but managed to bite her tongue.

"Honey, you really know how to embarrass a girl, don't you?" said Meredith.

"What did I say?"

So far they'd garnered no useful intel at this event whatsoever, but that didn't mean Nathan was ready to give up. They might still learn something. If not, they had a spectacular free dinner to look forward to. Nathan caught another glimpse of Ari Hoffman, but this time his former colleague was entirely distracted. He said a few words to two solidly-built men with the ambassador. Nathan guessed they were with the Diplomatic Security Service. Hoffman moved a few paces away to take a phone call, and his expression said that something was terribly wrong. Nathan recognized pure panic.

"There is something very civilized about this country, though, isn't there?" Meredith added. "We just can't compete with their culture, all the way back to the renaissance. Am I right?"

"We ain't got no palaces like this one, that's for sure," said the senator.

On the other side of the room, Nathan saw several security agents in dark suits approach Dubois, who stood with his romantic partner and the Legrands. One of the agents whispered into their host's ear. Dubois took the information in, nodded quickly and then said a few words to Philippe before the four of them were whisked away through a side door. Nathan turned to Sophie to see if she'd noticed anything herself, but it didn't appear so. "I don't want to hold you up, senator," Nathan said to Brogan. "I'm sure you have plenty of people to meet."

"Always good to touch base with a constituent, especially so far from home."

"Thank you, sir." Nathan nodded next to Meredith. "Very nice to meet you as well, ma'am."

"Meredith, please!"

"It was a pleasure to meet you, Meredith."

"Likewise, to you both."

Nathan took Sophie's elbow and quickly led her away.

"I hope you did not vote for that man," Sophie said.

"Something is going on. I don't know what it is."

"Why do you say so?"

Several armed police entered the ballroom and then closed and locked the door behind them. Hoffman was now huddling with the ambassador and her people in a far corner. Nancy Cartwright's face was pale with fear. Whatever Hoffman had learned was not going down well. Sophie headed quickly toward the front, where the police were having an animated conversation over their radios. Throughout the room, murmurs of concern swept through the attendees. Nathan was a step behind Sophie, and wishing he was armed, when he heard the distinctive sound of gunfire coming from outside. These were automatic weapons, firing in waves and interspersed with the explosions of grenades. The ballroom erupted into chaos as screams rang out and the guests began to run, with the women struggling not to topple over in their fancy dresses and high heels. Some hid behind curtains along one wall while others dove beneath tables. Yet more made their way further into the palace. Nathan and Sophie were like salmon swimming upstream as they continued forward. Turning to look back, Nathan saw Hoffman hustling his group into another room.

After reaching the front door, Sophie identified herself and demanded to know what was happening. The two officers had little to say, other than that an attack of some sort was underway. They'd moved, one to each side of the doors just before bullets began ripping through the wood. "Please, stand clear!"

Nathan kept his back to the wall beside Sophie on the left-hand side. "Give me a sidearm!" she demanded of the officer beside them, but the man was too busy pointing his rifle at the doors to react. Sophie read his name badge "Office Masse. Do you really want to explain to your superiors why you disobeyed a direct order from a lieutenant in the GIGN?!"

More bullets peppered the doors from the opposite side, and then came the sound of heavy boots kicking at the lock. Officer Masse took a few seconds to unholster his pistol and hand it over. As a foreigner with no ties to the gendarmerie, Nathan knew he would not be given similar treatment. Instead, he looked around for something, anything, that he might be able to use as a weapon. Nearby was a row of flags on short poles roughly six-feet high, each one representing the country of a different guest at the ball. He saw France, of course, but then

Switzerland, Germany, Italy, England and then closest to him in the row, the United States. Nathan lifted this flagpole out of its holder. It wouldn't help him much against an automatic rifle, but in close quarters at least it was something. He moved back beside Sophie, who looked at him in disbelief.

"What?" said Nathan.

"All-American hero, eh?"

"I do my best."

The ballroom was now nearly deserted as most of the guests had retreated further into the palace. From somewhere deep inside, Nathan heard more screams and then the rat-tat-tat of gunshots. This was a coordinated assault. How many attackers there were, however, he obviously had no idea. From outside the ballroom doors, he heard more shouting, and gunfire and then a command to "Hold your fire!"

"Open the doors!" Sophie commanded. Neither officer complied, so she moved around them. "Lieutenant Sophie Journet, GIGN," she called out. "I'm opening up, don't shoot!" With no reply, she looked to Nathan for some encouragement, and then to the two officers, rifles still pointed at the doors. Who was on the other side now, friend or foe? They didn't know, but Sophie turned the lock and pushed one of the doors open slightly. "We're coming out!" Sophie shouted through the gap, then pushed it a little further.

"Police, don't move!" came a voice. "Hands in the air!"

Through the crack, Nathan saw two men in black clothing bleeding on the tiles in the foyer. Beyond them were five armed officers in full body armor. Sophie lowered her pistol to the ground and then raised her hands. When she pressed the doors further with one foot, all five guns were trained on her. Masse moved around her and through. "It's all right, she's GIGN," he said.

"What's going on, how many are there?!" Sophie demanded.

"There are more inside the palace," said one of the other men. "We're assessing the situation."

The scene reminded Nathan of battle in one sure sense, and that was the absolute chaos and confusion of it. Nobody seemed to know exactly what was going on. The officer who had spoken looked with skepticism at this American, clutching his flag. "Who is he?"

"This man is with me," said Sophie, though that didn't seem to dispel the doubts.

Two men on the team quickly examined the fallen attackers. Nathan noted the grenades strapped to their vests, and two AK-47s on the ground beside them. "These men are dead," said an officer.

"We'll proceed inside," said another.

"What about us?" Masse asked.

"You two stay here. Guard the door."

"Yes, sir."

The five other officers entered the ballroom and hurried through, heading toward the interior and the sounds of battle that still echoed through the palace halls. Sophie took off her high-heeled shoes and tossed them aside, then reached down and picked the pistol back up. "I'm going in with them," she said to Nathan. "I'm afraid you'll have to stay here."

Nathan understood, but that didn't alleviate the sting of being left behind. "Good luck."

"Merci." In Sophie's eyes, Nathan saw sadness and fear as she faced the realization that tonight there would be no good outcome. People inside this palace were dying, and in fulfilling her duty she faced the distinct chance that she might end up joining them. There was no time for extended farewells, however, and she headed off toward the interior herself, barefoot and with her single sidearm in one hand. Nathan put his flagpole down, leaning it against the wall to keep the flag from touching the ground. One had to show respect. The two remaining officers examined the perpetrators, leaning in but not too close. One of the officers saw Nathan eyeing the discarded assault rifles. "You, stand back."

Nathan raised his hands in the air and took a few steps further away. "No problem." His thoughts went to Sophie, but also to Philippe and Dominique. Indeed, he feared for the lives of each and every one of the guests. None of it made any sense to him. Who would want to shoot up a charity ball dedicated to improving the lives of orphans? This didn't seem to be a good look for a terrorist organization, but then death and mayhem were their tools. For now, the who's and why's would have to wait. His friends were in danger. "I want you to listen to me very carefully," he said to the officers. "I am a trained United States Army Ranger. I am going to pick up one of those rifles and take it inside to assist."

"Stand down!" Masse spun his own gun around in response.

Nathan raised his hands further. "I am not a threat. We are on the same side."

"Back away," the other officer growled.

"OK, OK, take it easy." Nathan turned and took a step, but as he passed the flagpole, he snapped it back up, spun around and swung it at Masse's knees, dropping him to the ground. Before the other officer had time to raise his weapon, Nathan hit him full force in the forearm, then again in the legs, and he crumpled beside his partner. In the flash of an instant, Nathan picked up one of the AK's and pointed it at the two downed policemen. "Just stay where you are. Let go of your weapons and let me see your hands." The two men, stunned by the speed with which they'd been overcome, didn't push their luck. From their positions on the ground, each of them lifted their hands in the air.

Nathan pointed his rifle from one officer to the other and back as he kicked their guns away across the floor. He only needed enough time to move inside without being shot in the back. Kneeling low, he patted down one of the attacker's vests until he found an extra magazine and then slid that into his pocket. Carrying this particular weapon, and dressed in civilian clothes, he would have to be very careful not to be confused for a terrorist himself, though he doubted many wore designer French tuxedos. "You two just follow your orders and guard the door," Nathan addressed the officers. "I'm going to head inside and assist." He moved backwards into the empty ballroom, then turned and raced through, smelling the first hint of smoke. Somewhere inside, the palace was on fire.

The next room Nathan came to was a long banquet hall, with tables set with fine china. Large windows on one side overlooked an illuminated courtyard. Both the dining room and the courtyard were deserted. In fact, the whole scene was now eerily quiet. He no longer heard gunshots, or grenades, nor screams or shouts. He moved to a door that opened onto the courtyard and stepped outside. From a second-story window, he saw the orange flicker of flames casting a glow on the exterior walls. Unless this fire was put out quickly, it could engulf the entire palace. Nathan knew that no fire crews would be allowed entry as long as a gun battle was raging. His first step was to locate the terrorists in this enormous maze of rooms. Nathan continued across the courtyard and through another door on the opposite side. Here he found himself in a library, with a large fireplace, floor-to-ceiling wooden bookcases, and a spiral staircase in one corner. Still no signs of any people. Nathan continued on through.

The next room was a private study, with an enormous wooden desk on one side. Nathan moved toward a door on the far side, but when he came around the desk he was startled by his first signs of life. Huddled on the ground beneath the desk were a man and a woman, both in server's uniforms. The man raised one hand in the air, struck by terror. "Please, Monsieur, don't shoot!" he said.

"Where are the terrorists?" Nathan said.

Unable to respond, the man lowered his hands and began to quietly pray. Nathan continued on until he came to a stairway. A small cluster of guests from the ball hurried down the stairs toward him and then froze momentarily when they saw this man with an AK-47. "Go!" Nathan waved them past. The guests ran by, searching for an exit and Nathan hurried up the stairs. He seemed to be moving in the right direction.

On the second floor, the smoke was denser. Nathan heard the crackling of fire, and then the electric lights flickered and went out. Holding his gun in one hand, he used the other to take out his phone and flip on the flashlight, then moved in the direction of the fire and into a small salon. On the ground, he saw the motionless body of a man in a bloodstained tuxedo. Nathan recognized him as a member of the American ambassador's detail, and spotted the man's pistol on the floor halfway across the room. Feeling for a pulse, he found none. It was likely the first of many casualties to come. The palace was so large, the rooms so plentiful, that the perpetrators could be almost anywhere, and with the fire, time was not on Nathan's side. He moved to a window, looking out on the courtyard again from the second floor. The flames were catercorner to where he stood and had spread to an adjoining room. Screams of terror now emanated from this second room, echoing off the courtyard walls. Nathan saw a figure appear in a window briefly and then move aside. It was a man, in black, with an AK-47 like the one Nathan now held. He'd located his terrorists, or at least one of them. He unlatched the window in front of him and swung it open before pointing his weapon at the spot where the man had just appeared, waiting for another chance. Instead of the attacker, Nathan saw flashes of gunfire and heard more screams and chaos. A stray bullet shattered the window beside him.

Nathan moved backwards and ducked low, beside a solid wooden cabinet. From what he could make out, it seemed that perhaps police were storming the other room. With a raging inferno engulfing the palace, they had no time to negotiate. At this point, all Nathan could do was stay low and avoid getting caught in the crossfire. Three stun grenades went off in quick succession, ringing in his ears. His thoughts went back to Sophie Journet, hoping she wasn't fool enough to storm the room herself, barefoot and wearing an evening gown. He was sure of one thing, this would likely go down as the worst first date in all of history.

Somehow, despite the madness and the noise, Nathan thought he heard something else, closer at hand. It sounded like a whimper, but only briefly and then it went away. Was he hearing things? The only other person in the room was clearly dead. Right? Nathan picked up his phone and shone the light all around. Nobody else was there, but then he heard it again, the distinct sound of a woman in distress. It was coming from inside the cabinet just beside him. Nathan moved around to the front, where he was faced with two large wooden doors. He reached for a handle and pulled one open. Inside, curled up in a ball, was a woman in a black evening dress. She eyed Nathan in wide-eyed terror, certain that her time on earth was up. The woman was the American ambassador, Nancy Cartwright.

"Ms. Ambassador, I'm going to get you out of here!" Nathan's words had no discernible effect. The ambassador's debilitating fear left her unable to respond in any fashion. Nathan put down the gun and slid his phone into his pocket, leaving the room lit only by the flickering flames. Next, he reached in and scooped the ambassador out. He hoisted her with both hands and headed back in the direction from which he had come, through the next salon and into the darkened stairwell. He had to feel his way with his feet and one elbow against the wall as he made his way down. When he reached the dining room, he was able to see through to the ballroom. The gunfire upstairs had ceased. One side or the other had apparently come out victorious, but Nathan's job at this point was to get the ambassador to safety.

On the other side of the ballroom, he moved into the foyer, where the two police officers were now gone. Exiting through the front door, Nathan was hit with the blinding light of high-powered spotlights. "Don't move!" came a command. Nathan stopped where he was, the ambassador still in his arms.

"It's all right, they're civilians!" came another shout.

Nathan continued forward. "Don't shoot, I have the U.S. ambassador!" When he neared the spotlights, he saw a row of armed police standing behind them. Further back was a fire truck, with more arriving, as well as several ambulances. Nathan was met by officers in full tactical gear, pointing their weapons at him.

"Lower the woman to the ground and put your hands in the air!"

Nathan did as commanded, easing Ambassador Cartwright onto the lawn and then raising his arms. Two officers quickly approached, one covering him while the other patted him down. "He's clear!" It was all a blur of motion as he was escorted away, leaving Cartwright behind under the care of paramedics. Nathan was taken to a command post of sorts, behind an armored truck, where a police captain was speaking on a radio with officers inside. Helicopters hovered in the air above.

"We've got two officers down and multiple civilians!" a voice came over the radio.

"Is the threat neutralized?" replied the captain.

"We need to evacuate! Send in the fire crews!"

"Is the threat neutralized?!" the captain repeated, but this time there was no answer. From the front of the building, civilians began streaming out the door and across the lawn, some of them injured and bloodied.

"You'd better get the fire crews in there if you want this palace to survive," said Nathan.

"What the hell went on in there?" the captain asked him.

"I don't know. I wish I did."

The captain looked to an officer beside him. "Escort the fire crews, let's get water on those flames!"

"Yes, sir." A sergeant began to organize his men as ambulance crews tended to the injured. Fire trucks were positioned closer to the outside of the building and their ladders rose skyward as the firefighters sprung into action, dousing the visible flames. Other crews were led inside, moving past the guests and servers who continued flowing out. Nathan kept his eyes open for Sophie Journet, though he knew she wouldn't emerge until the danger had passed. He wanted to go back in himself to search for Domi and Philippe, but finding them in the darkness and chaos inside would be a nearly impossible task. He pulled out his phone and tried calling but it went straight to voicemail.

Exiting the palace next, Nathan saw Senator Jed Brogan and his group among the crowd, looking dazed but unharmed. Not far behind came a wounded Ari Hoffman, supported with one arm by the ambassador's husband, Allen Cartwright. Nathan raced across the lawn to help, taking his former colleague on the other side. Hoffman appeared to have been shot in the right leg, with his pants soaked in blood. "What happened Ari?" said Nathan.

"What the hell are you doing here, Nathan?"

"That's not important. Who shot you?"

"The terrorists!" said a distraught Cartwright. "They were after my wife. We've got to go back. We've got to find her. She's inside, I don't know where. Somebody has to help me!"

"Your wife is fine, I brought her out. She's unharmed."

"Nancy? Where?! Where is she?"

"With the police. Check with the commander on scene."

Allen Cartwright let go of Hoffman. "I need to find her." He rushed off in search of his wife, leaving Nathan to help Hoffman across the open space, past the police lines and on to the nearest empty ambulance. Paramedics loaded him onto a gurney.

"Ari, you've got to tell me what you know."

"I can't do that, Nathan. You're not with us anymore."

"Come on, Ari, it's me. We've got history."

"I'm sorry. Nobody knows whose side you're on these days."

"What does that even mean? What are you hearing?"

The paramedics wheeled the gurney around to the back of the ambulance and then slid Hoffman inside where they immediately went to work slicing open his pants and tending to the wound. "You're going to live, sir," one of the paramedics said to him. "But this might hurt." He applied some antiseptic, and the patient winced in pain.

"Come on, Ari," Nathan repeated.

"They seemed to be after the ambassador, from what I could tell," said Hoffman. "But I have no idea why."

The doors to the ambulance swung shut and the engine turned over before it pulled away, lights flashing. Nathan let this latest bit of information sink in. Why would a group of terrorists shoot up a charity ball, at a palace in France, to get to an American ambassador? There was so much to unwind here that Nathan didn't even know where to start.

Chapter Twelve

Two days after the attack, Nathan entered a cafe on a winding cobblestone street in the Latin Quarter. He arrived in the early afternoon, after the lunch rush was over, and was seated at a quiet table in the back. From media reports, Nathan knew that twelve innocent victims had died at the Chateau de Fontainebleau and nearly fifty more were injured, including guests, servers, police and firefighters. Philippe and Dominique Legrand had not been among them. Neither had Sophie Journet. When Nathan first made contact again with Sophie, she hadn't sounded so eager to speak with him. Indeed, she'd hung up almost immediately, and then texted from an unknown number to set up this meeting. Now he ordered a mineral water with lime and settled in to wait. Ten minutes later, he saw Sophie come through the front door. She scanned the cafe and then made her way to his table.

"Thanks for coming, Sophie." Nathan stood, but from her cold demeanor, he got the sense that she wasn't so pleased to see him.

"You have some explaining to do, Nathan," Sophie replied.

"Nice to see you, too."

They each took a seat as a server arrived to deliver Nathan's mineral water.

"Bonjour. Un café, s'il vous plaît," said Sophie.

"Bien sûr." The server moved off toward the bar.

"I was very worried about you," said Nathan. "For the first few hours, I had no idea if you'd survived."

"I hear that you rescued the American ambassador."

"I wouldn't go that far. I carried her out, that's true."

"Why, then, does your government not trust you?"

"We already went over that. I'm starting to think that maybe you don't trust me, either. Is that what this meeting is about?"

Sophie crossed her arms as she looked him over. "You know how these things go. We must deal in concrete facts."

"In this business, is there any such thing?"

"You entered our country using a false passport. Elias Mansour was the name, so I am told."

"You're checking up on me now? Who are you talking to? The CIA? Is that it?" Nathan looked toward the door, half expecting to see some of his former colleagues come through. "Are you going to have me arrested?"

"I could. In fact, I probably should."

"Why don't you, then?" The conversation was becoming heated. Sophie had a job to do, and laws to follow, and yet he hadn't expected this of her. They had a history, working together. Now she was implying that they might no longer be on the same side.

"Why are you making this so hard on me, Nathan?"

"That's not my intention. I only want to get to the bottom of it all, just like you do."

"You're not even in France legally. Go home, Nathan. Leave this to us."

Nathan wasn't sure how to respond. Giving up now was entirely out of the question, as far as he was concerned. He wasn't about to make any promises to the contrary. "I'll do my best to stay out of your way," he said.

Sophie narrowed her eyes in frustration.

"Is there anything you can tell me?" Nathan asked. "Anything useful?"

"After what I have said, and you are asking for my help?"

"I'd like to think we'd be helping each other."

"I'm sorry, Nathan. You are lucky I have not had you deported."

"That is something, I suppose."

"Please do not make me regret it."

When the server came back around, Nathan paid for his mineral water and the pair of them stood to leave. Out on the sidewalk, there were no kisses on the cheek this time around.

"Goodbye, Sophie," said Nathan. She looked him over one last time and then walked off without a word. Nathan pulled out his phone and dialed Philippe.

"Nathan!" Philippe answered. "I hope you're managing to stay out of trouble."

"You know me, trouble follows wherever I go."

"I think you are the one who follows trouble."

"Hey, Philippe, I'd like to speak to you about a few things. Do you have the time?"

"Always for you, Nathan. I'm at the office all day."

"I'll be there in half an hour. Is that all right?"

"Perfect. See you."

"Thanks." Nathan hung up and then caught a ride share out to La Defense. He entered Philippe's building, passed a security check and took an elevator up to the top floor. An administrative assistant showed him into a conference room with sweeping views of the city where he was told to wait. It only took about ten minutes before Philippe entered, his larger-than-life personality on full display.

"Nathan!" Philippe moved across the room as Nathan rose from his chair, and then gave his friend a hearty bear hug. "What a relief, we made it out alive, the both of us! I blame myself for inviting you."

"How could you have possibly known what was coming? It was a charity event, for orphans!"

"Yes, true, who could possibly predict such a thing?" Philippe took a step back to look Nathan over. "You have had a difficult week, no?"

"Rougher than most."

"Come, let's move to my office, it is more comfortable."

"Sure." Nathan followed Philippe out the door, down the hall, and into a plush suite, with oak paneling and dancing yellow flames in a gas fireplace. The style seemed out of place in this building of modern glass and steel, but it did convey the ambiance of a chateau, fit for one of France's premier champagne brands. Two leather chairs faced the fire, and Philippe gestured to one of them.

"Sit, please, what can I get you?" said Philippe.

"Nothing, thank you, Philippe. I'm here for information, that's all."

"Information? From me? What kind of information?"

Nathan took one chair and Philippe sat in the other. "First, tell me, how is Domi holding up? Is she taking it OK?"

"She's a strong woman. Much stronger than me. Thank you for asking. I will share with her your concern."

"I still don't know what happened to you two. I saw you in the ballroom and then you disappeared, along with Dubois."

"Yes, it is a good thing that Domi and I were with Laurent when the madness began. He has bodyguards, you know, always with an evacuation plan."

"Maybe you ought to consider hiring a few more of your own."

"Ha, no," Philippe shook his head. "That is not the life for me. At the office, yes, security is warranted. Sometimes when I travel. As a general rule, I prefer not to live my life that way. To me, it is suffocating."

"All right, so where did Dubois' people evacuate you to? It seems the terrorists were spread throughout the building."

"His men were well prepared. We were escorted below ground, into a warren of tunnels. We waited in a private chamber. I felt quite safe. Of course, we were more worried about your safety, and the lives of the others. Such a tragedy, what happened. I am only relieved that you and your friend managed to survive unscathed."

"Sophie is as tough as nails. You think Domi is strong, you have no idea."

"Yes, I can imagine. Tell me, Nathan, is there something… how shall I say this? Something newsworthy between you and this Sophie?"

"Newsworthy?" Nathan scoffed.

"I am confident that you understand my meaning."

"No, Philippe, nothing newsworthy. I'm still not ready for anything newsworthy."

"Pity. She is a remarkable woman."

"It seems to me that you are avoiding the topic at hand."

"What is the topic at hand? Domi and I sheltered in the basement. What else can I tell you?"

"I want to know the *whys* of this whole thing. I need to understand it."

"What can I possibly do to help you understand it? I do not understand it myself. None of it! Why do people do these sorts of things to each other? This is your area of expertise, is it not? I have no idea."

"There's always a reason. Maybe that reason doesn't seem logical to you or me, but it is logical to the people who pulled it off."

"I am a businessman, Nathan. Terrorist attacks are not, how do you say, *in my wheelhouse*?"

"No, but you are acquainted with some of the people involved."

"Involved? What do you mean by this? Victims, yes, we were all victims. All of us were under attack. Involved? No, I wouldn't say so."

"I'd like to know a little bit more about Laurent Dubois. How well do you actually know him?"

"Laurent?" Philippe crinkled his nose. "We cross paths from time to time. You know, Paris society, it is not such a large pool of people."

"Why do you think he chose orphans as his charity? Was he an orphan himself?"

"No, no... I can't imagine. He went to the best schools. Dubois, he is a man of the aristocracy. Orphan? Never. He is a generous man, that is all. He hopes to provide others with some of the good fortune that he had as a child. Laurent Dubois is a good man. I hope you are not meaning to imply otherwise!"

"I'm not implying anything at all, Philippe, I've never even met the man. I'm merely following all the leads at my disposal."

"Ah, leads, you sound like a detective."

"I am starting to feel like one. I don't suppose I would be able to speak with Dubois, do you think?"

Philippe placed his elbows on the arms of his chair and touched his fingertips together. "Speak with him? About what, exactly? He was in the basement, like me. We saw nothing."

"I'd like to know if he has any enemies, for starters."

"We all have enemies. When you are rich, you collect them along the way."

"Hence the bodyguards?"

"Of course. Listen, my friend, I do not mean to be inhospitable, but I have work that needs my attention. Is there something specific that I can assist you with? Otherwise, I am afraid I will need to cut our visit short."

"Can you arrange a meeting with Dubois for me?"

"Dubois?" Philippe seemed troubled. "I cannot promise. I will have one of my people look into it. Would that suffice?"

"Of course."

Philippe stood from his chair. "Give my regards to Sophie, would you? And if you want my opinion, I think that something newsworthy is in order."

Nathan rose to his feet and embraced his friend with both arms. "Thanks, Philippe, I will keep that in mind." He took a step back. "Give my regards to your better half, as always."

"We will have you over for dinner one night. Perhaps you can bring somebody special along."

"You don't give up easily."

"I am French, what can I say? We are romantic."

"All right, Philippe, I'll show myself out."

"Remember, Nathan, you are not a detective. I believe it is best to leave this case to the professionals."

"That's what people tell me." Nathan walked out of the office, closed the door behind him and headed down the hall. He took the elevator to the ground level and then caught the metro back into the city center. He had a lot to digest. First was the question of why these terrorists attacked a charity ball to begin with? So far there had been no claim of responsibility. In a more typical situation, if a terrorist group was trying to make a point about something, they would take credit for such an attack right away and maybe post some sort of manifesto explaining their righteous indignation that led to the slaughter. They might be extremists on either side of the political spectrum, but they always felt entitled to their rage and justified in their actions. That meant they wanted the world to know who was responsible. In this case, the authorities had the dead bodies of several attackers, and a few more in custody but they weren't talking as far as he could tell. Nathan was reliant on public reporting, but nothing about the men's identities or motives was being released. Ari Hoffman had thought that the men were after the American ambassador, but how did he really know? It seemed as though they were after anybody of elevated social stature that they could get to. It might very well have been Laurent Dubois in particular that they were trying to kill. Like Philippe had said, wealthy businessmen accumulated enemies along the way. As the host, the attackers would have known Dubois would be in attendance. If he was on their hit list, this would have presented a good opportunity. Nathan wanted to run this past the man himself, but without Philippe's help, he doubted he'd be granted an audience. One other issue needled Nathan in the back of his mind. It was a minor thing on the surface, but it still bothered him. This mysterious drug lord, The Fox, was supposedly an orphan, if you could trust the dubious source. The charity ball was being held for orphans. It was certainly an odd coincidence. Maybe he'd look into this orphan thing, and pull on the string a bit to see where it might lead. You never knew unless you tried.

Chapter Thirteen

Occupying a seat in the center of a metro car, Nathan had gone just a few stops toward the city center when he noticed two men standing near the forward doors. What set them apart was the fact that one of them was trying to awkwardly sneak surreptitious glances in Nathan's direction. Before each stop, the man would quickly look to Nathan, and then speak a few words to his companion. Both men wore business suits under dark overcoats. The man who watched Nathan was in his late 20s, tall and thin with a mustache and a blue knit beanie on his head. His companion was stocky and older, perhaps in his mid-40s, with a fleshy face and a brown wool scarf wrapped around his neck. It was clear to Nathan that these two were following him. The question was, for who? It might have been that Sophie, or someone else at the GIGN, decided that it was best to keep a close eye on him. That seemed to be the most likely answer. Another possibility was that they were associated with the Bou Zadjar cartel. Nathan was directly responsible for the death of one cartel member, the arrest of two others, and the comatose state of a fourth. He would no doubt be at the very top of their hit list by this point. Whoever these two men were, Nathan wasn't particularly eager to find out. When the train pulled in at the Argentine station, he rose to his feet and walked toward the rear doors. Immediately, the younger man alerted his colleague. So far, at least, they didn't seem to be aware that he'd blown their cover.

When the doors opened, Nathan stepped off the train amongst a small crowd and headed calmly toward the escalators. He rode up toward the street level, not looking back. He knew they were there, somewhere behind him. If they were cartel members, they might just shoot him at any moment, but Nathan figured they were more likely to wait for a quieter opportunity; one with fewer witnesses and an absence of security cameras.

When he reached the top of the escalator, Nathan emerged onto the bustling Avenue de la Grande Armée. A light snow fell as he pressed his hands into his pockets, bent his head low, and hurried up the broad sidewalk toward the looming Arc de Triomphe. He weaved around pedestrians who were heading in the opposite direction as he tried to come up with a plan. It shouldn't be too hard to lose the heavier of the two men, he didn't seem to be in the best of shape. The younger man, however, might be able to keep up if Nathan made a break for it. In the end, however, he couldn't come up with any better ideas. When he reached a narrow side street, he turned right. As soon as he was around the corner and momentarily out of view, he took off running. Nathan raced one block to the next corner, where a white delivery van blocked the street. He slid around the side and came upon a teenager moving toward him on an electric scooter. The boy slowed as he approached the van, steering to his right to squeeze past. Nathan waved his hands in the air to distract him. "Hey, hey!" he hollered.

"Quoi?" said the boy.

"Pardon!" Nathan grabbed the handlebars with one hand and knocked the kid off with a shoulder. Taking a quick look backward, he saw his pursuers huffing it up the sidewalk in his direction with the younger man in the lead. They were getting close when Nathan hopped on the scooter, pushed the throttle button, and zipped off down the street. When he came to another intersection, he looked back again. His older pursuer was now bent over, hands on his knees and heaving deep breaths. The other man had not yet given up, but Nathan gave him a quick salute with his right hand, then turned to the left and sped away, weaving around a few more cars as he went until he emerged at a long, narrow park, the Jardins d'Avenue Foch. Continuing on a walking path, he turned left again, then joined the sidewalk along Avenue Foch. He was nearly back to the Arc de Triomphe when he leaned the scooter against a wall and weaved through the pedestrians on foot, this time at a brisk walk until he came to a tunnel, where he followed along with crowds of tourists heading underneath the traffic circle. When he came out at the far end, he was in the roundabout, with the monument towering above.

Nathan joined a line for tickets at the base of the arch, paid the entry fee, and followed along with other visitors into a stairwell, where he went up and up and up, round and round, 284 steps to the top before he emerged onto the roof. Throngs of people lined the railings, jockeying for position to take in the sweeping views of Paris. Moving toward one edge, Nathan saw the maze of narrow streets below him as well the broad avenue, the Champs Élysées. In the near distance rose the Eiffel Tower. For Nathan's purposes, this spot he'd chosen to hide out was anything but ideal. It did have the benefit of being very public. They weren't likely to attack him if they somehow made their way up here. On the other hand, he was trapped in a location with just one entrance and exit. He'd thought about just heading back to his hotel but if they were still on his tail he didn't want to lead them there. Instead, he decided to hang out here for half an hour or so until he felt the coast was likely clear. In the meantime, he made his way around to all four sides of the rooftop, taking in the scenery himself. When he was ready to leave, Nathan headed toward the stairwell. Before he reached it, he spotted the younger of his two pursuers walk out. The man took a look around and quickly saw Nathan. Both men froze, staring directly at one another. A moment later, the heavier man appeared, wheezing and out of breath. They said a few words to each other, but nobody moved. Nathan had two choices. He could either fight his way out, or he could try simply asking what they wanted. In the end, he decided to give the latter option a try. He made both of his hands into fists before approaching the men, just in case. "Who are you and what do you want?" he walked up to face them.

"Relax, Grant. Masterson sent us," said the heavier man, with an American accent.

"Why am I not surprised?" The fact that he was still alive at all meant that at least he wasn't on the CIA hit list himself, yet.

"We need to talk," said the younger man.

"Why should I?" Nathan answered.

"Look, we don't want to get nasty," said the younger man. "Think of it this way, your country needs you. We are under assault, and we believe you might have information that could help us understand why. If that's not enough of an incentive, we could always put some pressure on our French colleagues to have you arrested."

"For what?"

"Do you need to ask? We know all about what went down at the auto shop."

"Am I worth all this trouble?"

"That's not our decision. You know how Masterson can be when there's something he's after. Very tenacious."

"Yeah, tenacious enough to go after an innocent man."

"Who says you're innocent?"

"I wasn't talking about myself." Nathan gritted his teeth. He didn't want anything to do with these two, but talking was the only way to get them off his back. "Let's go find someplace a little more private." Nathan gestured toward the stairway.

The man smirked. "Just remember, this is for your country."

"Sure."

The three of them headed downwards. When they reached the ground level, they egressed through the tunnel beneath the roundabout and then continued down Avenue Foch and entered the park once again. Nathan had to figure the CIA would catch up to him eventually, but he certainly wasn't happy about it. Masterson would feel like Nathan owed him something, though Nathan felt betrayed by the agency he'd once served.

The heavier man was still out of breath. He motioned to a park bench. "Take a seat," he said.

Nathan sat in the middle with one man on either side of him. "You really ought to exercise more," he said.

The older man took a moment to regain his composure. "Masterson wants us to bring you in," said the younger man. "He's not pleased with how things went down in Algeria. He wants a full debriefing."

"I'm not thrilled with how it went down, either."

"You tipped off the subject," said the older man. "He's in hiding now. We haven't been able to locate him. No phone, no devices. Did you tell him to do that?"

"The man is innocent."

"So you say," the younger man replied. "Who made you the judge?"

"Masterson did, when he sent me after him. What do you guys expect, that I'm going to get on a plane with you and head back to Langley? It's not going to happen."

"Like I said, we can make things hard on you," said the older man. "We can have you arrested. Extradited."

"What for? Some made-up bullshit? I've committed no crime, and even if I did, that's up to the local authorities to decide."

"We've seen video footage of you roaming the Chateau de Fontainebleau with an AK-47. What happened Grant, you take on some terrorist tendencies?"

"Oh, you're not going there..."

"Why not?" said the younger man. "First you tip off the man responsible for the death of the Secretary of State, and then you join a terrorist attack on a charity ball? It all looks like a pattern to me. We should have had you arrested already."

"Why haven't you?"

"We wanted to give you a chance," said the heavier man. "To come back and talk it out with the deputy director, man to man."

"You can tell Masterson to go fuck himself." Nathan rose to his feet and took two steps away before turning back around to face them. "If you think I'm a terrorist, tell the French authorities. Otherwise, leave me the hell alone."

"You're making a big mistake, Grant," said the heavier man.

"Graham Masterson is the one who made the mistake. I'm the one trying to clean it up." Nathan turned again and walked away through the park, overcome with fury. He'd wanted to punch these two in their smug faces. He tried to calm himself as he continued back to the Champs Élysées and then on toward his hotel. The question that ran through his mind now was, whose side was Graham Masterson actually on? Was he really this incompetent? Nathan understood that every field had maybe twenty percent of people in them who were very good at their jobs. The rest either got by the best they could, or outright faked it just to keep their positions. With enough confidence and bravado, the fakers could climb the ladder just as fast as anyone, sometimes faster. That went for lawyers and doctors, contractors and corporate types. Apparently, it went for CIA deputy directors as well. Back in Texas, where Nathan grew up on a ranch, things were different. For a rancher, your degree of competence translated directly to the success and viability of your operation. You had to know what you were doing, and execute. Somehow Graham Masterson had reached the upper echelons of the CIA, but he clearly did not know what he was doing. Perhaps he'd let his ego get the best of him in his quest for power and control. The alternative, that Masterson was on the side of the terrorists himself, was something Nathan wasn't ready to honestly consider. One always had to take into account the worst-case scenario, however.

This meeting with Masterson's emissaries did complicate things somewhat. Nathan couldn't be sure if they were bluffing or not. It was entirely possible that they would follow through with their threats to tie him in with the terrorists. One thing in his favor: his date that night at the charity ball was a well-respected officer with the GIGN. Another thing was that he'd carried the American ambassador out of the building to safety. He couldn't imagine that the French authorities would take such accusations against him seriously. More than anything, it was just an annoyance. The agency was watching him, and would continue to do so. He hadn't heard the last of them, of that he was sure.

By the time Nathan returned to his hotel, his heart rate was beginning to come back down. He had to put these two goons out of his mind and carry on. He still needed to figure out how these seemingly disparate threads all tied together. He wasn't going to get any help from the CIA, of course, but not from the

French authorities either. Nathan would need to sort this all out on his own, somehow.

Up in his room, Nathan took a seat near the window, looking out on the gray skies of Paris. What was his next step? He came back to that coincidence that still nagged at the back of his mind. Orphans. What did this have to do with orphans, if anything? He couldn't use his phone anymore, for research or anything else. What else would explain why these CIA operatives were able to locate him on the top of the arch, after he'd already managed to shake them? Sophie knew his number, which meant the GIGN had it, which meant that the CIA was liable to get it, too. He pulled the phone from his pocket and powered it down. He would only use it in emergency situations from now on.

Back down in the lobby, Nathan went to the hotel's business center and used the password the clerk had given him and logged on to one of the computers. He opened a browser and searched for orphanages in France. A small handful were listed on historical sites, but none of these were currently in operation. Most of them shut down by the early 1950s, in favor of foster care. Orphans these days were sent to live with families, but depending on the age of The Fox, he very well could have grown up in one. Those facilities that had previously existed were spread out in rural villages throughout the country. One in particular caught Nathan's attention. The location was outside Marseille. It operated during the Algerian War for Independence, through the end of 1962, housing children whose parents were killed in the war. These children were a mix of French and Algerian. The Fox had direct ties to North Africa. Could there be a connection here? The name of the place was the Chateau Saint-Martin. The building itself still existed, now operating as a boutique hotel. The high-speed train would take four hours to get down there from Paris. He checked the timetable and found that they departed twice per hour. With no credit cards at his disposal, Nathan would need to buy his ticket at the station with cash, but he was able to reserve a room at the hotel and print some maps of the area. When he was done, he returned to his room and started to pack his things. If he left now, he'd be there by early evening.

Chapter Fourteen

The chateau was a two-story, country farmhouse. The word chateau actually made it sound much fancier than it was. The building had seen better days. Nathan's cab pulled up a gravel drive in the last fading light of day. He examined the chateau's crumbling, gray stucco facade. Blue wooden shutters graced the upstairs window frames, with chunks of plaster missing around the edges. A rusted rain gutter hung askew from the roof, ready to fall off entirely with the next downpour. Despite the state of repairs, there was still a bygone majesty about the place. All it needed was a little TLC. The taxi came to a stop and Nathan climbed out, collected his bag from the trunk, and paid the fare in cash. When the cab pulled away, he was left standing alone at the front door. No bellhops here, that was for sure. He took a quick look around. No snow here this far south, either, but there was still a crispness in the air. The house was surrounded by fruit orchards, but the trees were untended and probably hadn't produced a decent crop in decades. A small outbuilding was constructed of warped wooden planks, several of which were missing. In front of that was a dilapidated tractor with four flat tires resting amongst the weeds, dead and brown at this time of the season. Nathan had to wonder what type of clientele wanted to stay in a hotel like this one. He imagined Brits flying down for a weekend to fantasize about living the simple life in Provence, with lavender fields and picturesque ancient villages. Perhaps the experience of staying in a worn-out dump like this might disabuse them of such ideas. Nathan tried to picture what the place might have looked like sixty years earlier, with orphaned children running through the orchards and tracking mud into the house. It certainly must have been livelier back then. He hoisted his bag and entered the building.

The first thing that struck Nathan about the interior of the place was the number of cats. He didn't see any people at all, but directly ahead was a small desk with a calico cat lazily napping on top. To his right was a sitting area, with several lounge chairs and a small couch arranged in front of a lit fireplace. Two more cats occupied spots on the furniture. None of them gave Nathan a second look. The whole atmosphere was warm and cozy, with potpourri providing an aroma of dried orange peels, cinnamon and spice. To the left, a corridor led back toward what must have been the kitchen, and further, a stairway led to the second floor. Nathan moved to the desk where he saw a bell sitting beside the cat, who eyed him now with mild curiosity. Nathan dropped his bag on the ground and then reached out to tap twice on the bell, sending the cat fleeing off the desk and down the corridor. From the opposite direction, Nathan heard heavy footsteps approaching across the wooden floorboards. A woman's voice called out, "Oui, oui! J'arrive! I am coming!" A moment later, the owner of the voice appeared. She was large and round, with gray hair tied back, wearing a bulky gray sweater and floor-length green skirt. Her face was made up with bright red lipstick and pink rouge. Nathan guessed she must be in her late 70s. That meant she'd have been in her early teens when the orphanage closed down. If she'd lived in the area that long, she'd remember it at the very least, and likely some of the former residents.

"Bonsoir madame," Nathan said, "I would like to check in."

"Yes, of course, welcome! You must be Monsieur Mansour."

"That's right." This alias was certainly blown at this point, but his only other option was his American passport and so he passed across the Lebanese document when the woman asked, then signed the register with his assumed name.

"Deux nuits?" she said.

"Yes, two nights." The truth was, Nathan had no idea how long he might stay: as long as it took to dig up some information or hit a dead end and move on. That could be one day, or maybe one week. He didn't have any other promising leads to get to, so he might as well be prepared to settle in and make the most of it. He could actually use a little downtime, strolling through the orchards of rural Provence and sitting beside the fire with a few cats for company. Maybe this wouldn't be so bad, regardless of the outcome.

The proprietor typed his information into her computer and then slid his passport back. "The charge will be one-hundred eighty euro per night. Would you prefer to pay cash or card?"

"Cash, thank you." Nathan handed her some bills.

"My name is Madame LaRue. My husband is Claude. If there is anything we can do to make your stay more pleasant, please do not hesitate to ask." She printed a receipt and handed it to him along with his change.

"Thank you."

"You are here in Provence for business, or for pleasure? Perhaps just a relaxing holiday?"

"A little of both. I'm researching some of the quaint hotels in the area for a blog that I write. I love these old buildings, they have such history. Perhaps you can find the time to tell me about the history of the Chateau Saint-Martin?"

Madame LaRue looked uneasy. "You do not expect a refund? Some free nights?"

"No. No free nights."

She absorbed his answer. "These young people these days, they post on the internet and think they can stay for free!"

"Not me, no, I'm happy to pay full fare. I'm interested, that's all."

"Well, of course, then. I'm sure we can find the time. Breakfast is included. Dinner is available for an extra charge if you desire. It will be served in one hour. Would you require assistance with your luggage?"

"No, I can manage, thank you very much."

"Of course." She reached out to lift a room key from a row of small boxes mounted on the wall behind her. "You are in room number two. Up the stairs, second door to your left along the hall. If you need anything else at all, Mr. Mansour, please do not hesitate to ask."

"I will be sure to do so, thank you very much." Nathan took the key in one hand and lifted his bag with the other, gave a nod and then moved to the stairwell and on up. At the top of the stairs, he turned down the narrow hallway to the second room and then unlocked the door and continued inside. The décor was typical French country, with wood-paneled walls, an antique wooden bureau, a tall wardrobe, desk, and a queen-sized bed covered in decorative pillows. A plush lounge chair was positioned in the far corner near the window. Nathan tossed his bag on a luggage rack and looked out on the orchards behind the house in the last fading light of day. Did orphans once occupy this very room? Was this the view The Fox grew up gazing upon? Nathan would unpack his things and then he needed a shower and a short nap before experiencing the cuisine of Madame LaRue.

An hour later, Nathan was seated in the dining room, clean and rested. Only two other tables were occupied, one by a young couple with Parisian accents and the other by a retired husband and wife from Great Britain. This second pair were discussing properties they'd scouted that afternoon, comparing the advantages and disadvantages of each as a potential second home. All of the places required a fair bit of work. It seemed to be a theme. The younger couple didn't say much at all, rather they spent their time staring dreamily into one another's eyes. Nathan guessed they hadn't been together for all that long.

The couple who ran the place, the LaRues, shared duties in serving their guests. Madam LaRue worked away in the kitchen while her husband, Monsieur LaRue, waited on the tables. He was also in his seventies, with shaky hands and a slight stoop, but he managed not to spill anything. Monsieur was assisted by a younger woman, perhaps from the nearby village, or maybe a granddaughter. She bused the tables and filled the glasses, both water and wine. In between, she helped Madame in the kitchen. It was a set menu, with the first course being a French onion soup accompanied by a sliced, round loaf of bread in a wicker basket. The main course, or plat principal, was rabbit stew with bacon and vegetables. Both were excellent, along with the wine that went with them. It was all enough to leave Nathan reconsidering his first impression of the place. In fact, at this point he almost wanted to settle in here and just forget about the outside world altogether for a while. Following the main course came a salad, then cheese, and finally small chocolate-filled pastries for dessert along with coffee. Madame LaRue went all out and did not disappoint. Nathan wondered how she kept this up, night after night. Perhaps it was a labor of love.

After dinner, there wasn't much for Nathan to do. Anything, really. He went into the sitting room and found a bookcase full of novels. Most were in French, but he managed to pick out a copy of *The Great Gatsby* in English and then settled down on the couch beside the fire. He scratched the head of one of the cats as he took another look around. What he wanted was to see if he could find any documents stored on the premises that dated back to the orphanage. Ideally, there would be a safe somewhere, or maybe just an old desk, with lists of all of the children, their origins and dates of birth. If not here, then maybe in the local library or government offices. These were the types of information one could never find online. You had to put in the time and pound the leather. You had to show up yourself and dig them up. He could wait until everybody was asleep and then go poking around in the LaRue's private office but that would be unseemly. He'd stoop to that as a last resort. His first choice was simply to ask. For now, the LaRue's were busy cleaning up the dinner dishes and preparing the dining room for breakfast. Nathan eased back on the couch and opened his book.

In my younger and more vulnerable years my father gave me some advice that I've been turning over in my mind ever since. "Whenever you feel like criticizing anyone," he told me, "just remember that all the people in this world haven't had the advantages that you've had."

This didn't seem like such bad advice at all, Nathan thought. He was halfway through the first chapter when Monsieur LaRue appeared, shuffling into the room. "Bonsoir!" he said.

"Good evening." Nathan watched as he went to a small woodpile beside the fireplace, lifted two small logs and arranged them on the dying flames.

"The weather is changing, yes?" said Monsieur LaRue. "The nights, they are very cold."

"Indeed. Do you run your hotel year-round, or will you close soon for the season?"

"Year-round, I am afraid. The holidays, they are very busy for us. After the new year, it is quiet. Some British, they like to escape the gray skies. You are British?"

"Lebanese."

"Ah, Lebanese! Your winters are warmer than ours, no?"

"A little bit, I suppose. Nothing to complain about."

"Yes, but you have plenty else to complain about." Monsieur LaRue shook his head. "Your country, it seems to hold such promise."

"Perhaps someday we will fulfill it."

"One can always hope. Good evening to you, sir."

"And to you."

Monsieur LaRue moved back out of the room the way he had come. Perhaps it was merely temporary, but here in front of the fire, with his book and his cats for company, Nathan felt a sense of peace descend upon him. He opened the cover once more and picked up where he left off, transporting himself to another world, very far away.

In the morning, it was high time for Nathan to get whatever information he could from the LaRues. He'd had a pleasant night, and a good sleep, but now he needed to make some progress in his continuing quest for the truth. He showered, shaved, and put on a clean pair of slacks, a collared shirt and a sweater. His shoes were brown leather boots, good for hiking around the farm when he needed fresh air. He left his room and went downstairs for breakfast, where the British couple was already enjoying eggs, bacon, toast, croissants and coffee. The Parisian pair had yet to make their way down, apparently. Nathan helped himself to the buffet, filled a cup with coffee and found a seat before digging in.

"I say we narrow it down right now, just cross one option off our list," the British woman said to her husband.

"Yes, but which one? They all have their charms."

"Pick one. Which is at the bottom of your list?"

He thought it over, pained by the prospect of having to choose. "Aureille," he finally said.

"Why?"

"Too much work. It would be a nightmare, you have to admit."

"But the village, it's so charming!" she protested.

"Trying to find the right contractors in a tiny village like that? Forget it. Definitely cross off Aureille."

"But what about Miramas? You know that one is far outside our budget."

"Perhaps we can talk them down. It's worth a try, don't you think?"

The couple didn't seem to be making much progress, but Nathan was more interested in the whereabouts of Madame LaRue. Instead, their young helper came into the room to check the coffee and the buffet. "Bonjour Monsieur," she said to Nathan, then disappeared briefly before returning with a fresh pan of fried eggs and placing them on the buffet table. Nathan rose from his seat and went to refill his plate.

"What do you think?" the British husband said in Nathan's general direction.

"About what?" he answered.

"Me and the missus, we're looking to buy a property in the area. Maybe you overheard our deliberations?"

"I did, yes." Nathan returned to his seat with his eggs as the server left the room once more.

"We've got our eye on a place with a ton of character, in the quaintest little village you ever saw, tucked right up into the hills. Medieval fortifications, the works."

"And?"

"And the place is a wreck. The price is OK, don't get me wrong, but the amount of work we'd have to put into it… I'm not sure we'd ever get it done."

Nathan knew which one he would choose. No doubt about it, he'd take the project house, and then he'd lose himself in doing as much of the work as possible on his own. In fact, the idea sounded tempting. Maybe that was what he needed to finally clear his head and move on with life? He hadn't ruled out the idea of a wooden furniture business back in Virginia, where he could work with his hands and breathe the aroma of sawdust in the air, but here in this quaint hotel in the South of France, Virginia seemed far too close to all of the demons he sought to escape. The fact that CIA headquarters was just up the river from Alexandria was enough to make Nathan never want to go back there at all. This idea, to put all of his focus on renovating a home in one of the most stunning locales on earth, away from the hustle and bustle of modern living… it had an undeniable appeal. Perhaps he might give it some serious consideration once his current quest was complete. For now, he looked the couple over. "How good is your French?"

The wife smirked as she looked at her husband. "He hardly speaks a lick."

"Well, excuse me! She learned a few things back in secondary school, but I wouldn't be puttin' on airs."

"I'm just saying, as outsiders, without full command of the language?" Nathan cut back in. "I agree with your assessment that finding the right contractors would be difficult. You'd probably be biting off a whole lot more than you expect."

"See what I mean?" the husband said to his wife. "We'd end up spending more. The place is a money pit! No wonder they're so eager to offload it."

"Fine!" said the wife. "We'll cut Aureille off the list. Are you happy?"

"I'll be happy when all of this is over and done with. All of this searching is wearing me down."

"Let's just make an offer on Miramas, then."

The husband took a deep breath. "You mean it?"

"I mean it. Come on," she looked at her watch. "Yvette will be here in ten minutes, we'd better finish up."

"I'm ready." The husband took a last drink of coffee and then put down his cup. "You have a nice day, Mr….?"

"Mansour."

"Very nice to meet you. We're the Lankershims, Harry and Louisa."

"Good luck with your offer."

"Thank you. I suppose we'll see you at dinner and tell you all about it."

"I will look forward to an update."

The Lankershims headed out of the room, leaving Nathan alone. He filled up one more cup of coffee as the young woman returned to clear the empty dishes. "That was a very nice breakfast, thank you," he said. The woman looked at him with wide eyes, then nodded quickly, lifted a few extra dishes and hurried out of the room. Nathan hadn't meant to startle her. She was more of a "back of the house" type, he decided, more comfortable behind the scenes. When he'd finished his coffee, Nathan went to the front room, where he tapped the bell that sat on the desk. After a long minute, Monsieur LaRue walked out looking disheveled while wiping a few stray crumbs from his mouth with a cloth napkin.

"Bonjour, Monsieur! I trust you found your way to breakfast?"

"Yes indeed, an excellent spread, thank you."

"How may I be of service to you?"

"I was telling Madame that I have an interest in the history of this place. She said she might sit down with me at some point to discuss it."

"I see, yes, well Madame has gone into town to do the shopping but I will let her know of your inquiry as soon as she returns."

"Perhaps you might have some information to share as well?"

"Me? No. I am afraid not. She is the one you'd want to speak with. I would only be wasting your time."

"Why is that? You must know a thing or two about the place?"

"A thing or two, of course, but my wife takes more of an interest in these things. Madame LaRue will return shortly. She prefers to have a coffee each morning at 10 o'clock. Perhaps you could join her then?"

"I will make a point of it. You can let her know to expect me."

"She will be overjoyed to hear it. Is there anything else that you might require?"

"No. Thank you. I will return at 10 o'clock."

Monsieur LaRue gave a quick nod of his head and continued back in the direction from which he had come. Nathan went upstairs, passing the Parisian couple on their way down. He entered his room to pull a camel hair overcoat from his wardrobe. He had some time to kill, he might as well stretch his legs. He slid on the coat, found a knit cap in one pocket, and pulled that onto his head before exiting the room, descending the stairs and moving on out the front door. The day was cool and misty, with a quiet calm about it. Nobody else was in sight. Nathan heard the low drone of a tractor operating somewhere in the distance. He smelled smoke from the fireplace and felt the sting of frost in his lungs. It was a good morning to get his heart rate up. He looked left, then right, before setting off down a dirt track that moved past the chateau and on through the groves of fruit trees, whose bare branches reached out toward the sky like skeletons. The road wound through the property, past a gate, and then on over rolling hills covered with rows of dormant grapevines. Nathan felt oddly at home here in this rural setting, as though he could finally breathe again after a very long time. This was what he knew, what he'd grown up with on his parents' ranch in Texas where the nearest neighbor was a mile away and a man could feel refuge in the knowledge that this little chunk of planet earth was his own. He thought again of the prospect of acquiring a property here himself. Would he go stir-crazy, this Texan plunked down in a culture so drastically different from his own? Or might he lose himself in such a project, renovating an old property and forcing himself to live entirely in the present? Maybe it was just a fantasy but there was certainly an appeal to it.

As he continued along, Nathan passed a few more homes here and there. Some were better maintained than others, but finally, he came to one that was abandoned. The windows were boarded up, with the roof half caved-in on one side. He stopped on the road to eye it more carefully. "I wonder how much I could pick that up for?" he said to himself. This one was a major project, of the scope that he couldn't hope to live in at all without a good six months to a year of work first just to get it in halfway decent shape. At the very least he'd need to redo the roof, the floor and the windows. Unlike the British couple, however, Nathan wasn't here to scout properties. His current focus was clear. He had to find out what the hell was going on with the Bou Zadjar cartel, what they had to do with the assassination of the Secretary of State, the attack on the Chateau de Fontainebleau, and orphans. And of course, the identity of a man known as The Fox. Nathan wasn't the type to leave a job unfinished. He couldn't walk away from this one until it was done. He took a look at his watch and then headed back toward the Chateau Saint Martin. With a little luck, Madame LaRue might give him some small clue to lead him forward.

When Nathan arrived back at the hotel, it was nearing ten o'clock. He came inside, stuffed his hat into his pocket and then hung his coat on a hook by the door. After ringing the bell on the desk, he waited for a minute with no response before moving into the living room, where he took his place on one of the couches beside a cat he hadn't seen before and settled in to wait. From the rear of the house, he heard rattles and thumps, and dishes being put away. It wasn't long before Madame LaRue appeared, shuffling into the room.

"Monsieur, good morning to you! I do hope you are having a pleasant stay with us so far."

"Indeed, I feel very much at home here, thank you."

"That is wonderful to hear." Madame LaRue. "May I offer you a proper coffee?"

"Of course, I would like that very much."

"Come. Follow me."

Nathan did as he was told and Madame LaRue led him to the back of the house and into the kitchen, where she motioned for him to sit at a table by the rear window. The place was worn but spotless, with gleaming pots and pans hanging from hooks above the stove and a drying rack in the sink lined with clean dishes. On one counter was an espresso machine, and Madame LaRue set to work grinding some beans and then loading the coffee into the filter and packing it down. She placed the filter into the machine and twisted the handle before placing a small cup underneath and pressing the button. A hissing noise emanated from the machine along with a burst of steam and then a stream of black coffee flowing into the cup. "I prefer une noisette," said Madame.

"That would be fine."

Madame LaRue took a small metal pitcher and filled it with milk before placing a metal nozzle inside to steam it, then added a dash of the hot milk to the coffee and placed it on the table in front of Nathan.

"You French certainly know how to live," he said.

"And why not?" said Madame LaRue. "We're only given one chance, c'est vrai?"

"Yes, that is true."

Madame made a second noisette and then joined Nathan at the table.

"You and Monsieur LaRue do seem to work very hard," said Nathan.

"Well, this was our dream for a very long time. Be careful what you wish for, is that not what they say?"

"They do. It does seem to be good advice."

"You want to know the history of this place?" She motioned one hand around the room. "Is that what you said?"

"Yes, that's right. How long have you owned the chateau? Is it something handed down through your family?"

"My family? No. My family, they were not property owners. We come from Montpellier. My father owned a small grocery. Monsieur LaRue, he comes from Toulouse. I was already twenty-two years of age by the time we relocated to the area."

"I see, so you've only lived here for fifty years or so?"

"Exactly. That makes us outsiders. One must have roots going back many generations to be accepted in this place."

"Are you treated poorly?"

"Not poorly, no, but the local inhabitants, they are dismissive."

"How long have you owned the hotel?"

"We acquired the chateau ten years ago. Prior to that, we operated a bakery in the village."

"Those are some early hours, running a bakery."

"They are, indeed. That I do not miss."

"I heard somewhere that this place was operated as an orphanage during the Algerian war. Is this true?"

Madame LaRue raised her eyebrows. "You cannot be after *that* dismal history. What sort of publication are you writing for, Monsieur? Travel you say?"

"Yes, I write a blog. I like to tell the untold stories. You know, the darker secrets."

"I am afraid I know very little about that period. This was not a pleasant time, no, not at all. I do not believe my visitors would like to dwell on such things. Sometimes the past is better left alone, would you not agree?"

"Perhaps, but I am intrigued. Might you have some old records left behind? Maybe some lists of occupants?"

"Nothing. If I'd found any, I would burn them. This is a country hotel, Monsieur. We prefer to not be associated with the sufferings of children. Is there something else you would like to discuss? The chateau was originally constructed in 1896. The property has operated fruit orchards for more than a century. Why focus on a few short years in the middle?"

"You're still a working farm, then?"

"Monsieur LaRue and I lease the orchards now, though I can't say they are very productive. Our tenant farmer tells us that all the trees should be torn out and replaced, but that costs money, and these days money is in short supply. It, unfortunately, does not grow on trees." Madame LaRue looked at her watch. "Now, if you don't mind, I have chores that need attending."

"Of course, go right ahead." Nathan hadn't learned a single useful piece of information. So far this entire excursion was proving to be a waste of his time. "Madame, I do have one more question," he said.

"Yes, please," she paused.

"Is there anybody else who might know more about that time period? Maybe somebody else in the village?"

Madame LaRue took a deep breath. She didn't want to go there at all, but her hesitancy was offset by an ingrained desire to accommodate her guests. "Our helper, Genevieve, perhaps you could speak with her grandfather."

"He was here at that time?"

"Monsieur Blanchet was an orphan himself. He grew up in this house."

Nathan perked up. "I see. Yes, I would very much like to meet him, if that would be possible."

Madame LaRue regretted having mentioned it at all, but she nodded her head. "I will speak to Genevieve when she returns."

"Thank you, Madame." Nathan downed the last of his coffee and held out the cup. "Where would you like this?"

"You can leave it on the table. Thank you."

"No, thank you, very much." Nathan placed the cup back down and headed out of the kitchen. In the core of his heart, he felt a glimmer of hope. At last he seemed to be getting somewhere. Every journey is taken one step at a time, and after a long pause, Nathan was moving forward once again. He wouldn't get his hopes too high, but at least this was progress.

Chapter Fifteen

Genevieve drove a rusted blue Fiat hatchback, circa 1996. Nathan was astonished that the car hadn't entirely disintegrated, yet somehow it held together. She took the driver's seat and Nathan climbed in on the passenger side. When Madame LaRue had approached her assistant to ask this favor, the younger woman hardly said a word other than a quick *oui* and a nod of the head. She wasn't in a position to deny a request from her employer, but that didn't mean Genevieve was happy about having to escort this guest to her private family home. It was obvious to Nathan how much of an imposition this was but that couldn't be helped. If her grandfather grew up in the orphanage, Nathan had to speak with him. Genevieve would simply need to put up with it.

As they started down the lane toward the main road, the young woman kept her eyes focused straight ahead. Nathan tried to think of something to say that might put her more at ease but nothing really came to mind. This was a girl who did not seem particularly happy with her lot in life, trapped in a small town with few good prospects to improve things. He knew the score. A place like this could be suffocating for a younger person. No matter how scenic it might be for a British retiree, this was the kind of place that the dreams and aspirations of youth died a slow death, day by day, year by year. One was either built for this life or not. He'd faced a similar choice himself. In Nathan's case, he was fortunate enough to have the means for a college education. He'd gotten out when the going was good.

To fill the uncomfortable silence, Genevieve switched on an old AM/FM radio, tuning in a contemporary music station. They headed toward the village of Pont-de-Crau. Entering the outskirts, Nathan imagined that her family home might be a source of some minor embarrassment. Perhaps that was why the young woman was so uneasy about bringing him home, or maybe it was just the fact that he was an older, foreign man, invading her personal space. When they finally pulled up to a small, single-story home, it was actually in fairly nice shape. The house was white, with a red-tile roof, fresh paint and a well-maintained yard. Genevieve parked in a driveway out front and shut off the engine. "Nous sommes arrivés," she said before getting out of the car. "We've arrived." Nathan exited his side and then followed her to the front door. Entering the house, Genevieve hung her car keys on a hook and then called out. "Bonjour, Maman!"

"Bonjour!" came a voice from somewhere inside.

"J'ai amené un invité!"

A moment later, a woman in her 40s appeared in the hall, drying her hands on a dishtowel and eyeing Nathan with surprise.

"Hello," he said. "I hope I'm not disturbing you."

The woman looked from her daughter to Nathan and back, trying to determine who he was and why he was here.

"Monsieur is a guest of the hotel. He would like to speak with grand papa."

"Elias Mansour is my name." He held out a hand and the mother hesitated for a moment before she shook it.

"With grand papa? You would like to speak with my father?"

"Yes, Madame, perhaps I should have called first. I apologize. I understand this must seem rather sudden. I am writing about the history of the hotel and I am told that your father was raised there."

The woman attempted to process the information before nodding. "This is true." She offered a hand. "I am Madame Roche."

"It is a pleasure to meet you."

"Come inside."

Nathan removed his overcoat and hung it on an empty hook by the door and then followed her down the hall and into the kitchen, with Genevieve just behind.

"An article, you say? Please, have a seat." Madame Roche motioned toward a kitchen table. "Can I offer you some tea?"

"Thanks, you're very kind." Nathan took a place at the table while Genevieve buried her head in her phone and left the room.

"My father, he is not used to receiving visitors. He is an old man, you know, he leads a quiet life."

"I don't need much of his time, but I would like to speak to him if it is not too much trouble."

"Those were not easy years. Who could want to hear such stories? Perhaps it is best to leave the past alone."

"That is exactly what Madame LaRue had to say. I find that period fascinating, though, don't you? I think it is important to document the memories of those who lived through it while we still have time."

Madame Roche shook her head. She wasn't buying it. Nathan understood that she was the gatekeeper. Unless he convinced her that his intentions were noble, he stood no chance of meeting with her father. But what could he say? Not the truth, of course, but he needed to win her confidence. "This is a beautiful part of the world you live in," he tried to butter her up a little.

"I will tell you, it is not an easy life here. Not unless you come from money. Then the world is all yours."

"Have you been here all your life?"

"Yes, all my life." Her voice betrayed a twinge of regret.

"Your grandfather, though, he came from Algeria?"

Madame filled an electric kettle with water and flipped it on. She took down two mugs from a cabinet above. "Yes, his parents lived in Algeria. But they were French!" This was an important distinction for her.

"What took them to North Africa?"

"What took them?!" She looked at Nathan as though he was a complete moron. "Their profession, of course! My grandfather was a bureaucrat, working for the colonial government."

"And your grandparents were killed in the war?" Nathan knew how personal his questions were, coming from a complete stranger, but he wasn't in the mood to dance around the subject.

"They were killed, yes." Madame Roche dropped a tea bag into each mug. "I am sorry that I have no cakes. I can offer some baguette with butter and fruit jam."

"The tea will be fine, thank you."

"You are American, yes?" she turned to him with defiance in her eyes.

"Yes, that's right," he admitted.

"Why do you care about this Algerian war? It has nothing to do with you. Nothing at all!"

"I'm sorry." Nathan was tempted to simply get up and walk out the door, but he hadn't gotten what he came for and he wasn't about to give up that easily. "I know what it is to lose someone to war. The gut-wrenching pain of it, when somebody is taken from this earth before their time. I'm sorry for your losses."

"Me? I was not born! It is my father that I am concerned with. He does not need to be reminded. He leads a quiet life. Why resurrect the past? I think you should have your tea,

Monsieur, and then go back to your lovely hotel. Forget about the past. Live for today."

Nathan appeared to be at an impasse. To get to the grandfather he had to get past the mother, and she was not giving an inch. The water came to a boil and Madame Roche poured some into each mug before placing them on the table along with sugar, cream, two teaspoons and a small empty bowl for the used teabags. She sat to face him, fulfilling some perceived obligation to be a generous host while not so secretly hoping he would leave as soon as possible. Nathan took the string from the side of his mug and dunked the teabag up and down. He was pondering his next move when he heard an odd thumping noise moving through the house, louder with each tap. Madame Roche appeared slightly dismayed and hurriedly rose to her feet but it was too late. A man appeared in the doorway. He was in his mid-70s, small and wiry, and he walked with the help of a solid wooden cane.

"Papa, you should rest!" said Madame Roche. "What are you doing up?"

"I heard a visitor. I thought I would see for myself."

"Good afternoon. My name is Elias Mansour. It is a pleasure to meet you." Nathan stood from the table and offered a hand.

"What nationality is that?"

"Lebanese, though I grew up in America."

"I see." The man moved the cane from his right hand to his left and then shook Nathan's. "My name is Pierre Lacroix. Please, call me Pierre."

"It is an absolute honor to meet you."

"What brings you to Provence? My granddaughter tells me that you are a guest of the hotel."

"Yes, that is correct. I am here to write a travel article with a focus on history."

"Papa, we don't want to interrupt your afternoon nap," said Madame Roche. "Please. Monsieur Mansour was just about to leave."

"It looks to me that he has not yet had a sip of his tea."

"I'm in no hurry," said Nathan.

Madame Roche was running out of options. Instead of trying to keep them apart any longer, she breathed a sigh of defeat before moving to the cabinet to take down one more mug. While her father pulled out a chair and joined Nathan at the table, Madame Roche dropped a teabag into the third mug, filled it with water, and then placed it in front of her dad. She retook her seat, cheeks burning lightly, but she said not another word.

"I understand you spent your childhood at the Chateau Saint Martin," Nathan said to the man. "I'd love to hear about that."

"The Saint Martin?" Pierre seemed shocked by the query, surprised that anybody would take an interest in those days. "That was so very long ago." His eyes took on a faraway caste as he thought back.

"I don't mean to pry, but I'm wondering if you might tell me what that was like, living there with a houseful of orphans?"

"I see, well..." he struggled to come up with some way to answer that question. "You know, my parents were both killed, murdered in our home by the neighbors they had spent years associating with. I was very young, but one does not get over a thing like that. Never. Not to this very day."

"I am truly sorry for your loss, and for all that you've had to endure."

Pierre took the teabag from his mug and placed it in the empty bowl before using a spoon to add some sugar. He poured in some cream, and as he stirred his tea, Pierre's daughter looked on with a worried air, desperate to protect him but knowing she was powerless at this point to pry the old man away. "I had some happy days there at the Saint Martin. It was not all so bad, you know, once I had adjusted. The first six months were very hard. I cried every night, but the human race is very adaptable. It amazes me what one can adjust to over time. You see, we were all in it together, all of the children, suffering together and finding our way in a world without our mothers and our fathers. We were not alone, we had each other."

"I would love to hear about some of the others. Do you remember their names?"

"Names? Oh, no, we had no use for names. Not in the usual sense. We were reinventing ourselves as we went along. We invented new names and gave them to each other."

"Nicknames."

"Yes, that is right, what in English you might call nicknames."

"And what was your nickname, if I may ask?"

Pierre laughed at the memory. "Ha! They called me L'etoile."

"The star."

"That is correct, the star."

"And why did they call you that?"

"At night I used to sit up by the window, gazing at the stars. I was sure that my parents were somewhere up there, watching me back."

"Do you still think so?"

"Of course. Why would I change my mind after so many years? Soon I will see them again, only this time I will be an old man. They are forever young. Let me show you! I have some photographs." He put his hands on the table and struggled to stand.

"No, no, papa! I will fetch them. You stay where you are." His daughter got up from the table and moved quickly out of the room. Nathan had a few sips of tea while they waited, and a minute or so later Madame Roche returned with a small cardboard box, setting it on the table in front of her father. His eyes lit up as he removed the lid. Clearly he was not bothered by this trip down memory lane. Quite the contrary, he seemed to enjoy having somebody to share his stories with. Even Madame Roche appeared relieved by the way he was taking it. Pierre smiled as he lifted out the top photo. It was faded with age, but portrayed a young couple arm-in-arm and dressed in their Sunday best. They appeared to be in their mid-30s; the same as Nathan was now.

"My mother and my father," said Monsieur Lacroix, holding the photo closer for Nathan to see.

"They were a beautiful couple."

Monsieur Lacroix peered at it again with a faraway look in his eyes. "Yes, beautiful."

"What about the Saint Martin? Do you have any photos from when you lived there?"

"The Saint Martin? Yes, yes..." Pierre flipped through a few items in the box and then pulled out a photo of an older woman wearing a black nun's habit. She stood in front of a chalkboard in what appeared to be a classroom. "Here is Mother Maria. She was in charge of my education."

"Was this in a school?"

"Our very own school. I believe the building still stands, in front of the chateau."

"The shed?"

Pierre looked confused. "Shed… I do not know this word."

"Never mind. Tell me, are you still in contact with anybody from that time in your life? Do you know what became of the other children?"

"No, no, not in sixty years."

"Do you know if any records exist? Anything that might show their true names?"

A blank look crossed Pierre's face and he didn't answer the question. Instead, he withdrew into himself, as though a veil had descended between them. The older man flipped through more of his photos, no longer attempting to share them. Nathan craned his neck to see what was there. An older man sat at a desk that looked like the same one that Madame LaRue used to check him in the night before. The next photo showed a group of eighteen children standing in front of the chateau. The building was in much better condition in those days, at least on the facade. On one side of the group was Mother Maria and on the other was the man from behind the desk. The children in between were a mix of ages and genders.

"Do you mind if I see this one?" Nathan reached out a hand and Pierre looked up as though he was surprised to still see him there. Nathan very carefully lifted the photo from the box. "Are you in this one?" he asked.

Monsieur Lacroix reached out with one weathered finger. "Here." The boy he pointed to looked to be roughly ten years old. He was skinny back then, too, and wore loose pants that were a few sizes too large for him, held up by a large black belt. His shirt was white, with a buttoned collar. The young Pierre had a serious expression on his face, and stood straight upright.

Nathan scanned the faces of the others. Nine were boys, with seven girls, ranging from perhaps four years old to around sixteen. "What year was this?"

"Nineteen sixty-three. We had only just lost the war. Of course, I was living at the chateau for two years already."

"You had no other family who could take care of you?"

"My father had one aunt, living in America," said Madame Roche. "She refused to take him in."

"My aunt, she was very young then," said Monsieur Lacroix. "I did not blame her. She had her own life to live."

"In 1964, a local couple adopted my father. He has lived in the area ever since."

"And he married here?" Nathan asked.

"Yes. My mother passed away some years ago."

"I am sorry."

Madame Roche gave a slight nod. "Your readers, they want to know about these things?"

"I don't know, but for me it is all fascinating. I hope you don't mind." Nathan held the photo closer and looked carefully at the faces of each of the nine boys. One of these might possibly be the leader of the Bou Zadjar cartel. Or more likely still, it was none of them. He looked back to Monsieur Lacroix. The older man reached for the next photo as a smile crossed his lips.

"These two, they were always trouble," said Monsieur Lacroix. The photo showed two of the boys, with their arms around one another and fierce expressions on their faces. "Inseparable. Where one went, there went the other."

Nathan looked them over. These two were perhaps eight years old. One had slightly darker skin, with brown curly hair. His eyes displayed an uncanny worldliness for a boy his age, as though he'd already seen it all. The other boy had straight blonde hair in a bowl cut. He was a little bit larger, with a round, pudgy face. "What do you remember about these two?" Nathan powered on his phone and took a photo of the snapshot.

"I remember that they gave our Mother Maria fits. They didn't like to follow the rules. More than once they ran away, only to be dragged back by the local gendarme under great protest."

"Were they adopted as well?"

Monsieur Lacroix shrugged. "When I left that place, I did not look back."

"But you still have these photos. It's a part of who you are."

"Yes, I have the photos, but I have not looked at them for a very long time."

"Do you remember what you called these boys?"

Lacroix tilted his head as he thought back, taking a moment to replay those ancient days through his mind. "In the beginning, this one was very quiet," he pointed to the smaller boy. "For that reason, we called him *The Mouse.* It was only later that we realized how cunning he could be."

"In what way?"

"The other boy was the brash one, but *The Mouse,* he was responsible for the planning. Whatever they got up to, stealing rations from the kitchen or sneaking cigarettes from the groundskeeper, it was this one behind it."

"At the age of, what, seven years old? Eight?"

"Mais oui, Monsieur."

"I see, and what was the other boy called?"

Monsieur Lacroix looked to the blond child. "Yes, I remember quite well. This one was sneaky, always getting away with something. We called him, *The Fox.*"

Chapter Sixteen

By the time Nathan was able to catch a ride back to the chateau with Madame Roche's husband it was past the dinner hour but Madame LaRue fixed Nathan a sandwich with gruyere, ham and caramelized onions on a toasted baguette. The French made even a grilled cheese sandwich seem special. The British couple had departed, as had the Parisians. As far as Nathan could tell, he was the only guest remaining. He considered calling Sophie to tell her what he'd found. She might be able to help in some way. At the very least he could bounce his thoughts off her, but then, at this point he was gun shy when it came to sharing anything with anybody. This was a puzzle he needed to solve himself, without the GIGN or CIA coming along to screw the whole thing up. He'd made good progress. Nathan would keep at it, plugging away for now on his own terms.

In the cozy living room, he read some more of *The Great Gatsby* and chatted briefly with Monsieur LaRue when he came in to put some wood on the fire. Looking around the room, Nathan pictured those two little troublemakers running rampant, The Mouse and The Fox. He'd already done the math. If they were roughly seven years old in 1963, it meant they'd be in their mid 60s now. Drug kingpins didn't often live that long, let alone in secret. This Fox was obviously very careful. He no doubt had help on the inside, with payoffs to the right politicians, or police officials, or army generals. That was even more reason for Nathan to keep this close to the vest. In the morning he would make his next move. For now, he opened the novel and picked up where he'd left off.

I believe that on the first night I went to Gatsby's house I was one of the few guests who had actually been invited. People were not invited—they went there... Sometimes they came and went without having met Gatsby at all, came for the party with a simplicity of heart that was its own ticket of admission.

By ten p.m., Nathan was upstairs and tucked into bed beneath a warm down comforter. He slept well, had breakfast early, and then caught a ride-share to La Mairie in the Ville de Saint-Martin-de-Crau, the city hall in the nearest village. If any records were kept from the 1960s, Madame LaRue assured Nathan that he had the best chance of finding them here. The building itself was white with a red tile roof, rising two stories and with a clock tower on top. Inside, he found a young man in a white-collared shirt sitting behind a desk. This man informed Nathan that the person he wanted to see was Madame Carre, who looked after the village archives. Madame Carre reported to work at 9 a.m., which was still nearly one hour away. Nathan left the city hall and found a small cafe up the block where he ordered a café crème and read a local paper to kill the time. In a village this size, he drew some attention merely by his presence. This came in the form of a few extended looks his way from curious villagers and a comment or two that he wasn't meant to understand, but nonetheless did.

"Another speculator from the north," one customer commented to another.

"Madame LaRue is going to price us out of the market," the other lamented.

"You two be quiet," said the proprietor. "You have no right to complain. With the value of your properties these days, you can retire in luxury!"

"I will never sell," said the first man. "Never! They will bury me on the property, next to my mother and my father."

Nathan was tempted to respond, to let them know that he spoke fluent French, but then, they didn't seem to care. After all, he was reading the newspaper in their language, or perhaps they hadn't noticed. When the 9 o'clock hour drew near, he threw some euro coins onto the table. "If you change your mind about selling your place, please inform Madame LaRue. I would love to take a look," he said to the customer, in French. The man was too stunned to respond.

Nathan downed the last of his coffee and headed out the door. Back at the city hall, he was informed that Madame Carre had arrived. After a short wait, he was escorted into a small, stuffy office full of crowded bookshelves. An older woman with a full head of gray hair sat behind a desk piled with binders of old newspapers. One binder sat open in front of her, and the woman read an article through a pair of glasses perched on the end of her nose. When she reached a stopping point, she looked up.

"Here is the man to see you," said the clerk.

"Elias Mansour is my name."

"Hello, Monsieur, how may I help you? Please, have a seat."

Nathan plopped himself down in a chair facing the desk while the younger man retreated back the way he had come. "I'm interested in the orphanage at the Chateau Saint Martin. Madame LaRue tells me that you might have some records dating from that time?"

"The orphanage?" Madame Carre repeated the words as though in awe. "Nobody has spoken of that in many years, as far as I am aware. What is your interest? You are searching for a lost relative, perhaps?"

"No, nothing like that. I'm writing a travel article about the history of the chateau and how it came to be such a quaint hotel.

I thought my readers might enjoy a little background on those years."

Madame Carre raised her eyebrows. She didn't seem to be buying Nathan's logic. "I see."

"Do you have records stored here that might help me? You are the village archivist, correct?"

"Yes, Monsieur, I am the archivist. I will need to research your request. This will take some time, to go through the files and see what we have."

"How much time?"

Madame Carre shrugged. "I cannot say. Maybe one day, maybe one week."

"It is somewhat time sensitive."

"Your readers, they need to know right away?" she scoffed.

"I have a deadline, you understand."

Madame Carre slid a notepad and a pen across the desk. "I will contact you. Please, write down your information."

Nathan knew how these small-town municipal employees operated. This woman would be in absolutely no hurry but without knowing where to look himself he couldn't very well rifle through the files on his own. He jotted down his email and phone number and slid it back across the desk. He considered adding a few hundred euros in cash as an incentive but then he couldn't tell how Madame Carre would take it. Instead, he breathed a sigh and then stood. "Thank you, Madame."

"I will be in touch," she replied.

Outside on the street, Nathan ran the whole situation through his mind once more. Only one person stood out to him as a prime suspect. Laurent Dubois was the right age. He was wealthy enough to be the head of a major drug and weapons smuggling cartel, and he had a soft spot for orphans. It was almost too obvious. A guy like Dubois, though, would have a background that was easily looked into. A little research ought to provide some clues. Better yet, he could call Philippe Legrand to add a little urgency to his request for a meeting. Nathan turned on his phone and dialed but it went to voicemail.

"Philippe, it's Nathan. Call me back when you have a chance." Nathan hung up the phone. If he left it on he would likely be tracked wherever he went but if he turned it off he might miss a return call. That went for Philippe, but also for Madame Carre. He opted to leave it on and take his chances.

Back at the chateau, Nathan went up to his room and sat in a chair by the window. On his phone, he scrolled through everything he could find about Laurent Dubois. The man's adult history seemed carefully curated. He was quite wealthy, as Nathan already knew. The man had a hand in all sorts of industries, including finance, technology and manufacturing, but there was not one single company alone that appeared to be the primary source of his money. Instead, he ran what was called Dubois Holdings, which operated as an umbrella corporation for all of his other enterprises. Was the Bou Zadjar Cartel among them? Nathan searched through images for the earliest photo he could find of Dubois. The best he could do was a shot of the man in his mid-20s, standing on a pier on a warm summer day and holding a fish in his hands, posing proudly for the camera with his catch. The big question, of course, was whether or not this man's face matched that of an eight-year-old boy from the Saint Martin Orphanage some twelve years earlier. Nathan went back and forth from one photo to the other. The hair color seemed right, and the cheekbones were similar. The forehead, and the spacing of the eyes, it all seemed plausible. This was no home run but he couldn't rule it out either. The boy in the photo could be Laurent Dubois, but then again perhaps not.

The available bios of Dubois didn't seem to help much, at first. He was said to have come from a humble background and made his own way in the world. His mother was a schoolteacher and his father a bureaucrat. But then Nathan came to a paragraph that sent his pulse racing. When Laurent Dubois was only a young child, his family relocated to Algiers. Two years later his parents were killed in the war. Both of his parents. Laurent Dubois was an orphan. Nathan put his phone down and looked out the window at what was quite possibly the same view the young Laurent admired all those years before. Nathan's phone rang. It was Philippe Legrand returning his call.

"Hello, Philippe, thanks for calling me back," said Nathan.

"Of course, what can I do for you? Let me see, you are calling about Dubois?"

"Yes, indeed. Were you able to set up a meeting for me?"

"I left that task to Claudette. She is very busy you know, though I believe she made an attempt."

"No success?"

"Sometimes these things take time."

"Look, I don't mean to be demanding, Philippe, but can't you just call the man and ask him yourself?"

Legrand cleared his throat, stifling any annoyance with this pestering American. "This is important to you?"

"I wouldn't ask otherwise. Tell him I'm a freelance journalist. I'm writing an article and I'd like to interview him."

"And what, by chance, is this article about?"

"Orphans."

There was a pause as Legrand thought it over. "I will see what I can do."

"Thank you, Philippe. You are very good to me."

"I will be in touch."

Nathan hung up and sat back in his chair. What if he did get a meeting with Dubois? What would he even ask? If Dubois was involved, his primary goal would be to hide it. With some luck, Nathan would at least get a little bit closer.

Chapter Seventeen

Dubois was in Monte Carlo. For Nathan, that meant a five-hour train ride, connecting through Marseille. Somehow, Philippe Legrand had worked his magic. Nathan was scheduled to have dinner with Dubois and his wife at a place called the Buddha Bar, across the garden from the famous Monte Carlo Casino. According to Philippe, Dubois had substantial financial interests in Monaco, including several large commercial developments that consisted of retail space, restaurants, and high-rise apartments. Asked where Dubois originally came upon his fortune, Philippe was cagey. "Sometimes it is best not to pursue such questions too intently," he'd said.

"You're implying criminal activity?" Nathan wanted clarification.

"Nobody with this amount of money is completely above-board, Nathan. You know that."

"Do you include yourself in that assessment?"

"Let me just say, no comment."

"I'm not interested in somebody who cooks the books to save on his tax bill. I'm interested in more serious infractions."

"I'm already starting to regret setting up this meeting. What exactly do you intend to ask Dubois, and for what purpose? You know, I have put my reputation on the line for you."

"I appreciate that. All I can tell you is that the cause is noble."

Philippe was not at all convinced. "Your date from the charity ball, she is an officer with the Gendarmerie Nationale. Are you working with them?"

"Look, Philippe, you're going to need to trust me on this one. Have I ever let you down?"

"You know what they say. There is always a first time."

"Just try to relax. I will do my very best to protect the name of Philippe Legrand."

Philippe seemed to realize that there was nothing to be done at this point on his end. The meeting was set. He'd have to live with the consequences, whatever they turned out to be. "Please promise me one thing. If things do not go as you plan, will you at least give me some warning?"

"You will be the first to know."

Nathan hung up as his train sped through the countryside. He had some time to formulate a game plan. Mostly, he just wanted tidbits of biographical information out of Dubois, at least to start. If he could definitively identify him as The Fox, Nathan would be more inclined to pass this along to Sophie and the GIGN. Getting anything more useful out of Dubois by himself would involve a careful dance. One thing in Nathan's favor, he had years of experience with the CIA, recruiting foreign assets. If there was anything to pry out of Dubois, Nathan was well trained to get it.

When he arrived in Monte Carlo, the station was just a short distance from Nathan's hotel. A chill breeze swept through the air as he buttoned his overcoat, hoisted his duffel on one shoulder and walked the three blocks before checking in just after 6 p.m. He would have enough time to shower and change before meeting Dubois at 7:30. What did one wear to a meeting with a billionaire drug and weapons smuggling kingpin? Nothing in Nathan's bag of wrinkled clothing was likely to suffice. Adjacent to the lobby, he spotted several high-end shops, with at least one selling men's clothing. After receiving his room key from a hotel clerk, Nathan entered one of the shops and took a quick look at a handful of suits on display. It didn't take long for a sales associate to come to his assistance.

"Looking for anything in particular?" said the clerk.

"How fast can you have this tailored?" Nathan lifted a charcoal suit to take a closer look.

"We can have it ready for you by tomorrow afternoon."

"How about if I need it in an hour?"

The man gave Nathan a pained expression. "That would be difficult."

"But not impossible?"

"Nothing is impossible, Monsieur. For a price."

"Let me try it on."

Nathan found his size and was in and out of the dressing room in a matter of minutes. The fit was reasonable, and the sales clerk took measurements for Nathan's inseam and sleeves. After taking the suit back off, Nathan picked out a white shirt and gray tie. He paid and then took the shirt and tie with him but left the suit for the tailor and then went up to his room for a shower. A little over one hour later, he was trying the clothes on in front of a mirror. As he cinched up his tie, he had to admit, he didn't look half bad. He took a black belt and dress shoes from his bag and slid those on, along with his watch. The last touch was the camel hair overcoat that he'd owned for years. It wasn't fancy, but it would do. He headed out for dinner.

The Buddha Bar was easy to find. It was located in the casino complex, along with more high-end watch stores and clothing boutiques. This place just smelled like money. If you didn't have it, you weren't welcome here, but if you did? Well, then, the world was yours. The building itself looked like another French palace. Nathan made his way up an elegant set of stairs and on inside, where he dropped off his overcoat at a coat check. He took a number tag from an attendant and then passed through another doorway into what could best be described as an elegant ballroom with a Southeast Asian theme. The throbbing sounds of techno music provided a soundtrack. The place was bustling with diners at their tables and servers swirling through the room in what seemed like a choreographed dance. Red and purple light reflected off the walls and ceiling to give it a contemporary air, with enormous chandeliers hanging from either side of the room and a DJ on a balcony in between. Against the facing wall was a fifteen-foot-high bronze statue of the Buddha himself.

"Can I help you, sir?" a young hostess asked Nathan.

"I am here to meet Monsieur Laurent Dubois for dinner."

The hostess looked on her reservations list. "You are the first in your party to arrive. Would you like to wait in the bar?"

"Yes, thank you." As Nathan moved further into the room, he got a better look at the place. The bar was directly beneath the DJ balcony, and two grand staircases led to more private tables upstairs. Nathan took a seat at a barstool and ordered a Scotch before glancing around at the other patrons, some at dinner tables and others scattered around the bar area. He saw plenty of gold lame, and designer dresses, boob jobs, Botox and six-figure watches. These people needed a place like this, in order to dress up and show off for each other. Nathan tried not to judge them. He'd been around wealth many times, most recently at the Chateau de Fontainebleau. Rich people weren't so much different from anybody else, just with a whole lot more money. That meant that both their virtues and their vices were accentuated. One could do a lot of good with a large pot of money, if so inclined. Or, one could afford to behave very badly, often in the service of accumulating even more. The question for this evening was, what kind of man was Laurent Dubois? Nathan knew what he expected to find. Dubois would be loathsome and unscrupulous, the type who found satisfaction in exerting his raw power over others. He would be cunning, with no moral compass. These were the traits necessary to run such a criminal enterprise as the Bou Zadjar Cartel. The charity ball, of course, was all intended to boost his standing among the rest of the French elite. This was what Nathan expected anyway, but he had learned over the years to avoid making raw assumptions. Still, he was somewhat surprised when the man he recognized as Dubois walked into the bar, along with a woman of roughly the same age and no added security in sight. Dubois wore a double-breasted Navy suit with a medium blue shirt underneath and a yellow tie. The woman, whose long, gray hair was combed back and hung just beneath her shoulders, wore a green cashmere sweater and loose, khaki pants. If Nathan were asked ahead of time who Dubois' female companion might be, he'd have described a woman forty years his junior, with platinum blond hair, wearing the latest designer clothing and a sparkling array of jewelry. In fact, that was exactly the type of woman Dubois was with the last time Nathan had seen him. This woman wore all jade: earrings, necklace and bracelet, none of it expensive. She was having a little bit of fun, matching the Asian theme. Nathan liked her already.

When the Dubois' followed the hostess into the bar, Laurent's eyes rested on Nathan, who finished off his Scotch. Laurent reached out. "Monsieur Grant. You come highly recommended."

Nathan shook the outstretched hand. "Philippe is very kind."

"This is my wife, Iliana." Laurent turned toward her. "May I introduce to you, Monsieur Nathan Grant."

"It is a pleasure." Madame Dubois leaned in to present her cheeks and Nathan kissed them, once on each side.

"I hope we haven't kept you waiting," said Dubois.

"No, no, I was enjoying the ambiance of the place."

"The kitsch is amusing, is it not?" said Iliana.

"It reminds me of my younger days," said Laurent.

"He spent some years in Bangkok," Iliana explained. "Back when he was poor, and happy."

"And you are not happy now?" Nathan asked him.

"Oh, I can't complain."

"You can try, but nobody will listen," said Iliana.

"With you in my life, what's to complain about?"

Iliana looked to Nathan. "You see? He is well trained."

Laurent turned to the hostess, who stood by with menus in hand. "Come, let us find our table."

The hostess led them up the grand staircase to a table along the balcony rail with a view of the entire establishment, upstairs and down. Nathan sat on one side, with Laurent Dubois directly across from him and Iliana beside her husband. None of this was anything like what Nathan had expected. He'd thought they would be dining in a private back room, surrounded by heavily armed thugs who kept a careful eye on Nathan's every move. Instead, he was sitting in an open restaurant with what seemed to be a perfectly normal couple. Laurent Dubois did not give off the vibe of a criminal mastermind, and in fact he didn't even exude the aura of wealth that was so evident all around them. Nathan felt a strange sense of disappointment. This whole meeting was starting to feel like a waste of his time before it even began, though he knew that it was too soon to draw any firm conclusions, and besides, even if Dubois was not The Fox, he was connected to that same milieu of former orphans. He might still know something. On another level, Nathan was relieved. He didn't like the idea of Philippe Legrand being friends with a sociopath.

"My husband tells me you attended the ball, at the Fontainebleau."

"Yes, I was there."

Iliana gave a shudder and then shook her head. "So terrible. I don't understand the world today. Why must people do these things?"

"I wish I could answer you."

"Iliana was away that evening, visiting family on Mykonos."

"When I heard what was happening, I was so terrified! I was sure they were after my husband." She looked to Laurent beside her and they held hands on the table. Nathan was not about to ask who Dubois' escort was that evening. After all, it was the French way. What concerned him more than Dubois' personal life was whether he had any inside information on who exactly had attacked the ball, and why.

"Monsieur Grant is not here to discuss that tragedy," said Laurent. "He is here to discuss orphans. Isn't that correct, Monsieur?"

"Yes, that's right. I'm working on an article."

A server stopped back at the table to take their drink orders and Nathan opted for a mojito this time while the Dubois' ordered a bottle of champagne. At a table nearby, he saw the server seating a couple who had been near him in the bar. Both were in their mid-30s and exceptionally fit. The man's biceps bulged beneath a designer sport coat. The woman wore a knee-length, sleeveless dress, her own muscles toned from many hours in the gym. As they took their places at their table, both took surreptitious glances at Laurent Dubois, and Nathan himself.

"Do you enjoy sushi, Monsieur Grant?" Iliana asked.

"Absolutely."

"Wonderful." Without consulting the menu, she rattled off a selection sushi rolls to the server, who nodded and moved away.

"You come here often," said Nathan.

"Oh, yes, you could say it is in our rotation," said Iliana. "When we are in Monte Carlo."

"You spend much of your time here?"

"Well, at this time of year the weather is not so bad," said Laurent. "But let us get back to the orphans."

"Next to his business interests, it is my husband's favorite topic," said Iliana.

"But of course!" said Laurent. "Is it so wrong that I try to leave the world a better place?"

"No, dear, I would never imply such a thing."

"I understand that you were an orphan yourself?" Nathan asked Laurent. "Can you tell me about that?"

"Me? No, that is ancient history. I am more interested in helping those young survivors of today. Did you know, in the northern Syrian province of Idlib alone there are currently 1.2 million orphans. Can you imagine that? Worldwide the United Nations estimates that there are 153 million of them! These are children in desperate need, Monsieur Grant."

"I had no idea there were so many."

"India, 31 million. Africa, 59 million. Any light you can shine on this situation would be of help."

"I do think my readers would be interested in your personal story. It would humanize things, more than just these numbers that are so hard to comprehend. Besides, you are a success story, an inspiration that shows how one can overcome the most difficult of circumstances."

"My story, it is far from typical. More likely, these children become child laborers, or worse."

"Tell me, though, if you don't mind, how did you lose your parents? Was it in the Algerian war?"

"The war, no?" Laurent shook his head. "My parents were not involved in the war. In fact, they were not French at all."

"Laurent Dubois, that sounds like a very French name to me."

"My given name, my real one, was lost to history I am afraid. Dubois was the name of my adopted family. They named me Laurent. I was found as a baby, you see, in the bottom of a small boat, adrift in the Mediterranean Sea. Nobody knows where I came from. Nobody knows what became of my parents. Did one fall from the boat and the other jump in to rescue them? Did they both fall overboard? The questions have haunted me for a lifetime, Monsieur Grant. That is why I prefer to live in the present, as much as I am able."

This was far from the story Nathan had heard about Dubois already, that his parents were typical French bureaucrats. Perhaps it was true, but then he might be trying to mythologize his origins, to create a more romantic story. "Have you tried a genetic analysis?"

"He is North African with a little Greek," Iliana chipped in. "That's what they say."

"It does not tell me much of anything about who I really am," said Laurent.

"I see. And what can you tell me about an orphanage called Chateau Saint Martin?"

"I have never heard of it."

"Never? It operated in Provence in the early 1960s, as a home for children orphaned by the war."

"As he said, my husband prefers to focus on the present day," said Iliana. "To help the children currently in need."

"Of course. I wonder, however, if Monsieur Dubois might fill in some further details on his own story. You were found in the bottom of a boat, like the legendary Romulus and Remus, but what came after that? How were you discovered? Who raised you?" Nathan realized that nothing the man told him could be taken for granted. In fact, it all sounded unlikely.

"I was rescued by Corsican fishermen and taken to the local Gendarme. I have no memory of those days, of course, I was much too young, but this is what I have been told. A young family took me in for the first year, but when it was too much for them I was adopted by a merchant and his wife in the capital city of Ajaccio."

"Birthplace of Napoleon Bonaparte."

"That is correct, you know your history Monsieur."

"The merchant who adopted you was named Dubois?"

"Yes, I took his name but I have never been entirely accepted in this country. I am considered a perpetual outsider, without a proper pedigree."

"Success in the business world does help," said Iliana. "When you have money, everybody wants to be your friend."

"My wife, she is one hundred percent Greek. No mystery on her side."

The server returned with their drinks while another placed multiple platters of sushi on the table along with two plates of spicy tuna tacos and one of crispy calamari. When the champagne was poured, Laurent raised his glass. "To our friend Philippe, I am only sorry he was not able to join us."

"To Philippe," Nathan tapped his mojito glass to each of theirs and took a drink. Looking over the menu, Nathan chose the Angus tenderloin steak, while Iliana ordered Thai red shrimp curry and Laurent opted for Peking duck.

"Tell me, Monsieur Grant," said Laurent, "What brings you to our part of the world? I don't suppose it is an article about orphans."

"I've always had a soft spot for France. I lived in Marseille for three years through my previous employer. This time it is a shorter visit."

"And you are a journalist?" said Iliana.

"I'm not sure if that is what you call it these days. I have a blog, travel and history. It pays the bills and allows me to roam the world."

"I envy your freedom," said Laurent. "No responsibilities to tie you down? It sounds like a fabulous life."

"It is at that, but tell me, do you maintain contact with any orphans from your generation? Perhaps you have some friends who endured similar hardships as children?"

"Friends? No." Laurent chuckled at the question. "None of my friends endured hardship at all. The people I associate with now were born with silver spoons in their mouths, as you say. Their only hardships were being sent off to boarding school. Of course, I was very fortunate myself. Fortunate, indeed. With my adopted family, I was able to create a future."

"It seems that you've managed to amass quite a fortune." Nathan sipped at his mojito. "Or so I've been told."

"Nothing was handed to me. I worked as a fisherman, in my younger days. I was able to buy a boat. Then I bought another, and another. Soon, I was running cargo to the mainland and back. It all grew from there."

"In a port like Ajaccio, you must have come across your fair share of smugglers, yes? It seems perfectly located between Africa and Europe."

Laurent's face flushed red. "What are you implying, Monsieur Grant?"

"Nothing, nothing at all." Nathan seemed to have touched a raw nerve. "I just thought that such people might have made your life difficult. Is that fair to say?"

Laurent eyed Nathan warily. "This line of questioning has not one thing to do with orphans, Monsieur."

"No, you are correct. I apologize." A tension now hung over the conversation, but safer ground wouldn't give Nathan the answers he was after. "Tell me this, if you don't mind: Why do you think a group of terrorists would attack a charity ball for orphans? Do you have any idea? Perhaps the authorities might have given you some indication?"

Laurent's eyes narrowed. These questions weren't much better, apparently. "A travel blog. Is that what you said? Your readers, they have an interest in terrorist attacks?"

"This is more for my own personal curiosity."

"Who are you, Monsieur Grant? I will give you a choice. You can level with me, or this dinner is over. I do not appreciate being set up under false pretenses. Legrand should know better."

"Please don't hold Philippe responsible for any offense I may have caused."

Iliana drank her own champagne quietly. The muscles in Laurent's shoulders stiffened as he leaned forward. "Who are you?" he repeated. "You may as well tell me. I will find out either way, I can assure you."

Nathan didn't doubt it. He was only surprised that Dubois' people hadn't dug up more on him already. Or maybe they had. He looked back to the couple at the table nearby, quite certain by this point that they were private security. Dubois and his wife may have liked to pretend that they were just an ordinary couple, out for dinner on their own in a local restaurant, but that was all just a facade. Businessmen this wealthy didn't go anywhere without protection. The truth of the matter was that Dubois most assuredly knew a whole lot more about Nathan than he was letting on. "I'm former CIA, now retired," he admitted.

"*Retired*?" Dubois scoffed. "Please, do not insult me any further."

"It's true. I'm no longer with the agency."

"And yet you accuse me of being a smuggler of some kind?! What is your game, Monsieur Grant?"

Nathan's intelligence training told him to put the target at ease, to create a personal connection if possible. That prospect was now out the window. Likewise, implied threats would only put Nathan's own life in danger. He seemed to be running out of options as he tried to figure out a way to climb out of this hole he'd apparently dug for himself. "Old habits die hard, we say. I was a witness at the Chateau de Fontainebleau. I'd like to know what it was all about." Nathan looked from Laurent, to Iliana, and back. "I apologize, Monsieur. My intentions are noble, I can assure you."

While Monsieur was glowing with anger, Madame seemed oddly amused as she sampled some of the sushi, unwilling to insert herself into this conversation.

"This is not the job for a private citizen," Monsieur Dubois continued. "The authorities are responsible for solving such crimes." Before Nathan could respond, Dubois snapped his fingers at a server, who hurried to the table.

"Oui, Monsieur?"

"We have had a change of plan. Please prepare our dinners to go," Dubois replied.

"As you wish." The server turned around and headed back toward the kitchen.

"Don't leave on my account. I am sorry to have wasted your time." Nathan stood, giving a light nod to Iliana. "Madame."

"Good evening," she replied.

Nathan gave a nod next to Monsieur Dubois and then turned and headed toward the stairs. As he started down, he took one last look back to see the fit couple watching him go. The man immediately looked away, but Nathan made eye contact with the woman for a brief moment. In her fierce blue eyes he saw the depths of a cold and calculating predator. That look sent a shiver down Nathan's spine as he descended toward the ground floor.

Continuing toward the front, he retrieved his overcoat and slid it on, then went out the door and past a large white Rolls Royce Phantom waiting by the curb. In the driver's seat sat a uniformed chauffeur, and beside him, another burly security guard. No matter how much they liked to pretend otherwise, Monsieur and Madame Dubois were billionaires through and through. Nathan made a mental note of the registration plate: BL-432-ML. Next, he checked his watch. It was still early. There was no sense going back to the hotel right away, just to sit in his room. Besides, he hadn't been able to finish that mojito, nor his tenderloin either.

Directly across the park was the Hotel de Paris Monte Carlo, adjacent to the casino. Nathan headed over. Parked out front here was a Lamborghini Huracan, beside a McLaren 720S, beside a Ferrari 488. He almost turned around in search of someplace more within his budget, but then, you only lived once and besides, he still had some of Philippe's loan burning a hole in his pocket. The building itself was in the same Belle Époque style as the casino beside it. Nathan walked up the front stairs, looking over his shoulder as he went and half expecting one of Dubois' goons to be following him. He spotted nobody of interest, just a lone valet standing by the curb.

After passing through the hotel lobby, Nathan entered Le Bar Americain. The place had a 1920s ambiance, as though straight out of *The Great Gatsby* itself. Instead of taking one of several open tables on the floor, he went to the long wooden bar and slid onto an empty stool. A bow-tied bartender was immediately at his service, dropping a napkin in front of Nathan. "Bonjour, Monsieur," he said.

Being in a bar called Le Americain, it seemed to Nathan that only one drink was fitting. "I assume you serve Jack Daniels?"

"Oui, Monsieur, bien sur."

"I'll take it neat with a splash."

"Of course." Behind him along the wall, hundreds of bottles were lined up on shelves stretching nearly to the ceiling. The bartender reached to pull down the Jack Daniels and then poured two ounces into a glass, added a few drops of water and placed it on the napkin. "Voila. Will there be anything else?"

"A food menu, if you please."

The bartender reached for a menu and placed it beside the whiskey, then moved away toward another pair of customers further down the bar. Nathan looked over his options. He could have blue lobster spaghetti in black truffle juice for 130 euros. Or there was the caviar selection with buckwheat blinis for 286 euros. Nathan scrolled further down the menu until he came to the cheeseburger with fries, for 39 euros. That would do. He didn't need any reminders that he was currently unemployed. At some point soon, he would need to address the issue. Nathan was thirty-six years old and nowhere near retirement age. One way or another he'd need an income at some point soon. As he waited for his cheeseburger, he sipped at his whiskey and thought about his current situation. The U.S. government had entire agencies dedicated to chasing down this type of conspiracy, along with all of the resources that entailed. There was the CIA, of course, and the FBI, along with Homeland Security, the Diplomatic Security Service, the National Security Council, and then of course, Nathan Grant, sitting here at a fancy bar in Monte Carlo, waiting for his cheeseburger and fries. What had he even accomplished so far? Laurent Dubois seemed to be a dead end, as far as he could tell. The same went for the orphanage. Maybe he knew that The Fox was raised there, but he still didn't know the man's identity, nor did he have any idea what was behind it all. Why was the Secretary of State assassinated? Why was the charity ball attacked? Were they even connected? The only reason Nathan was still pursuing any of it was pure stubbornness. He'd always had that in him. Nathan didn't like unfinished business. When you started something, you carried on through to the end. Of course, another part of it was more personal. Nathan reached a hand up and felt through his shirt the gold wedding band that hung from a leather strap around his neck. Chasing after international smugglers and assassins was not a bad hobby if you had something you wanted to forget. Nathan found some unlikely joy in it all. This pursuit was dangerous, and often foolhardy, but it made him feel alive. He took another sip of whiskey and thought about what sort of an actual job he might be suitable for. Nothing much really came to mind. Definitely not an office job, that would suck the life out of him. For now, he'd enjoy his 39-euro cheeseburger and try to push these thoughts aside for a little while longer.

Nathan turned to scope out the other patrons around the bar. The tables were roughly half occupied, including a few small groups, some couples and a pair of gentlemen in dark suits. Further down the bar sat two women in their 20s, dressed to party and showing too much skin for a high-end establishment like this. Nathan thought they might be professionals, then wondered if such women were even allowed in here at all. The nearest one gave him a sly smile. He turned away as the bartender placed Nathan's food on the bar, along with utensils, salt, pepper and ketchup.

"Anything else you need?" said the bartender.

"Is there a local beer you'd recommend?"

"The Monte Carlo Amber, brewed here in Monaco."

"One of those, please."

"Yes, sir."

While the bartender poured the beer, Nathan started in on his fries and then took a big bite of his burger. It was not half bad, but in a place like this one he'd only expect the best. He was pouring some ketchup on the fries when he heard animated murmurings coming from a small group seated at the tables. He looked over to see them staring with rapt attention at their phones, or looking over each other's shoulders as they viewed something of great interest. Whatever the news was, it seemed to spread through the room in a wave, from one table to another. Each party in turn was soon reading their phones, aghast. As the bartender placed Nathan's beer on a coaster before him, Nathan went straight to the headlines on his own phone and there it was, breaking news. The Vice President of the United States was dead, gunned down during a fact-finding trip to the U.S.-Mexico border. The whole incident was caught on video and Nathan watched it just like everyone else in the room, or no doubt everyone else in the world. There was the Vice President standing with a group of dignitaries near the wall, and then a burst of gunfire, followed by screams and chaos. Nathan shut it off and put his phone down. So much for all of those agencies responsible for sorting out this mess. He was tempted to get up and head straight back to his hotel, but then, he'd already passed up one dinner tonight, he wasn't about to let two of them get away. He lifted his beer and took a sip. Again, not bad at all. He ate another bite of his burger. Maybe in the morning all of this would somehow make more sense

Chapter Eighteen

Unfortunately, things didn't look any clearer in the morning. Nathan had spent all evening reading news of the assassination and watching multiple videos of the attack. Now he sat at a table in his hotel room, having a breakfast of two eggs over-medium, potatoes, ham and toasted baguette, along with a café au lait. He took a sip of the coffee and leaned back in his chair to take in his view of the Mediterranean, stretching to the horizon.

What authorities did know of the attack so far was that the shots had come from the southern side of the border, through open slats in the tall steel fence posts. Security around the Vice President would have been tight, as usual, with Secret Service operating on both sides, along with Mexican cooperation. Tragically, the Federal Police south of the border was infiltrated with corrupt officers, working in tandem with one of the Mexican cartels. The government tried to overcome this by deploying a special operations team from the Mexican Navy, but in this case it hadn't made a difference. Besides the Vice President, the ensuing gun battle took the lives of eight others on the American side and an unknown number of combatants and innocent victims alike on the Mexican.

Eating his breakfast half a world away, Nathan attempted to draw connections between the three attacks, including Secretary Parsons, the Chateau de Fontainebleau, and now this. The Parsons attack involved a drug cartel active in North Africa. The Fontainebleau may have involved the same group, though Nathan couldn't say. From public reporting, this latest assassination seemed to involve a Mexican cartel. The fact that such groups were resorting to extreme violence wasn't surprising, that was par for the course. What surprised Nathan was the enemies they were willing to provoke. The American government went to war for twenty years in Afghanistan over a terrorist attack. What resources would they bring to bear over something like this? The risk/reward ratio for the cartel involved seemed completely out of whack, but then they weren't likely dealing with logical actors.

When he was finished with his breakfast, Nathan placed his dirty dishes in the hall and then went back into the room to pack. It was becoming clear that his involvement in these matters was finished. It had all moved far beyond his pay scale, which of course was currently $0.00. He had nothing left when it came to operative leads. The time had come to leave the whole thing to the professionals, just as nearly everyone he'd come into contact with had suggested. The most reasonable course of action would be to head back to Virginia where the condominium he was paying a monthly mortgage on sat empty. He could settle in and start looking at job prospects in ernest. There had to be something he was willing to do for the right paycheck. All the same, winter in the greater DC area would be cold, clammy and gray. He was pondering the idea of returning to his dive master job in Thailand when his phone rang. Checking the number, he saw that it was Madame Carre, from the Saint-Martin-de-Crau city hall. He very nearly didn't answer. In his mind, he was already thousands of miles away, scuba diving in the warm Andaman Sea. Of course, curiosity got the best of him. "Hello, this is Elias Mansour," he picked it up.

"Good morning, Monsieur," Madame Carre replied. "I located some files for you, though I do not suspect they would be of much interest."

"That's fine, thank you, but I've changed my mind. I won't be needing them anymore."

"No? And after I spent half of an afternoon searching through old boxes just for you! Of course, I understand, they are only names, nothing more."

"Names are good," Nathan couldn't help himself. His interest was piqued once more. "Whose names exactly, the children?"

"Yes, the children. Names, dates of birth, arrival date, any known relatives. I can forward them in an email if you would like."

"That would be fine. Thank you, Madame."

"Pas d'problem. Goodbye, Monsieur."

"Goodbye to you."

By the time Nathan was finished packing, the email had come through. He sat in his chair by the window and opened the file. It consisted of a separate page for each year. Just as Madame Carre had said, the children were listed based on their dates of arrival. The first time through, Nathan focused on the boys' names, but none stood out. He didn't recognize a single one, though of course he could research them all one at a time to see what turned up. Assuming, of course, that he was still in this thing. Was he? Nathan went through the lists again, this time looking at the girls' names. He came to one arrival from 1961 that stood out. This was a six-year-old girl by the name of Aurelie Carre. If she were still alive, that would put her at 67 years old today. It almost seemed too startling to be true. Could it possibly be? He dialed back Madame Carre.

"Yes, Monsieur, did you receive the files?" she answered.

"I did, thank you. I have a question. Would you mind telling me your first name?"

There was a long pause on the other end. Madame Carre knew exactly where this was headed, and she didn't much seem to like it. "My given name is Aurelie."

Now it was Nathan's turn to take a moment. "You were raised there, at the chateau. Is that right, Madame?"

"I prefer to look forward, not back."

"That does seem to be a theme around here, but I would very much like to ask you about those times. I believe it is important, for the historical record. Would you perhaps indulge me with an interview?"

A heavy sigh could be heard on the other end. "If you must insist. Twelve noon tomorrow in my office, if that suits you. I will speak to you on my lunch hour."

"Thank you, Madame, I will see you tomorrow." Nathan hung up the phone. He was heading back to Saint-Martin-de-Crau. Despite his best intentions, he *was* still in this thing, whether that was a good idea or not. It was that same old stubbornness driving him forward. Nathan just couldn't seem to let this go.

The following day at twelve noon sharp, Nathan sat across the desk from Madame Aurelie Carre. Where she'd previously shown those signs of bluster associated with the negligible power of a low-level bureaucrat, she now appeared chastened, uneasy over the secret of her upbringing having been discovered and fearful of whatever additional memories Nathan's questions might dig up. She didn't particularly want to sit for this interview, she'd made that clear, and yet here they were. She hadn't refused. Nathan knew, however, that he'd need to go easy. His first goal was to gain her confidence, to soften her up. Maybe she was reticent, but by and large, people like to talk about themselves and to make some sense of the lives they've led. What Nathan needed to do was take a genuine interest. Questions about The Fox and The Mouse could come after. "Tell me, Madame," he pressed *start* on an audio recording app and placed his phone on the desk between them. "The name Carre, that came from your parents?"

"Yes, of course!" Madame was annoyed already, as though this question were far too obvious to bother wasting her time with.

"What can you tell me about them? Do you have any memories of those early years? Perhaps you can start with their names?"

At this, Madame Carre's eyes glassed over. "I have not thought about those years in a very long time."

"I understand."

"I am not, what do you say, the sentimental type?"

"You are a strong woman. I can appreciate that. You had much to overcome. I see you are married," he glanced at a wedding ring. "Any children?"

"Two. A girl and a boy. Our daughter, she lives in Paris. Our son is a vintner in Bordeaux."

"You must be very proud. Tell me, was there a reason you kept your original family name?"

Madame Carre's expression flashed skepticism once more as she considered whether or not to answer. Eventually, she acceded. "My name was the only thing that my parents left me. Nothing could make me give that up. Nothing!"

Nathan nodded. He could see how hard this conversation was for her, probably the first time she'd been asked these questions in fifty years. "Let's talk about the Chateau Saint Martin. What were your years there like? What sort of environment was provided?"

"Environment?" Madame Carre scoffed. "We were a house full of traumatized children! What would you expect?"

"Did you get along with the others? Maybe you've kept in touch?"

"No. Frankly, I do not understand your interest."

"I think the history is fascinating. It is such a human story, of loss and perseverance. I was able to speak to one other man who was raised there, perhaps you remember him? Pierre Lacroix?"

Madame Carre blinked twice but did not answer.

"Were you there at the same time?"

"Pierre."

"Yes, Pierre. He told me that you referred to each other by nicknames."

"L'etoile. That's what we called him."

"Yes, that's right!"

"Always gazing at the stars. Pierre was very small. Malnutrition, I believe. He was very kind."

"He still lives nearby, have you seen him?"

"No," she shook her head. "Not for many years."

"He has a daughter. She works at the chateau now."

This seemed to be news to Madame Carre, but she didn't respond to this either.

"Monsieur Lacroix showed me a photo of some other boys. Perhaps you remember them as well?" Nathan lifted his phone from the desk and opened his photo app, scrolling through until he found the shot of the two young boys, arm-in-arm. He passed the phone across and Madame Carre took it in her hands, staring at the image wistfully. A light smile slowly crossed her lips, the first evidence of joy Nathan had seen in her. "You remember them?" he asked.

"Of course."

"Monsieur Lacroix tells me they were called The Fox and The Mouse."

"Oui, oui, I do remember."

"I wondered if you might recall their given names?"

Madame Carre took her time. "The Mouse," she said finally. "No, it does not come to me. But the other boy…"

"The Fox?" Nathan was so close, his adrenaline surged. The leader of the Bou Zadjar cartel's name was about to be revealed, if only Madame Carre could remember.

"Jacques. I believe his name was Jacques."

Nathan leaned back in his chair. There it was. Jacques Orleans. It matched an entry from the files that she'd already sent to him. Birthdate March 15th, 1958. Birthplace unknown. Nathan had already spent hours searching online for any information he could find on each and every name on the list. He'd found some tidbits here and there that may have pointed toward the former orphans, but nothing concrete as of yet. As for Jacques Orleans, he'd located scores of them, but not one of those was of the correct age. To track down The Fox, he would need something more. "What do you remember about Jacques?"

Nathan saw a twinkle in Madame's eye at this question. "Oh, Jacques, he was a trouble maker," she said. "Always up to no good."

"What sort of trouble?"

Madame Carre shrugged. "The usual mischief. He gave Mother Maria fits, that one did. Running away all the time, stealing extra portions of food. Nothing serious."

"How about The Mouse?"

"How do you think? He was quiet as a mouse."

"Why do you think those two were so close?"

"Well, they were the same age. Both lost their parents in the war. Everyone needs allies in life, do they not? I think one would done anything for the other, no matter what. It was a strong bond."

"Whatever happened to them? Do you have any idea?"

"No. The Mouse, he was born in Algiers, as far as I knew. Perhaps he went back there."

"And Jacques?"

"Jacques... I believe he came from Corsica."

Nathan's ears perked up. "Are you sure?"

"Yes, yes, quite sure. He used to speak of it often, what a wonderful place it was, and how much he longed to return. In the end, he got his wish."

"He went back there?"

"Yes, yes. An aunt agreed to take him, his mother's sister. I was so sad the day that Jacques left. I suppose he was my very first love." Madame Carre was deep into nostalgia now as she allowed herself to revel in the memories. "He kissed me once, you know. Behind the barn, when nobody else was watching. My very first kiss."

Nathan barely heard what Madame Carre was saying anymore. Instead, his mind was busy connecting dots. The Fox was Jacques, and Jacques was Laurent Dubois. Just the night before, Nathan had dined with one of the most notorious drug and weapons smugglers in all of Europe, poking around for clues to the man's past. If this was true, then Nathan was a marked man. His head turned toward the window. They might be watching him even now. Outside he saw a peaceful, tree-lined street, with a few cars passing by at a leisurely pace. Parked along the opposite curb was a white van with no markings. "Thank you, Madame, I appreciate your time."

"That is all?" She was surprised.

"Yes, that's all." Nathan was standing to go when he saw a flash of movement exiting the van. It was a male figure, in a long, gray coat. In his hands was an automatic rifle. "Get down! On the ground!" Nathan cried out as he dove behind Madame Carre's heavy oak desk. She was too stunned to respond, watching him in confusion. Seconds later, the windows shattered in a maelstrom of broken glass as the sound of gunfire rang out. Nathan curled up into a ball, shards raining down upon him. He was unarmed and pinned down, with nowhere to go. But what of Madame Carre? When the shooting paused, he poked his head around the desk to see. Aurelie Carre was sprawled out on her back, her body riddled with bullets, eyes staring blankly to the heavens. The boy she'd once loved, her very first kiss, had in the end sent her to her grave. More shots rang out and wooden chips flew from the desk as the assailant sprayed it with lead. The man was at the window now, knocking out what remained of the panes with his boot and the butt of his rifle. He was coming to finish the job. Nathan scanned what he could see of the room, searching for anything he might use to defend himself. He saw the open door leading to the hallway. If he simply stayed where he was, his assailant would be upon him in a matter of seconds. If he made a break for it he'd be fully exposed and likely mowed down, but if Nathan moved fast enough, he might just make it. Nathan jumped to his feet and bolted for the door, entering the hallway and turning the corner just as the attacker let loose a fusillade. These bullets ripped through the wall, with one clipping the back of Nathan's right calf as he sprinted down the hall, through the foyer and out the front door. The man would be chasing him, but Nathan didn't look back. Instead, he turned on the jets and bolted up the block before bursting into a small boulangerie, where an older woman was buying a loaf of bread. She and the sales clerk looked up at Nathan in alarm as he moved around the display case and into the kitchen. Hurrying through, he lifted a long knife from a counter and continued out a rear door and into an alley. From here, he rushed straight across and through the back door of another shop on the opposite side, finding himself now in a hardware store.

Nathan heard screams coming from the boulangerie. As he moved forward into the hardware store he took a quick look around, searching for anything else that might be useful. It was an unfair fight, no matter what. His attacker had a military assault rifle. Nathan had a knife. Scanning the shelves, he saw paint buckets and sandpaper, screwdrivers and drills. None of it was up to the task at hand. At the end of the first aisle, his eye caught some small spools of colored electrical wire. He grabbed one of these and slid it into a pocket, just as the man burst through the rear door after him with his gun in the air. Nathan ducked around the end of a parallel aisle and sped back toward the rear. As he reached the end of this aisle, the assailant came around to meet him. Nathan was two feet away with the barrel of the gun swinging toward him but he lunged forward, driving the knife deep into the man's left shoulder. With momentum hurtling Nathan forward, he tackled the man and sent them both crashing to the floor. The gun skipped out of the man's hands and slid to rest a few feet away. In the background, Nathan heard more screams coming from the front of this store, but his focus was solely on what was now a wrestling match to the death. The man was larger than Nathan and stronger, but Nathan was on top, with his left hand pinning the man's wrist to the floor and his right forearm pressing across his attacker's windpipe. His advantage would not last long. The assailant reached up with his left hand and pulled the knife out of his shoulder. Nathan lunged again and pinned the man's left arm back to the ground. He bared his teeth and bit hard into the man's forearm. His assailant let out a scream, then reached down with his right hand and grabbed a handful of Nathan's coat, lifting him up and tossing him away. Nathan jumped to his feet and ran once more as fast as he could, down the aisle, out the front door and away.

After cutting left down another street, Nathan wound through the alleys of the old village, working his way back to where they'd started, to the white van parked across from city hall. The rear door was still ajar. Nathan quickly slid inside where he found several crates stacked beneath a green canvas tarp. Sliding under the tarp, he pressed himself up close to the wooden crates. His breathing was heavy and his heartbeat was pounding, but Nathan willed himself to relax. He had to be invisible in here, unnoticed by a man who would not expect this move. It only took a few more minutes before the rear door swung wide and he heard the assault rifle being slung into the back. The door slammed shut. Next, the assailant entered the driver's side door and took his place behind the wheel. Nathan heard the engine turn over and felt movement as they began driving up the block. He would be patient. He wanted to get outside of town before he made any move. The gendarmes would be on their way, and Nathan didn't want to be tied down in red tape and explanations. He could wait until they were a few kilometers outside of the village, or better yet, he could see exactly where this guy was headed. Nathan opted to remain hidden until the vehicle came to a complete stop and the engine shut off. He'd have one chance to get this right. If he managed it, this guy would never see him coming.

As they moved down the road, Nathan carefully reached into his pocket and pulled out the spool of electrical wire. He took hold of one end and then unwound three feet of wire from the spool. After fraying the insulation with a fingernail, he bent the wire back and forth, around and around until he'd managed to snap this section off. Next, he wound two loops around his right hand and two loops around his left, leaving a two-foot strand in the middle, pulling it tight as a test before letting one side go and settling in. They continued onto what seemed to be a motorway and went for roughly an hour before taking an exit. From the timing, Nathan realized it might be the outskirts of Marseille. If this city was their destination, they would be getting close to the end of the line. He heard the cacophony of an urban environment, with horns honking and sirens wailing. Very, very carefully, he slid the tarp off his body. The back of the van was cloaked in shadow, but he saw the two front seats ahead of him, and the windshield beyond. The passenger seat was empty. Behind the wheel, Nathan spotted the back of his attacker's head. The man was oblivious to the danger that lurked within. As slowly as he could, Nathan slid further forward until he was directly behind the driver's seat. He rose slightly and looped the wire around both hands once more. From a gap between the seats, he was able to catch a glimpse through the front window. They pulled up to a garage door at some sort of industrial warehouse and the driver pushed a button on an opener. The door began to slide up. When the van was clear, he drove on through. Here they were, their destination. Nathan's heartbeat raced once more with the knowledge that he was about to take the life of another man. If Nathan failed in this attempt, the man would kill him. Plain and simple. One of them would die within the next few minutes, and Nathan was determined that it not be him.

The van pulled up beside a delivery truck and the driver shifted into park. Before he'd even shut off the ignition, Nathan popped up and threw his arms across the seat, looping electrical wire over the man's head and cinching it tight around his throat. The man bucked and flailed, trying to reach backwards with his arms, all while his seatbelt kept his body strapped in place. The man had no chance. As soon as Nathan got the wire around his neck, it was game over. The man still struggled with a desperate desire to live but Nathan held tight as his air ran out. The more he resisted, the less time that would take. In just over a minute, he'd passed out cold. Nathan held on this way for another few minutes to make sure before finally loosening his grip. He placed two fingers on the man's neck until he found where the carotid artery should be, just below the jaw. The man had no pulse. He was dead.

Back into the van's cargo hold, Nathan found the assault rifle laying on one side. He lifted the rifle, checked that the safety was off, and then opened the rear door and climbed out of the van. Nobody else was in sight. Stacks of wooden crates lined one wall. From somewhere on the opposite side of the warehouse he heard another door opening and closing, along with two voices. "Ahmed!" a man called out. "You take care of that son-of-a-bitch?"

Moving around the side of the delivery truck, Nathan saw the two men now, standing fifty feet away near an office door. One was borderline obese, wearing casual pants and a sport coat. The other was of average build, in pair of worn blue coveralls. Their faces dropped as they saw Nathan, weapon in hand. "No, that son-of-a-bitch is about to take care of you." Nathan was clean out of compassion, if he'd ever had any to begin with. He pointed the weapon and fired, taking down one man and then the other. They dropped to the ground, groaning with their last breaths as Nathan moved past them and burst through the door and into the office. It was empty but for two desks, cluttered with papers, a printer, and two laptop computers. Against one wall was a stack of crowbars. He lifted one and took it back into the warehouse where he set the gun down and proceeded to pry open one of the crates. When he got the lid off, he slid it to one side and looked in. Carefully packed inside were six Mistral 3 surface-to-air missiles. Each one was six-feet long and capable of being fired in the field from a man-portable launch system. These were manufactured in France. That meant, for the Bou Zadjar Cartel to have their hands on them, somebody very highly placed was providing assistance.

Nathan continued from one crate to another. What he found was a smorgasbord of weapons, from rifles to grenade launchers, missile launchers, mortars and ammunition. The Zijiang M99 sniper rifles were Chinese made. Nathan had come across those before during his Army Ranger days, on the battlefields of war-torn Syria. This was a popular weapon on both sides of the conflict, including both the Kurdish rebel forces and fighters with the Islamic State. Whoever provided them wasn't taking sides. Any war was good business to a weapons smuggler and that included Laurent Dubois. Here in front of Nathan was enough weaponry to take the man on all by himself, just the way he liked it. Maybe along the way he'd actually discover what the hell this was all about in the first place.

Chapter Nineteen

Nathan loaded everything he thought he could possibly need into the van. That included a Kalashnikov AK-74M assault rifle with a GP-34 grenade launcher attached and plenty of ammunition to go with both. He also threw in one of the Zijiang M99 sniper rifles, a pair of binoculars, a bullet-proof vest, and enough slabs of C-4 explosive to blow up a small city, along with a box of detonators. He hid the three dead bodies in the back of the delivery truck and found a padlock to seal it shut. He didn't have to worry about surveillance cameras. The last thing international smugglers wanted was a record of their exploits. Nathan still took a quick look around just to make sure before climbing into the van. He turned over the engine and pressed the garage door opener. When the door rolled up, he drove on out, closed the door behind him and eased into traffic. He was in Marseille, as expected, near the commercial port. After two years assigned to this city with the CIA, Nathan recognized these surroundings. For the moment all he cared about was putting some distance between himself and the recently deceased. Slowly and carefully he drove toward the city center and then out the other side.

In the suburban neighborhood of Croix-Rouge, Nathan pulled into the parking lot of a Hyper Casino supermarket and drove around until he found a similar van, this one yellow and parked near the rear. Nathan pulled in next to it and shut off his motor. He'd felt a stinging pain in his right calf ever since Saint-Martin-de-Crau but with all of the excitement he hadn't had the time to examine it. Now he bent low to take a look. A bullet had torn through his pant leg and clipped his flesh but it wasn't serious. Blood ran down his lower leg, soaking his shoe. It needed some attention but he could manage it himself. For now, he took a look inside the van's glove compartment where he found among other things a pair of screwdrivers, a crescent wrench and a pair of pliers. There was also a fully loaded 9mm SIG Sauer pistol for good measure. He took the pliers and a screwdriver and exited the vehicle. First he took off the license plates from his van and then the one beside him. At any moment the other driver might return, so he worked as expeditiously as possible. When he had them all off, he swapped them. Nobody seemed to give him a second look. Most likely, they simply didn't want to get involved. He was putting the tools away when the other van's driver returned with a loaded cart of groceries. Would the man notice that his license plates had changed? Nathan said a cheerful hello. The other man gave a gruff nod and moved his groceries into his van, then climbed into the drivers' seat and drove off, taking Nathan's plates along with him. Nathan locked his van and headed into the store. Once inside, he grabbed a cart and went first to the pharmacy where he loaded up on first aid supplies, including rubbing alcohol, gauze pads and bandages. Next, he stocked up on food. All he really needed was enough fuel to keep him going. That meant bread, cheese, a few salamis and some apples. He needed a clear head while he came up with a plan but given that this was France, he couldn't resist a nice bottle of red wine. Unsure where he might find an opener, he chose a bottle with a twist-off cap and then made his way to the checkout counter.

Back outside, Nathan spotted a small phone store in the same shopping center and carried his bags inside. It didn't take long before he'd bought a brand new phone with a new SIM card. His old one was somewhere in the rubble of Madame Carre's office at the Saint-Martin-de-Crau city hall. When Nathan returned to his parking space, he loaded his bags into the van and then continued driving further toward the outskirts of the city until he saw a quiet hotel with parking in the rear. He pulled around to the back, parked his van where it couldn't be spotted from the road and went inside. Nathan used his Lebanese passport to check in, paid cash up front, and then went to his room where he took off his pants and then cleaned and dressed his wound. He was lucky, the bullet had only grazed him, but it still stung as he wiped down the gash with a damp gauze pad and then applied antiseptic. When he'd bandaged it, he put his leg up on a pillow on the bed while he reclined against the backboard. He needed three things; food, rest and a plan. He'd already lined up the first two. It was the last one that was going to be a challenge.

Beside Nathan on the bed was his shopping bag from the phone store. He opened it up and took out the phone, removing it from the box that it came in and then slipping in the new SIM. The phone needed charging, so he plugged it into an outlet beside the bed and then lifted a remote control and turned on the television that hung on the opposite wall. He navigated through the channels until he came to a news channel in English. The coverage, as expected, was all about the assassination of the Vice President, with footage of a flag-draped coffin being unloaded from a military cargo plane at Joint Base Andrews. A panel of pundits was debating who might have carried out the attack and why. The theory that held the most sway was that the Mexican drug cartels were upset over increased border enforcement and the seizure of an ever larger percentage of their shipments north. They were taking their fight to a whole new level. The question of the hour was, what would the U.S. government do in response? A full-scale invasion of Mexico appeared to be on the table. A slightly more likely scenario was for the Americans to pinpoint which cartel was behind it, if possible, and then send in a special operations team to completely wipe them out. Considering that this was an ally, the U.S. might first pressure the Mexican government to take care of it themselves. Their Navy special forces were capable. No matter which of these options was chosen, somewhere in the heart of Sinaloa the surviving members of a drug cartel were about to take an ass-whupping. This attack on the Vice President was a declaration of war. To Nathan, that was exactly the reason he didn't buy any of these theories. No drug cartel would declare all-out war on the United States. Why commit suicide when they already had a good thing going? None of this made any sense to him at all.

Nathan shut off the television and then climbed off the bed, moving around to the dresser where he pulled his food out of a paper grocery bag. He took a long baguette and broke a piece off, then pulled it apart before stuffing in slices of cheese and salami. After making two such sandwiches, he found a plastic cup in the bathroom and then opened his bottle and poured a cup of wine. Returning to the bed with his booty, he retook his position with his foot propped up. As he munched on a sandwich in his right hand and washed it down with fine French wine in a plastic cup in his left, Nathan did his best to sort things out in his mind. What he needed to find, at least as a start, were the commonalities between the three attacks that had occurred so far. There was Parsons, and then the attack on the chateau, and finally the Vice President. The first and third had plenty in common. Both were assassinations of top administration officials. The chateau attack was a less obvious connection. Why shoot up an entire charity ball? Just for the American ambassador? That didn't seem likely. So far, Nathan couldn't be sure that the chateau attack was necessarily related.

Nathan quaffed another gulp of wine and focused on the VP attack. All indications were that it was carried out by the Sinaloa cartel, which made Nathan think it was much more likely some other group instead with more to gain, perhaps a competitor. What better way was there to wipe out an adversary than to get the full weight of the United States military behind the effort, free of charge? All they had to do was make it look like the Sinaloa boys were behind it and Uncle Sam would sweep on in and destroy them. The culprits under that scenario could be another drug cartel looking to expand their territory. Nathan's mind came back to the Bou Zadjar cartel. North America was awfully far away. Could they intend to broaden their operations that far? It was hard to believe, but Nathan didn't have anything better to go on. What he did know was that whether Laurent Dubois was behind these plots or not, he did seem to be involved at least in the first two. Besides, Dubois was The Fox, and The Fox wanted Nathan dead. All of it meant that it was time Nathan paid him another visit and not for dinner at the Buddha Bar. This time, Nathan would get some answers or die trying.

The first step was to figure out where Dubois might be found without tipping him off. Nathan had no idea if Dubois was still in Monte Carlo but he knew the man spent time there. It was time to head back and do some poking around. With a little bit of luck, he might find some trail of crumbs to lead him to his quarry. In the meantime he had another sandwich to eat, after which he would take it easy and get a good night's rest. One had to take advantage of such opportunities when they presented themselves. Once this whole thing got going, a good night's sleep might not be an option for a while, especially running this operation as a one-man show. Beginning first thing in the morning, Nathan Grant would switch into full-fledged hunting mode.

Chapter Twenty

The drive back to Monte Carlo from Marseille was only two and a half hours, which meant that Nathan arrived mid-morning. He found a hotel with an underground parking garage and hid the van away on the lowest level. It was too early to check in, but he booked a room at the front desk and then left his bag in the back of the van, along with his armory, before walking to a small cafe with a view of the Buddha Bar. Nathan sat near the window while he had a café au lait and a chocolate croissant. He didn't expect Dubois to show up now, but he wanted to scope out the scene, to get an idea of who came and went. Nathan's first strategy was to identify employees of the Buddha Bar so that he might offer them a small cash incentive to notify him when Dubois and his wife came in. The problem there was that he'd have to give out a phone number or email address. What was to stop an enterprising server to go straight to Dubois with the information, handing over the phone number in exchange for an even more generous tip? After all, they knew Dubois. Nathan was some stranger, offering a one-off payment. The more he thought about it, the more he realized this was probably a bad idea. What else, then? He couldn't just sit in this cafe for two weeks, hoping that Dubois and his wife eventually made an appearance. Unfortunately, Nathan didn't seem to have much else to go by. He was a former spy, not a private investigator. His expertise was in getting people to spill secrets, or turning adversaries into assets, but in this case he didn't have the bankroll of the U.S. government behind him. He couldn't offer tens of thousands of dollars for the right piece of information. He would need to improvise.

As he munched on his croissant, Nathan caught up on the news on his phone. Mexican special forces had launched a major operation against the Sinaloa cartel, along with an assist from the United States Air Force. So far, American ground troops were staying out of it but the available images coming out of the conflict looked like full-scale war. Drone attacks and missile strikes leveled an extensive list of targets, including several remote compounds where cartel leaders had hidden in plain sight for years. Operations were also carried out in Mazatlan, San Miguel de Allende, and even several locations on the outskirts of Mexico City. The Western Hemisphere hadn't seen destruction on this level since perhaps the American Civil War. Nathan watched video of the hulking wreck of what had previously been an apartment building. Outside, mobs of protesters vented their fury, burning American flags as a journalist on the scene spoke of civilian casualties. Whoever was really behind this whole plot must have been reveling in their handiwork.

When he'd finished his coffee, Nathan decided to take a walk. The Buddha Bar wouldn't open for hours yet and he needed to stretch his legs. He slid on his overcoat and headed out the door, taking a gray beanie from one pocket and pulling it onto his head. The weather was cool and damp, with dark skies threatening rain. Nathan always was drawn to water, so he wound his way through town and down the hill toward the port. He'd been here before during the Monaco Grand Prix, when these same streets were filled with Formula One race cars hurtling around the turns in a roaring spectacle of speed. Now it was just a quiet day on the cusp of winter, with the summer tourists long gone. Nathan liked it better this way. At the bottom of the hill he came to a marina, with mid-sized yachts lined up in their slips. He eyed them, one after another, fantasizing about what it might be like to own such a boat. There were sailboats and powerboats, both old and new. These weren't the vessels of the super wealthy. The owners of these boats would be better described as comfortably well off, but Nathan knew that any boat at all was likely to be a money pit. Things always went wrong and needed fixing, but if you could afford it, owning a 30-foot pleasure craft in the Port of Monaco seemed like a nice life.

As Nathan continued along, the slips, and thus the boats, were larger. These would be owned by upper management, perhaps the CEOs of a few mid-sized companies. It was only after he'd crossed another road and continued on to the next boat basin that Nathan came to the super yachts. Now we were talking big money. These boats varied in size from roughly 150 feet on up and were tied to a quay that extended at a perpendicular angle out into the harbor. They had motorized tenders strapped to their decks, along with jet skis and some with helicopter pads. These would be owned the heads of large corporations, and maybe a professional athlete or two at the top of their game. A road ran out onto the quay, looped around in a U-turn at the end and came back, with a one-meter high concrete wall separating the two sides. Nathan followed it along and the farther out he went, the larger the yachts became. These were like small cruise ships, ready to whisk their owners away at a moment's notice to just about any port or harbor in the world that had the proper facilities. He was wondering if one of these yachts might be owned by the leader of a notorious drug cartel when he spotted a familiar car parked on the quay: a white Rolls Royce Phantom, registration plate BL-432-ML. Nathan stopped to take a better look. The vehicle appeared to be unoccupied. At the very least, nobody was in the driver's seat. The rear windows were tinted, however, and Nathan continued past at a relaxed clip. Aside from some other parked cars, the dockside was nearly empty, with hardly a soul around. Twenty meters further on, two uniformed crew members stood behind a van loading a cart with boxes of groceries. The name of their vessel was stitched on matching jackets: *Bon Vivant.* As he walked past them, Nathan eyed the rows of yachts on either side, tied to the quay at their sterns. Which one was owned by Dubois? Nathan wished he'd brought along the SIG Sauer, but then, what would he even do with it? If any of Dubois' men recognized him walking past, he was likely done for whether he was carrying the pistol or not. One thing in his favor was that Dubois would never expect Nathan to come after him like this. Nobody was that bold, or that stupid. Nobody but Nathan Grant, who felt that he had nothing to lose. If he failed in this quest? There was something to be said for leaving this world and all of its problems behind.

Moving further along, Nathan spotted the *Bon Vivant,* a respectable 100-foot sailboat but nowhere near as large as most of the others. The crew members with the cart were met by three more, who began transferring the groceries on board. Next came *Merci Madame* and *Party Time,* then *Hard Where?* and *Last Dance.* None of them were obvious until the very end. Last on the dock, and the largest by good measure, was a burnt orange mega-yacht with a helicopter parked on the bow. Two security guards stood watch on the stern and another could be seen on the bridge. The name, written in a cursive script across the transom, was *Renard Rouge.* Nathan knew exactly what that meant. Red Fox. The home port was listed below as *Ajaccio, Corsica.* He didn't linger. Instead, Nathan turned and casually headed right back the way he'd come. He hadn't expected it to be so easy to locate Dubois, but now that he had, it was time to formulate his next move. Of course, just because the yacht was here, and his car was here, didn't mean Dubois himself was on board. For all Nathan knew, he'd hopped a private jet for a tropical holiday in the South Pacific.

Directly facing the harbor across the main road was a modern six-story hotel called the Port Palace. Nathan moved inside and on up to the front desk where he was able to book a harbor-view room for two nights at $250 per night, also with underground parking for the van. There went another small chunk of Nathan's savings, but it was all for a good cause, right? He was acting in service of his country, even if they weren't prepared to give him any credit.

With the room arranged, Nathan trudged back up the hill to his current digs, checked out and drove back down to his new hotel. He left the bulk of his arsenal locked in the van but brought the SIG Sauer up to his room, along with a pair of binoculars, a DSLR camera with zoom lens, and his clothes. It was mid-afternoon by this time and with the calendar nearing the winter solstice that meant just a few hours of daylight left, but from here Nathan had a clear view of both the Rolls Royce and the *Renard Rouge*. He could settle in for a while and see who came and went.

First things first, Nathan checked the room service menu and ordered a croque monsieur and a bottle of sparkling water. Next, he arranged a chair near the window and took a seat, binoculars in hand. From here, the *Renard Rouge* was only a few hundred meters away at most. With a carefully placed block of C4 attached at the waterline, he could blast the boat to kingdom come. Of course, that would mean killing a whole lot of innocent people in the process. Nathan was not that cavalier. Somewhere on that yacht were stewards and deck hands and cooks, who all deserved to go home and see their families for Christmas. Not that Dubois was likely to give them the time off.

With his binoculars, Nathan watched several men in dark suits roaming the decks. They might as well have worn uniforms that said *Goon* printed on the back. For the next thirty minutes he didn't see much more action. No signs of Dubois or his wife. The Phantom hadn't moved from its parking spot on the dock. A light rap on Nathan's door signaled that his food had arrived.

"Room service!" came a voice. "Votre déjeuner, monsieur."

Nathan put the binoculars into a drawer and lifted the SIG Sauer from the dresser. He slid the gun into his waistband at the small of his back and then peeked through a peephole in the door. On the other side he saw a man with a white shirt and black pants holding a tray with a dome-shaped cover on top. There was no reason to suspect him, or to think that anybody at all knew Nathan was even here, but being careful was part of the reason he'd lived as long as he had. With one hand on the pistol grip, he used the other to open the door.

"Good afternoon, Monsieur. Your lunch."

"'Thanks, you can leave it on the table."

The man entered the room, placed the tray on a small table and then moved back toward the door where he stood to face Nathan with a short nod. It took Nathan a moment to clue in, but then he let go of the gun and reached forward into his pocket to pull out his wallet. Cash seemed so outdated but he had a five-euro bill so he slid that into the man's hand.

"Merci, Monsieur." The valet nodded again and then left the room. Nathan turned the deadbolt, retrieved the binoculars from his dresser drawer and went back to his chair. He placed the gun and binoculars on the table next to his lunch, sat down and slid the table closer, then lifted the cover from the tray to find his sandwich on a white china plate, along with some fruit salad, napkin and utensils. Beside it was a glass with ice and lemon, and a bottle of sparkling water. For a stakeout, this was quite civilized. Nathan poured some water into the glass and then munched on his sandwich as he lifted the binoculars to see if there was any further activity down below. All was quiet. He saw an elderly couple walking along the harbor with their dog on a leash. A man in a helmet and dark jacket rode past on a scooter. No matter how civilized this was, Nathan still didn't like sitting around. He was more a man of action, but simply barging onto Dubois' yacht and shooting up the place was not a solid plan, especially when he didn't even know if the man was aboard. Sometimes the slow and calculated approach led to better outcomes. Nathan would force himself to be patient.

Over the next few hours, not much changed. The sun went down and the streetlights flipped on, casting their glow upon the water. The vast majority of boats in the harbor were entirely dark inside. This wasn't yachting season, after all. As for the *Renard Rouge*, nobody had come or gone. Every thirty minutes he spotted the bodyguards making the rounds on deck but the rest of the time they stayed inside, out of the cold. If Dubois was on board, he seemed to be staying in. No Buddha Bar tonight.

By 9 p.m., Nathan's mind drifted to his van, sitting down there in the parking garage with the Kalashnikov and grenade launcher, and all the ammunition he needed for both. Perhaps if nothing happened by the wee hours of the morning, he would take a more proactive posture. For now, he stood and stretched, and then dialed room service once again to order dinner before the kitchen closed. Half an hour later, he was just digging into a plate of spaghetti carbonara when he saw a black Mercedes sedan drive slowly up the quay. The vehicle stopped at the very end and the driver got out. Nathan put his utensils down and lifted the binoculars, watching as the man walked around the car to the far side and opened the rear passenger door. Another man climbed out, holding a black overcoat tightly around his body.

He was short and pudgy, with a gray scarf around his neck, dark hair and Asian features. Swapping the binoculars for his camera, Nathan zoomed in and snapped a series of quick photos as the man moved toward the *Renard Rouge* and passed up a gangway and onto the stern where he was welcomed by two members of the security detail. The driver, meanwhile, unloaded two pieces of luggage and carried them on board. A few minutes later he disembarked, climbed into his Mercedes and drove off, leaving the quay quiet once more. Nathan checked the screen on the back of his camera, zooming in on the face of the new arrival. "And who are you?" he said to himself, trying to remember if he'd seen the man at the charity ball or anywhere else. He didn't look familiar.

Nathan opened a Bluetooth connection from his camera to his phone and was in the process of transferring the photos when another car pulled up onto the quay. Watching with his binoculars, Nathan saw another single man get out of the rear passenger door. His back was to Nathan, preventing a clear view of his face, but the man was taller and broad-shouldered with wavy brown hair. He wore a knee-length black overcoat on top of gray slacks and black shoes. The driver lifted a single suitcase from the trunk and they moved up the gangway. At the top, the newcomer turned his head and Nathan got his first clear view of the man's face. This one he recognized immediately. It was the junior senator from the great state of Texas, the Honorable Jed Brogan. "What the hell are you doing here?!" Nathan said out loud. Something mighty strange was going on.

Chapter Twenty-One

These new arrivals generated more questions than answers for Nathan, but they did provide at least one important indication. With visitors showing up, Dubois was likely to be on board. Of course, there were no guarantees. Nathan had yet to spot the man himself, but he couldn't just sit in this hotel room any longer. It might very well be that once the last of the guests arrived, the yacht would depart for ports unknown. Nathan's chance was now. Whatever conspiracy was afoot, the players appeared to have gathered. The time to take action had arrived.

For a lone operator, carrying out an assault on the *Renard Rouge* made for some particular challenges. He couldn't very well go waltzing up the quay with a Kalashnikov. They'd mow him down from fifty meters. Likewise, if he commandeered a smaller vessel and attempted to approach by sea, they'd blast him out of the water. He'd seen plenty of movies where James Bond-type characters donned scuba gear for such an operation but Nathan had no such gear and besides, he'd never be able to hoist himself onto the deck let alone with a weapon. He'd already ruled out the C4. He could try to create a distraction by setting explosives on an empty yacht across the harbor but that probably wouldn't buy him much advantage. Somebody on Dubois' security detail would still spot him coming. Nathan eyed the approach from his hotel window. The yacht was tied up on the right-hand side of the quay, stern to the dock with a wooden pier extending along the port side. The quay itself was around 100 meters long and if Nathan could get to it undetected, he could work his way out on the left side, low and out of sight behind the cement wall in the center. From his hotel, it was 100 meters to the quay itself, with 30 vessels and a row of parked cars blocking the view of anybody on board the *Renard Rouge*. It was doable.

This would not be Nathan's first firefight aboard a luxury yacht. On the previous occasion, the boat ended up at the bottom of the Adriatic Sea. At least this one was tied up to the dock. The bigger question, perhaps, was what Nathan hoped to accomplish with this foolhardiness? The truth was, he didn't really know. All he could say for sure was that the answers to all of his questions were on board that boat, and he was ready to do whatever he could to wring them from those involved. He would either find out what was really going on or very likely die trying. Simply forgetting all about it and moving on was not an option. Nathan was far too stubborn for that. He just couldn't seem to let it go.

Back down in the hotel parking garage, Nathan climbed into the back of the van and then slid on a bulletproof vest. He took a rifle and loaded a fresh magazine, then put two more into his pockets. He loaded a grenade into the attached launcher and clipped two more of those to the vest as well. One thing he had learned in his career was that once you had committed to an operation, hesitation could be lethal. He thought back to the city hall at Saint-Martin-de-Crau, with Madame Carre's dead body sprawled across the floor. He remembered the carnage of the attack on the Chateau de Fontainebleau. He pictured Secretary Parsons' plane going down in flames. Yep, he was committed.

Nathan donned his heavy overcoat on top of the vest, then lifted the Kalishnikov and held it underneath the flap on one side. Perhaps from a distance, behind a row of parked cars, it wouldn't be so obvious. He locked the van and exited the garage onto the damp, dark street along the harbor, crossing to the other side and then turning left along the walkway. All was quiet as he kept up a brisk pace to the quay, crossed to the left side, and dropped low beneath the wall. Crouching here, he put the rifle down while he stripped off the overcoat and left it in a clump on the ground, then used a strap on the Kalashnikov to sling it over his back. Nathan crawled forward on hands and knees, covering 100 meters of gravel road. Approaching the end, he very slowly raised his head up above the edge of the wall. He saw nobody on deck aside from one of the bodyguards standing by a railing along the bridge. The windows of the vessel were illuminated by interior lights and he heard the low thrum of the yacht's diesel engines Two deckhands appeared on the bow and began to hoist large rubber bumpers that hung from lines along the starboard hull. They flipped the bumpers up over the rail and onto the deck before moving out of Nathan's sight to the port side. They did indeed seem to be preparing for departure. It was now or never, Nathan understood. To maintain any advantage, he'd need to act with lightning speed.

Nathan eased himself back down out of view, slid the rifle off his back and clutched it in both hands, safety off. He took three deep breaths, picturing in his mind what he was about to do and then rose back to his knees, spun the weapon around and aimed at the man on the bridge. He fired two bursts of three rounds each and the man crumpled, flipping over the rail and dropping into the water below.

The stern of the *Renard Rouge* was only twenty meters away from Nathan and he launched a grenade straight at it. Seconds later it exploded against a door, shattering all of the windows in the rear cabin with shards of shrapnel. Propelling himself over the wall, Nathan rushed forward on pure instinct and adrenaline, flying across the gangway and onto the stern. Just inside the rear cabin lay two men in dark suits on the deck. One of the men was inert. The other was stunned but alive, with a pistol in his hand and a look of disbelief in his eyes as he tried to aim it. Before he had the chance, Nathan fired one round.

Moving further into the cabin, Nathan saw a long bar along with tables and plush couches. Everything was covered in broken glass, from the windows and drink glasses and smashed liquor bottles that crunched beneath his feet. From behind the bar he saw flames as the spilled alcohol burned blue and hot, rising up the wall to shelves where the remnants of more broken bottles lay askew. Nathan rushed toward a hallway leading forward. Before he could enter, two more armed figures appeared and Nathan ducked behind a bulkhead. He unclipped another grenade and loaded it into the chamber. Crouching very low, he swung around the corner and fired. Boom! Another blast, another two down. This was all going well so far, but he couldn't become complacent. He moved past the two men and kept on going. To get Dubois, he'd need to take care of every member of the security detail. How many that was, Nathan didn't even know. To hazard a guess, he'd thought eight at least, which put him just about halfway there. The next question was, where would Dubois and his guests hide out? Nathan would likely need to search the entire vessel and he didn't have much time. The Monte Carlo police were probably already on their way. He was ascending a stairway when three shots rang out from below and behind. Two bullets slammed into the back of his bulletproof vest, knocking him forward onto the stairs. It took him split second to recover, but Nathan managed to scramble on hands and knees up to the next deck, dragging his rifle along with him. He emerged in a grand salon, with opulent chairs and couches that looked like they belonged in a palace, not an oceangoing vessel. A sumptuous buffet was laid out on a side table and the soothing strains of Mozart drifted through the air.

Two terrified stewards crouched behind a small table. Floor to ceiling windows gave expansive views of the harbor to port and the hills of Monte Carlo to starboard. Nathan spotted the flashing blue lights of multiple police vehicles approaching at a rapid clip. This whole enterprise was starting to seem like a very bad idea.

Twin staircases with golden banisters wound up one deck higher. Nathan popped to his feet and bolted, straight up the staircase on the right. He realized by now that his chances of finding Dubois, or wringing anything useful out of his guests, were slim. His chances of getting killed in the process were significant. Even if he did come out alive, he'd most likely end up spending the rest of his life in a French prison. What had he been thinking? Maybe he had some sort of a superhero complex, falsely believing that he alone could save the day. Now that he was on board, he would try to make the best of what little time he had.

As Nathan reached the top of the stairway, he glanced back to see his pursuer emerging into the salon. In fact, there were two men, both armed with pistols. Nathan raised his rifle and fired again, driving them back into the stairwell before he continued on down a hallway. He came to a set of twin doors, closed and locked tight, kicking them hard once and then twice before they sprung open. On the other side was an enormous bedroom suite. The back of the cabin swept in a semi-circle with windows overlooking the bow, where the helicopter rested on the pad just below him. To Nathan's left, he heard noises coming from what was likely the en-suite. Pointing his rifle forward, Nathan kicked this door open next. Kneeling on the ground in the bathroom was a housekeeper, bobbing her head up and down as she prayed out loud.

"Santa María madre de Dios..." she said.

The next thing that Nathan heard was the engine on the helicopter firing up. He looked to his right and saw the rotors spinning. Senator Brogan was rushed across the deck and ushered on board, followed by the other guest. But where was Dubois? Nathan moved closer to the windows just as they shattered all around him. He dove to the ground to the sound of gunfire and then slid up beside the bed on his belly. The shots came from the hallway.

Loading his very last grenade, Nathan crawled around the bed, pointed it down the hall and fired. The explosion sent a shudder through the hull and Nathan jumped to his feet and ran forward toward the bodies of two men, their guns on the carpet beside them. As he continued past, Nathan saw movement. One of the men was still alive, though mangled and bloody. Nathan recognized him as half of the couple who'd watched over him from a nearby table at the Buddha Bar. The man gazed up at Nathan through a fog of pain. "Please..." he managed a whisper.

Nathan pointed his rifle between the man's eyes and pulled the trigger. His only mercy was in making it quick. He descended the port side staircase and moved forward on the lower deck. Through another window he finally spotted Laurent Dubois himself, climbing on board the helicopter along with his wife. His female bodyguard, with the fierce blue eyes, held Laurent's elbow as her boss took his seat and then she climbed in after him. With a whine of its engine, the aircraft lifted off. If Nathan could clip the rotors, he just might take the whole thing down. He burst onto the deck and raised his rifle, getting off three shots at the departing craft before his magazine ran out. The helicopter disappeared across the dark waters of the bay. He'd missed.

A thick column of smoke now rose from the stern and the wail of approaching sirens intensified as police and firefighters continued pouring onto the quay. They were gathered on the starboard side of the vessel at the stern. Nathan was on the port side, hidden from view. Moving to the rail, he saw the wooden pier below and an expanse of dark, open water just beyond. He threw his rifle overboard and into the harbor. Next, he took off his bulletproof vest, and then his shoes. With no time to spare, he climbed over the rail and then launched himself, out and over the pier, dropping thirty meters through the air. With a shock to his system, he plunged deep into the frigid water. When he came back up, he started to swim, straight out and across the harbor. If he was very lucky, nobody had spotted him. With all of the commotion focused on the quay, and the fire now consuming the stern, it seemed he might just make a getaway.

It was roughly two hundred meters to an opposing pier, across a quiet expanse of calm water. Nathan managed it, still fully clothed, in ten minutes. When he reached the dock, he swum around between two boats and then climbed out, shoeless and soaking wet, but alive. The flames on the *Renard Rouge* now engulfed the back third of the vessel as fire crews desperately fought to put it out. Nathan walked off the pier and then back around the crescent-shaped harbor to his hotel. He walked in without a word to the front-desk clerk, who stood at a window with some of the guests watching the action in awe. Nathan headed up to his room where he quickly changed into dry clothes and put on a pair of running shoes, then gathered his things and retreated to the parking garage. He climbed into the van and turned the ignition, pulled out onto the street and drove off at a cautious clip. He may not have gotten to Dubois this time, but at least he'd made a statement. Hopefully, he'd gotten inside the man's head. If Dubois was frightened, he was more likely to make a mistake. At the very least he now knew it was better not to mess with Nathan Grant.

Chapter Twenty-Two

Nathan headed northeast along the coast toward Italy. He needed to put some distance between himself and Monte Carlo. He crossed the border near Ventimiglia and continued on toward Genoa. Driving gave him time to think. His little stunt with the *Renard Rouge* hadn't accomplished much but at least he now knew that whatever was going on, Senator Jed Brogan was in on it. He also knew that if he wanted to locate Laurent Dubois, all roads, or perhaps boats in this case, led to Corsica.

When he'd gone a few hours, Nathan exited the motorway on the outskirts of the city and found a quiet place to park behind a warehouse. He left the engine on the van idling to provide some heat and then found room to stretch out on the floor of the cargo area beside his remaining weapons stash. The first thing he needed to do was swap vehicles. He couldn't afford to be driving around in a stolen one, though his options were generally poor all around. Stealing another one, or another set of plates for that matter, would just leave him in the same predicament. It would only be a matter of time before police were searching for the vehicle either way. If he'd known anybody in the area he might borrow one, but he didn't. He could buy a used one but his cash was already stretched thin. That left a rental, which would mean showing a driver's license and a passport, along with an electronic payment. Nathan didn't like any of that, but under the circumstances it seemed like the least bad choice. For now, he would try to get some badly needed sleep.

Back in his Army days, Nathan was trained to sleep in the most unforgiving of situations but here on this hard floor in the back of the van, he still struggled to nod off. In part he just had too much on his mind and not only this stuff about Dubois, and the senator, and Nathan's unlikely quest for justice. What really kept him up was more personal than that. He rested his head on his right forearm and listened to a light rain pattering on the roof of the van. It seemed an unlikely thing to be bothering him now, at this moment, but undeniably there it was. Today, he'd stormed the mega-yacht of a ruthless cartel leader with an assault rifle and a grenade launcher. He'd barely escaped with his life, and what was he thinking about as he lay here on the floor of a stolen van, squeezed in next to his hoard of stolen weapons? He was wishing he had somebody close in his life, somebody he could talk to, somebody he could love. For the past year and a half, he'd carried around the memory of his lost wife. He still missed her more than he'd thought was even possible, but he was also coming to realize an important truth. What held him back from getting on with his life, and opening the necessary space to allow in somebody new, was more than just grief. It was a hovering cloud of guilt at the very idea. This didn't come from Jenna, of course, she never would have laid that on him under such circumstances. These feelings were entirely of Nathan's own creation. To deal with them, he'd plowed himself into this current project to the point that he was taking unnecessary risks. Nathan was trying to forget something that could never be forgotten, but forgetting wasn't the answer. Accepting the truth of his current reality was the only path forward. Nathan needed to give himself permission to move on, still carrying Jenna in his heart of course, but with an eye toward the future. Acknowledging the finality of her passing felt like part of *him* was dying, but this was a necessary step in the process and the time had come to let her go. First, he would finish what he'd started here when it came to Dubois. He would keep on going until he reached the end, meting out whatever form of justice he could manage. After that, Nathan would be free to start over, to find his peace in whatever measure he was able. This understanding was like a burden lifted from his soul. Sometime very late at night, he finally managed to fall asleep.

A loud knock jolted Nathan some hours later. He opened his eyes with a start and peered around. He was still in the back of the van, but daylight shone through the front windows. Staggering to his feet, he hurried forward to get a better look. Outside, he saw a man in a knit cap and reflective yellow vest who held a clipboard in one hand while a cigarette dangled from his lips.

"Chi sei?" said the man. "Who are you?"

Nathan waved a hand in the air. "Sorry! Scusa!" He took his place in the driver's seat, clipped in his seat belt and threw the van into reverse. After a full night of idling, his gas tank was nearly empty but it was enough to get into town. As he pulled away, he saw other workers loading delivery vehicles backed up to the warehouse. He retraced his route to the highway and then headed into Genoa. Ten minutes later, he was cruising down a city street, keeping an eye out for a car rental agency. It was still only 7:30 in the morning. He pulled over and used his phone to find a place just one kilometer away, opening in thirty minutes. Nathan drove halfway there and then found an out-of-the way place to park. He walked the last of the way and then stood outside blowing hot air into his hands in an attempt to stay warm before a clerk finally arrived and let him in. Twenty minutes later, he was pulling out of the lot in a small blue van. He drove back to where he'd parked the first one, transferred his duffel bag and all of the cargo from one to another, and was off again. This time he drove another thirty minutes further east and pulled off the highway in search of a decent cafe. He was dying for a coffee.

It didn't take long to find a place that would do. It wasn't the greasy-spoon American diner he'd have preferred, but it was a cafe and it was open. Nathan parked out front and went inside. He was seated near the window where he ordered a frittata of bacon, eggs, cheese and veggies. First up, however, was a latte macchiato. Just the smell of the ground beans as they were pressed into the handle on the espresso machine warmed his very soul. These Italians, they knew their coffee. When it arrived, he held it to his nose and inhaled before he took a very small sip and then set it on the table to cool while he took out his phone. He opened a photo app and scrolled through the pics he'd taken the night before, eyeing Dubois' mystery guest as he stood on the dock beside his car. Could this be The Mouse? It didn't seem likely. For one thing, the man was too young. He appeared to be in his late 30s, or perhaps early 40s at the most. For another thing, his Asian features didn't match up with the boy Nathan had seen in the earlier photo. Nathan cropped this one so that only the man's face remained, saved it as a separate file and then opened a web browser and dragged the file into the search bar. A slew of images showed up, but as he went through them, none of the men in these pictures seemed to be Dubois' guest. At least as far as Nathan could tell. He took another sip of coffee and dialed the one person that he thought might be able to help him.

"Bonjour, c'est Sophie Journet."

"Sophie, it's Nathan."

"A new phone number every time."

"Where are you right now?"

"I am at headquarters. Where are you and what are you up to?"

"I need a favor."

"Always with your favors. The terrorists, they attacked again last night, did you hear?"

"No. What happened?"

"They tried to kill Laurent Dubois. In Monte Carlo, they set his yacht on fire."

"I'm sorry to hear that. Do you have any leads?"

"I can't discuss that publicly. Can you share some insights with me, perhaps?"

"This is the first I've heard of it. Look, Sophie, I'm sorry to have bothered you. I'm sure you're very busy."

"Now you have changed your mind? No favor? What's wrong, Nathan?"

"I just wanted to check in, honestly. I'd love to have dinner with you next time I'm in Paris."

"Where are you now, Nathan?"

"I'm just having a bit of a holiday. Take care, Sophie." Nathan hung up the phone. He'd realized what a massive mistake it would be to send her a photo of this mystery guest, standing on the dock beside the *Renard Rouge* mere moments before the attack. If they hadn't been able to place Nathan at the scene already, that would seal it. He might as well just call her again with a full confession. Instead, after breakfast, Nathan got back onto the motorway and continued heading east. Two more hours brought him to Livorno, a port city on the Tuscan coast. He paid cash for a ferry ticket to Bastia, on the island of Corsica. He didn't know exactly what he'd do there but he knew that Laurent Dubois called it home and that was good enough. With two hours to go before departure, he parked the van and walked around town, taking in sights that included an ancient fortification on the water. At 1 p.m., he drove the van onto the ferry and then went up to the passenger decks. Four hours later, he returned to his rental van and joined a long line of vehicles as they disembarked and exited the terminal complex. The drive to Ajaccio was another two and a half hours, from the northeast corner of the island to the southwest, right up and over a spine in the center. He topped off his fuel tank before getting started, then stopped for dinner in the village of Corte along the way, and rolled into Ajaccio at just after 9:30 p.m. to find a quiet port city, at night, in early December.

One night sleeping in the van was enough, so Nathan parked in the city center and walked the streets until he found a small two-star hotel near the water. He checked in with a bored front desk clerk and was given a room, where he changed and then headed out for a stroll before bed. He'd left his overcoat on the quay in Monte Carlo, but even with just a thick sweater the temperature was endurable this much farther south. Nathan wandered through narrow, cobblestone streets of the old town before emerging at the harbor where he saw yet more boats of all sizes, though nothing nearly as large as the *Renard Rouge.* In a place like this, everyone would know exactly who Laurent Dubois was. With a little bit of sleuthing, it shouldn't be too hard for Nathan to find out where the man lived, and more importantly, if he was on the island currently.

Back in his room, Nathan showered and then crawled into bed, where he crashed hard and slept solidly for nearly eight hours. When he woke, he dressed and went down to a small dining room for a continental breakfast of coffee, toast and pastries. Over an extra cup of coffee, he used his phone to scan satellite photos, familiarizing himself with the area. The airport was in a valley to the southeast. Private homes covered the hills less than one kilometer away, further to the east and north.

Directly across a sweeping bay to the west, a two-lane road hugged the coast as it passed exclusive homes along the water. This was where the wealthy elite lived. Many of these properties were likely the second homes of rich Parisians looking for a winter getaway. Nathan scrolled from one to the next. If Dubois owned one, it would have to be the largest. A few of these compounds looked promising, with massive mansions on sprawling grounds, complete with swimming pools and private docks, but one stood out more than the others for a simple reason. It had a helicopter pad. Tied up at the dock was a sleek speedboat with massive outboard engines. This place certainly deserved a closer look.

After breakfast, Nathan checked out of the hotel and drove his van out along the coast road. At the address in question, all he saw was a three-meter-high wall with a solid metal gate. He might have better luck surveilling the place by sea, but in the meantime he turned around and drove back out toward the airport and then wound up into the hills beyond. The homes here were modest, to say the least. This was where the working-class inhabitants called home. Many of the structures were abandoned and in disrepair, with peeling paint, cracked walls and collapsing roofs. Nathan took his time scoping out all of his options before he chose one. It was a small, one-story home on the edge of the hill, set back in a little notch and away from any others. Weeds grew in the yard. All of the windows facing the street were boarded up. Beside the house was an unattached garaged with a rusted padlock on the door. Climbing out of the van, he walked around to the other side of the home where he found a wooden deck, mostly intact. A valley of low scrub stretched out below, with the Mediterranean Sea beyond. In between, Nathan had a clear view of the Ajaccio Napoleon Bonaparte Airport. He went back to his van and returned with his pair of binoculars. A single runway ran north and south. On the west side was a passenger terminal with two commercial planes parked in front. To the north of the terminal he saw a separate tarmac with two private jets, one smaller twin turboprop, and multiple hangars with their doors closed. His rough estimate of the distance to the private jets was roughly 1,200 meters. That was well within the range of the Zijiang M99. What poetic justice it would be to kill The Fox with one of his very own guns.

Nathan turned back to the house where the windows were on this side boarded up as well. A single door leading to the back deck was closed and locked. He picked up a cinder block from the yard and swung it against the knob until he'd crushed the latch and the door swung open. Inside, the place was musty and damp. Nathan used the flashlight on his phone to explore the layout. He found an empty living room, a small kitchen with a wooden table and chairs, and a single bedroom with a bare mattress on the floor. This place suited his needs just fine.

Back around in the driveway, Nathan used the cinder block on the garage door padlock, too, snapping it off with the third try. Inside the garage, he found a stack of used lumber beside a rusty old Citroen that probably hadn't run in decades. Next to the car was an empty space with plenty of room to store his cargo. Nathan transferred the weapons from the van to the garage. It wouldn't have done well to be pulled over by the police with this cache in the back. He didn't want to take that chance.

Hanging from a hook on the garage wall was an iron crowbar. Nathan took that and the sniper rifle around to the other side of the house. Setting the rifle on the deck, he used the crowbar to pry the plywood off the window on this side, giving himself some indoor light and a view of the airport from the living room. When he was finished with that, he lined up the M99 toward the airport and positioned himself prone on the deck, holding the gun in his hands with the barrel resting on a stand as he peered through the scope. All was quiet on the tarmac with not a soul in sight. Laurent Dubois could come and go from the island by air or by sea. His helicopter didn't have the range to make it all the way from the mainland. The charred remains of his mega-yacht were resting on the harbor floor in Monte Carlo, and Dubois wasn't the type to take the ferry. All of that left his own private jet as his most likely mode of transportation. Whether he was coming or going, Nathan should be able to pick the man off from here, assuming his skills with a sniper rifle hadn't deteriorated too much. He would take his chances. Above him, he heard the sound of an incoming plane and looked up to see an Air France turbo-prop entering the flight pattern, then turn base and final, approaching the airport from the sea. He watched the plane land and taxi to a stop, then eyed a handful of passengers through the scope as they disembarked down a set of forward stairs and walked across the tarmac toward the terminal. It was hard to tell for sure from this distance, but Nathan didn't think he recognized anybody.

For now, Nathan had a few other things to take care of. He stood up and put the rifle back into the garage before closing the door. The SIG Sauer he placed in the van's glove box before driving back into town. By this time, Nathan had a shopping list going. First, he'd need a good down sleeping bag. This house had no heat. Then he'd need a padlock for the garage and some food. Despite the milder temperatures, he also wanted a new coat to replace the one he'd left on the dock in Monte Carlo. Sourcing these items in an unfamiliar city took some doing, but he managed it in a little over an hour and picked up a small electric lantern to boot.

Back at the house, Nathan retrieved the M99 from the garage along with some ammo and then clamped his new padlock on the door and pocketed the key. He brought the rifle, the pistol, and his binoculars into the house, along with his new sleeping bag, jacket, the lantern, and a fast-food burger and fries that he'd picked up on the way out of town. He pulled the kitchen table and a chair up close to the living room window and sat down to eat his dinner. He polished off his food in a few minutes and then there was nothing much to do but wait. An hour went by, and then another. By 5 p.m. the sun was already setting and the temperature dropping along with it. Nathan put on his new jacket. He considered smashing some of the furniture to pieces in order to have a fire in the fireplace. He'd seen a box of matches in the kitchen and the warmth might make this place feel downright cozy, but then he thought better of it. He wasn't sure the flue would be clear, for one thing. He didn't want the place to fill with smoke. A fire would also be a dead giveaway to all of the neighbors within 200 meters that the place was occupied. They'd smell it, and might even see the flames flickering through the window. Somebody might say something to somebody else, and the next thing Nathan knew, the owner could show up, or the fire department. No, it was better to keep as low a profile as possible.

Once again, Nathan found himself feeling antsy, but he vowed to be patient. The last time he'd gone off half-cocked, in Monte Carlo, it didn't end particularly well. There was no sense in repeating that disaster. By eleven p.m., the airport had been dead quiet for hours and Nathan was ready to call it a night. He placed the pistol on the floor beside the bed and climbed into the sleeping bag. This time, sleep did not come easily. Dubois could come or go at any time. Trying to sleep and yet listen for incoming planes was a challenge. Nathan also had his own escape to consider. Getting off the island after such an operation would be complicated. If he succeeded in killing Dubois, every ferry and plane to the mainland would be carefully scrutinized. He'd need to find another way. By some time past 3 a.m. he managed to nod off.

The following morning, after only a few hours of fitful sleep, Nathan got up and moved back into the living room. The first glow of dawn lit the valley below him as he lifted the binoculars and watched a ground crew fuel one of the commercial planes and load luggage in preparation for takeoff. Shortly afterward, another group of passengers was escorted across the asphalt and on board. When all was ready, the plane taxied to the far end of the runway and took off, lifting over the valley and climbing with a roar just in front of Nathan before disappearing over a ridge. The noise faded away into the distance.

A coffee would be nice, Nathan thought. Maybe some breakfast. It might take him a week before Dubois showed up, or more. Who knew? Nathan figured he'd better stock up on some more supplies. He was thinking about heading into town when he heard another incoming plane. This one was a jet. He couldn't see it at first, but eventually he spotted the small speck out over the sea. He kept his eyes pinned to the plane as it came in, dropping in altitude until it touched down and rolled to Nathan's end of the runway before turning off toward general aviation parking. This was a twin engine private jet: a Gulfstream similar to the plane Secretary Parsons had been on. That meant a range of up to 8,000 nautical miles, or enough to fly from here to nearly anywhere on earth. Nathan picked up his binoculars to get a better look and was just able to read the tail number emblazoned across the starboard engine. "November, Niner, Zero, Three, Echo, Delta," he said to himself, repeating it three times to help remember. November, he knew, meant this plane was American. He quickly grabbed the sniper rifle, loaded a cartridge, and moved out to the deck where he positioned himself prone with one eye to the scope and a finger just off the trigger. Once the plane was parked and the engines shut down, the cabin door opened and a set of stairs descended to the ground. Nathan carefully placed one finger on the trigger as he lined up the crosshairs on the open door. The morning was perfectly still. This should be a relatively easy shot, if the opportunity presented itself.

The first person to exit the plane was a flight attendant in a blue and white uniform with her hair up in a bun. She carried a small roller bag down the stairs, placed it on the tarmac and extended the handle before walking toward the terminal at a brisk pace. A ground crew set to work unloading some luggage, while a fuel truck pulled up beside the starboard wing. It took another few minutes before Nathan saw the first passenger. It was another man he didn't recognize, but then again, he was eyeing the face through a sniper scope from more than one kilometer away. It could be that he just needed a closer look to be sure. This man was small and thin, with dark curly hair, a narrow face and wearing a Navy-blue overcoat. It wasn't Dubois, in any case. A second man followed him off the plane, and this one Nathan did recognize. It was the junior senator from the Great State of Texas himself, Jed Brogan. "Well, hello again," Nathan said. Behind the senator came a younger man carrying a briefcase. A black car pulled up next to the plane and the three men climbed inside and drove away. "I'll bet I know where you're going." Nathan took his finger off the trigger and stood up. There was little use hanging around here for at least the next few hours.

Once he'd put the rifle back in the garage, Nathan snapped shut the padlock and then climbed into the van. He drove back down into town, had a quick breakfast in a warm cafe, and headed to the harbor in search of a boat that he might be able to rent. At this time of the year, all of the tourist operations were shut for the season. That meant he'd need to improvise. He could try to hot wire one but it might be reported stolen before he was finished using it. Instead, he worked his way up and down the docks until he saw a small powerboat, roughly 5 meters long, with a For Sale sign on the canvas cover. The boat had seen better days from the looks of the worn cover and the barnacle-encrusted hull underneath. If the owner took the same care when it came to maintaining the engine, Nathan wasn't convinced it would even start, but he couldn't see a better option at present. He pulled out his phone and dialed. "Hello, I'm interested in the boat you have for sale..." The man on the other end was asking 20,000 euro. "How about letting me take it for a test run?" Nathan asked.

"Yes, of course, we can take her together, this weekend."

"I was thinking that maybe I could rent it for the week, to see how I like it."

"No, no, not for a week. We go together. You see."

"Look, you'll never sell it to anybody else at this time of the year. I'll give you five hundred euro to rent it for a week. That should pay your slip fee for the month, at least."

The man thought it over. "One thousand euro."

"Seven hundred."

"Tell me, for what purpose do you intend to use?"

"I'd like to do some fishing."

"Now? This is, how do you say... very unusual."

"I'm an unusual guy, but I'll give you seven hundred euro in cash up front."

Again, the man took his time to consider the offer. "Seven hundred euro, one week, OK. You give me deposit. One-thousand-euro deposit. I return at end."

"No deposit. You can copy my passport."

"No, no..."

"I'm standing beside the boat right now. When can we meet? Seven hundred euro, cash. Do you want it?"

The man grumbled. "I be there one hour."

"Great. One more thing, do you have any fishing gear I can borrow?"

The man seemed dumbfounded by this question. What self-respecting fisherman didn't have his own gear? But then, 700 euros was calling. "On the boat."

"Perfect. See you here."

Ninety minutes later, Nathan was motoring out through the harbor with the pistol in his jacket pocket and the binoculars on the seat beside him. He'd paid up front and let the man take a photo of his passport: Elias Mansour from Lebanon. When Nathan reached the end of the breakwater, he pressed forward on the throttles and roared off across a wide, arcing bay. Despite the looks of it, the boat had some get-up-and-go. He headed west toward the seaside compounds of the upper class. The morning was clear and crisp, with the sun at his back. Nathan eyed the homes as he passed them, one after the other. These were impressive, no doubt, but not to the standards of Laurent Dubois. It took Nathan twenty minutes to reach the compound in question. At 200 meters straight offshore he eased the throttles closed and then drifted, cutting off the engine entirely. The mansion was situated on a hillside and set back some way from the water. In between the home and the private dock was a vast lawn, with flower gardens now dormant for the season. The helicopter pad, Nathan knew, was up to the left and behind. Parked at the dock was the same speedboat he'd seen in the satellite photo. It was long and sleek. Perfect for drug running, or for chasing down any interlopers. No people were in sight aside from a gardener, raking leaves in the yard.

Down along the inside of the boat's hull were two fishing rods and reels. Under a rear seat was a tackle box. Nathan didn't have any bait, but catching fish wasn't the point. He took a lead weight from the box and attached it to one of the lines, then cast it off into the sea and slid the rod into a holder at the stern. This ruse wasn't likely to fool anybody but at least he'd try. Returning to his seat, he lifted the binoculars and used them to scan the entire property, knowing full well that he was likely being watched right back. Breaching this compound by himself would be near next to impossible. If Nathan went over a wall, he'd trigger an alarm. If he tried to come in from the sea, they'd spot him a mile away. Even under the dark of night, his chances weren't good. It was better to stick to his airport plan, though at the very least he'd like to confirm that Dubois was in residence.

For the next few hours, Nathan pretended to fish. He moved the boat a few times in an attempt to keep them guessing, first up the coast a ways, and then a bit further out to sea. It was early afternoon when he saw activity on an upper deck of the mansion. Two men dressed in casual attire appeared. They stood near the rail as a server followed after with a tray of champagne. One of the men was the senator. The other was his companion from the plane. They each took a glass, made a toast and drank before being joined by a third man. This, at last, was Laurent Dubois. He greeted his guests and was handed a glass of his own. After chatting briefly, he turned his attention to the sea. For one moment, Nathan started as Dubois looked directly at him. Dubois could hardly have identified him from this distance, but that didn't stop a chill from running down Nathan's spine. It was as though the Frenchman were staring directly into his soul with a cold and calculating malevolence. Nathan put his binoculars down. He'd learned enough for now. Laurent Dubois was in town. The hunt was on.

Chapter Twenty-Three

Ominous clouds gathered on the horizon as Nathan reeled in his fishing line and stowed the rod in its place along the inside of the hull. A change in weather was on the way. From the looks of the rain squalls he saw in the horizon, Nathan estimated that he had twenty to thirty minutes to get his craft back into the harbor before things started getting rough. He turned the key and the engine sputtered to life. That was a good sign, anyway. As he swung the boat around and pointed the bow toward town, he took one last look at the Dubois compound. The three men had vanished from the deck and moved inside. Down on the grounds, two other men dressed in black pants and sport coats hurried across the lawn. They moved out onto the dock where one took his place behind the controls of the cigarette boat and the other busied himself untying the lines. That was a bad sign. Nathan pushed full forward on his throttle and the boat got up and went again, as fast as it was able. That meant maybe 25 knots. Dubois' speedboat could easily do three times that. Nathan could never outrun it. He'd need to find an alternative.

Racing back along the coast, Nathan searched for any place he might be able to come ashore. With no other harbor nearby, that meant ditching the boat on the beach and making a run for it. Looking back, he saw the cigarette boat in pursuit at half a kilometer and closing fast. Nathan spun his bow straight toward shore. He came in hot, approaching at full speed before throttling back at the last second and bracing himself for impact. The boat hit the sand and skidded halfway up the beach, throwing Nathan forward against the dash before it skidded sideways and finally came to a rest. The cigarette boat turned away along the shoreline but not before one of the men pulled out an assault rifle and began to fire, shattering Nathan's windshield as he jumped overboard and ran, zigging and zagging as he fled. In his ears was the zing, zing, zing of bullets flying past, crackling at the speed of sound. To hit a moving target from an unstable platform at this distance would challenge the best of marksmen, but they might get lucky. A row of properties lined the beach straight ahead and Nathan picked one, sprinting across the yard and continuing along the side of the house. At the opposite end he came to a driveway and beyond that, a wall with a wrought-iron gate decorated in an elaborate flower design. Grabbing hold of the iron flowers, leaves and vines, he was able to launch himself up and over, dropping to the other side along the coast road where a few solitary cars moved past. Nathan turned and headed toward the city, lifting a thumb in the air as he went. His heart was pounding in his chest but he seemed to have made it. Two or three cars passed without stopping before a black Range Rover pulled over. He didn't like the looks of this, but Nathan approached cautiously as the passenger side window rolled down. Looking back at him was a burly man in a dark green sweater. In his hands was a 9mm pistol, pointed straight between Nathan's eyes. The rear passenger door opened and another man got out, also armed and pointing his weapon at Nathan's heart.

"Keep your hands in the air and get in the car," said the second man.

"Sure," Nathan replied. "That sounds like a fine idea." He climbed in.

The man got in after Nathan and swung the door shut. The driver pulled a U turn and headed back toward the Dubois compound while the man in the front passenger seat kept his gun pointed squarely at Nathan's chest.

"I've got somebody who is quite eager to talk to you," said the front seat passenger.

"Talking is good," said Nathan. "I'm always up for a chat."

When they reached the Dubois property, the driver pulled up to a security camera just outside the gate and stopped. "We got him," he said.

"Good," a voice replied. "Bring him to the study." The gate rolled open and the Range Rover moved through. At the front of the house, Nathan was escorted inside and taken to a cozy room on the second story, facing the sea. Comfy chairs and a wooden table were arranged on an antique Persian rug, with a fire burning cheerily in a stone fireplace. Nathan's wrists were bound behind his back with a length of rope. A chair was swung around with the back to the fire and he was thrown into it. For the next few minutes they waited, Nathan and three armed goons. Outside, the storm swept ashore with wind and rain lashing the windows and the occasional crash of lighting illuminating the turbulent sea. No words were spoken until a door on the far side of the room opened and Laurent Dubois strode in with his two guests, followed by the female bodyguard whose fierce blue eyes burned with bitter fury. In her hands was a pistol and from her expression it looked like she wanted to use it.

"Monsieur Grant, we meet again," said Dubois.

"I think you still owe me a dinner."

"Is that why you're stalking me? All of this trouble over one tenderloin?"

"Don't forget the mojito."

"Ah, yes, the mojito."

"What the hell is he doing here, Dubois?" Brogan complained. "I'm not liking this."

Nathan turned his attention to the third man, still silently eyeing him. Up close, Nathan did finally recognize the man. They'd never before met, but he appeared in American newspapers from time to time. Farid Nasri was known to be exceedingly wealthy, with a hand in numerous commercial sectors, from mining, to paper mills, to steel production. Nasri kept a low profile as much as he could, eschewing the limelight, but that didn't stop him from becoming one of the largest political donors in America. He wasn't shy when it came to giving enormous sums of money to causes he believed in. One of those causes was Senator Jed Brogan, apparently.

"The senator offers a reasonable question," said Dubois. "What are you doing here, Monsieur Grant?"

"I was minding my own business when your thugs kidnapped me. Why don't you ask them?"

"Ah, yes, you were fishing. Isn't that right? What an odd coincidence to find you here in Ajaccio."

"Too bad the weather didn't cooperate. The fish were just starting to bite."

"This is becoming tedious. You work for the CIA I am told. I want you to tell me what you know about us."

"Why would I do that?"

"Because if you cooperate, your death will be much less gruesome."

Brogan looked away with unease but he didn't protest.

"Senator, are you going to let him threaten one of your constituents like that?" said Nathan. "I thought you were supposed to represent me?"

"You brought this on yourself," said Brogan.

Dubois snapped his fingers and held out a hand. The female bodyguard passed him her gun, with a gleam in her eyes. Dubois cocked the pistol and held the cold steel barrel right up against Nathan's temple. "It is time that you started talking."

"It would be a shame to ruin such a nice rug," said Nathan.

"I can afford a replacement."

"I'm sure you can. Look, Dubois, put the gun away. We'll talk."

Nasri stepped forward and put his fingers under Nathan's chin, curiosity showing in his expression. "So talk," he said.

"You were behind the Parsons assassination. What I don't yet know is why."

"This is a bold accusation," said Nasri. "What evidence do you have?"

"Not enough for a court of law, but I'm getting there."

"And so you are here on this fishing expedition," said Dubois. "Entertaining your preposterous theories?"

"I have heard a few interesting things about you, Dubois. Or should I refer to you as The Fox?"

Dubois recoiled. "Call me what you'd like, Monsieur Grant, it does not change the fact that you are going to die."

Nathan looked to Nasri. "And you must be The Mouse. Am I right?"

Nasri chose not to reply but the corners of his lips turned downward in a scowl.

"What is this all about?" Brogan complained.

"You tell me," said Nathan. "What are you planning here?"

Brogan looked to Dubois with growing impatience. "Why don't you just kill him already?! We're wasting time."

"What's your hurry?" Nathan asked. "You've got somewhere else to be?"

"Tell me, Mr. Grant," said Nasri. "Why do you think we had anything to do with what happened to your Secretary of State?

What could possibly be in it for us to perpetrate such a bold maneuver?"

"I'll tell you what I think, sure. I think you have ambitions to put the senator here into the oval office. You're one of his biggest donors, as far as I know."

"It is not a crime to support a political candidate, the last I checked."

"No, but it is a crime to murder his opponents."

"Get rid of him, now!" Brogan seethed.

"Calm yourself, senator, Mr. Grant is going nowhere," said Nasri.

"The secretary, the American ambassador to France, the vice president; all of them had presidential ambitions," said Nathan. "I think you're bumping off anybody who might stand in the way. Too bad you missed the ambassador, but perhaps you'll get another chance along the way."

"You seem to forget, Grant, the current officeholder is quite eager for a second term. None of these others you have mentioned would dare to challenge him. Neither would Senator Brogan."

"That is all true. Assuming, of course, that the President is around to run again."

"I've heard enough of this!" Senator Brogan paced back and forth in front of Nathan like a mad dog.

"From here you're off to Elba," said Nathan. "That means direct access to the President himself, doesn't it, senator? How are you going to do it? What's the plan?"

"You won't live long enough to find out." Brogan leaned close, his face screwed tight with rage.

"Is power really worth such a price, that you'd sell your very soul for it?"

A phone began to ring and Nasri pulled his device from a pocket and answered. "Yes," he said and then listened to the caller for a few beats. "All right, thank you." He hung up and turned to Dubois. "That was my pilot. He informs me that the worst of the storm is yet to come. If we don't depart with some haste, we might not make it out until tomorrow."

"I'm afraid that just won't do." Dubois gave Nathan another look and then turned to the others. "Such a wild imagination our friend has, doesn't he? Nobody would ever believe it."

"The Fox and The Mouse, growing up together at the Orphanage of Saint Martin and dreaming to take over the world. Life was cruel, then, wasn't it, to such innocent children? You planned for your revenge, but you are not so innocent any longer."

"Perhaps we never were."

"You'll never succeed in this, you know."

"I admire your conviction, Monsieur Grant, but you are the one who is heading to an early grave."

"How much is enough, Dubois? How much do you need to put your past to rest, to soothe your fury with the whole of mankind?"

"The world, Mr. Grant," said Nasri. "We need the world."

"You heard what the pilot said, we need to get moving!" Brogan cut in.

"Yes, the senator is correct." Dubois turned to his bodyguard with the fierce blue eyes. "Monsieur Grant came here on a fishing expedition. Why don't we give him what he came for? I believe the Americans have a saying, 'Swimming with the fishes.' Isn't that right, Monsieur Grant?"

"I believe we can make those arrangements," said the woman with grim satisfaction.

"You see, Monsieur Grant, Gabriella takes this quite personally. One of the men you murdered on my yacht was her fiancé. They were engaged to be married in the spring."

"My condolences but he got what was coming to him," said Nathan.

"As will you," said Dubois.

This time, Nathan didn't answer. He was too busy trying to figure out how to escape his predicament. So far the opportunity wasn't presenting itself. His hands were tied behind his back and armed guards were pointing guns at him.

"Take him out on the boat, tie him to an anchor and toss him overboard," Dubois said. "Alive."

"Yes, Monsieur," said Gabriella.

"I want to make sure Monsieur Grant has plenty of time to think about his life's failings as he sinks into the watery depths." Dubois turned next to his co-conspirators. "Come, let us depart."

"It's about time," said Brogan.

"Goodbye, Nathan Grant. I wish I could say it was a pleasure."

"That makes two of us."

Dubois, Brogan and Nasri strode from the room, taking two of the bodyguards with them. That left Nathan with Gabriella and two others. At least his odds were improving.

"Let's go, on your feet!" One of the men grabbed Nathan by the left arm and yanked him up. Another grasped his right arm. Gabriella stood behind, pointing her gun at the back of Nathan's head. They led him from the room and down a set of stairs before emerging into the yard under sheets of rain, continuing across the soggy lawn and down to the pier. The cigarette boat was tied up once more and Nathan was unceremoniously heaved over the gunwale where he landed with a thud in the cockpit.

Whoever had tied the rope seemed to know what they were doing. Despite his best attempts, Nathan wasn't having much luck undoing it. Gabriella jumped on board along with one of the men while the other untied the lines from the dock. Still holding her gun on him, Gabriella gave Nathan a solid kick to the gut and then leaned close. "I am going to enjoy this," she hissed before kicking him again, this time in the head and nearly knocking him unconscious. One of the men tossed her a dock line but as she caught it with one hand, Nathan thrashed at her with his legs, taking her out at the calves and sending her crashing down beside him. Nathan flipped himself on top of her with his thighs around her neck, squeezing tight as he looked down on her bulging blue eyes, overtaken with disbelief. Gabriella choked and struggled to breathe as Nathan pressed his full weight down on her, but the next thing he felt was a sharp crack on the side of his head and he toppled once more. Looking up, he saw one of the men standing over him with a pistol in his hand.

"I say we just shoot the son-of-a-bitch right now and get it over with," the man growled.

"No!" Gabriella shot back. "We do as we were told." She scrambled to her feet, one hand around her neck as she inhaled that precious air. Looking to Nathan, she pulled a leg back once more and swung it forward. When she connected this time, all of Nathan's consciousness drained away and the world faded to black.

When Nathan came to, the speedboat was bounding across the open sea in the thick of a rain squall. He was still tied up on the floor of the cockpit, bouncing up and down with each bump, only now his ankles were bound together and an anchor was strapped to his legs. He didn't have any idea how long he'd been out or how much time he might have left. The man at the controls pulled the throttles back to neutral and the boat coasted, rolling side to side in the maelstrom. "Let's get this over with," he said.

"The sooner the better," Gabriella concurred.

These two seemed to be the only thugs on board, as far as Nathan could tell. As they converged on him, he twisted violently back and forth, unwilling to go without a fight. They'd have to wrestle him overboard with everything they had. "Grab him!" Gabriella called out, but Nathan swung his legs upward, crushing the man under the chin with the anchor and sending him hurtling backward. As Gabriella lunged for Nathan, the boat dipped and swayed, causing her to stumble sideways and then trip. Nathan scooted himself forward and to one side, sliding up with his back against the inside of the cockpit. He bent his knees, lifting the anchor with his calves as he pulled his legs in close, then pressed hard with his thighs and slid up the cockpit wall to his feet. He now stood with his back beside the front dash. The male bodyguard was out cold. Gabriella's gun rested idle on a rear seat along the stern. She took one look at Nathan and then lunged for the gun, lifting it from the seat and spinning around to face him.

"I've had enough of this, it's time for you to die!" Gabriella roared into the wind.

"Why don't you go first?" Nathan replied. With his left elbow, he knocked the throttles forward. The boat lurched ahead and Gabriella stumbled once again. Nathan used his right elbow to turn the wheel and the boat veered sharply to the left, sending his adversary over the rail and into the sea with a splash. As the boat spun, Nathan nearly fell himself before pulling the throttles back with the crook of his arm. Thirty meters back, he spotted Gabriella in the water, struggling to stay afloat as she flailed her arms in a poor approximation of swimming until she slipped below the surface. As the craft bobbed and swayed, Nathan backed up close to the rail where a metal cleat was affixed. He slipped the rope that bound his wrists underneath one of the metal prongs and worked it back and forth, loosening the knot as he went. From the cockpit floor he heard low groans and detected movement as the man came to, but Nathan kept at his task. When the knot was loose enough, he pulled with both arms until a hand slid through. He untied his other wrist and set to work on his ankles and legs, first removing the anchor and then freeing himself entirely.

The remaining bodyguard's eyes slid open and he looked up in groggy confusion. Nathan bent down and lifted the man's torso, draping him over the gunwale. "You might just make it if you know how to swim," he said. "Unfortunately for your partner, she didn't." Nathan lifted the man's legs and then flipped him up and over into the sea.

Back at the controls, Nathan eased forward on the throttles once more and turned the wheel until the bow was pointing east toward the harbor. With some luck, he'd make it to the house on the hill before it was too late. Roaring off across the turbulent sea, he went with the swells, up the back of one and down into the trough of another, squinting through the cold rain. It took only ten minutes before he was pulling into the calm waters of the port. Nathan tied up at a vacant dock, ran up the gangway and out to the parking lot, fumbling his keys as he opened the door to the van and jumped inside. He fired up the engine, flipped on the headlights and the wipers and roared out of the lot, hellbent on getting to his sniper rifle if it wasn't too late already.

Weaving around a few slower vehicles Nathan narrowly missed a pedestrian, out on a dark and tempestuous night. He couldn't afford to crash, but the life of the President of the United States on the line. This was also quite likely Nathan's last remaining chance at revenge. He'd pushed his luck as far as it would go already with the CIA and the GIGN and local authorities in numerous jurisdictions. If he finished this and managed to get away it would be a miracle but he was too close now to let the opportunity pass.

After winding through the hillside neighborhood, Nathan pulled into the driveway at the little house. All was quiet. The rain was letting up some but the wind was still brisk from the west. Nathan had made some spectacular shots with a sniper rifle during training. He also had a long history of hunting with his father on their ranch in the Texas hill country. He'd never made a shot under these conditions, in the middle of a winter storm and with his heart pounding this hard, but there was a first time for everything. He unlocked the garage, grabbed the gun, and ran around to the deck on the other side of the house. Nasri's plane was still there, parked in the same spot as before. A black car was pulling up to the stairs. Nathan threw himself to the deck, lined up the gun and peered through the scope. He had no time to calculate the wind or the time to impact. These would be moving targets. Any Army sniper instructor would tell him it was nearly impossible. Nathan knew it would take an enormous stroke of luck to hit even one, let alone three. The driver got out, unfurling an umbrella and holding it aloft before opening the rear door. Through his scope, Nathan saw the profile of Laurent Dubois for a split second before his visage disappeared beneath the umbrella.

"Fuck!" Nathan yelled to himself. The driver escorted Dubois to the stairs and on up as Nathan heard the jet turbines spinning. He needed a clear shot. With one finger on the trigger, he waited for it until the very last moment. The umbrella came down and Dubois appeared. Nathan pulled the trigger. He waited the few seconds it took for the bullet to impact. Dubois ducked inside the plane. The shot had missed.

Looking at the fuselage behind him and then up toward the hills, the driver hollered toward the car and then ran back down and dove inside. He seemed to have figured it out. A madman in the hills was shooting at them. It took another moment for Nasri to emerge, followed by Brogan. They ran up the stairs in a panic and into the plane as Nathan fired three more shots. Not one hit their mark. He pointed the gun at the next best thing, which was the starboard engine on the tail. The magazine on the M99 held five rounds. That meant one more left. Nathan fired his last shot. The stairs on the plane swung up and it began to move forward, heading for the taxiway. He'd missed again.

There on the tarmac one kilometer off, The Fox and The Mouse and The Senator were off, slipping through Nathan's grasp. His heart sank at the thought of letting them get away, but he had one more chance. Leaving the rifle where it was, he hurried back around to the garage. There on the floor amongst his cache of weapons was a single Mistral 3 anti-aircraft missile and launcher. He'd very nearly left the system behind in Marseille. The launcher was designed for a crew of two. It was nearly impossible for one man to lift it skyward, aim and fire, but Nathan was a man possessed. He would manage, somehow. He quickly pulled the launch system out into the driveway and positioned it beside the van, then went back for the missile itself. At six-feet long and weighing nearly 100 pounds, he was just able to hoist it with both arms, carry it to the launcher and slide it into the tube. Even now he heard the roar of engines as the Gulfstream sped down the runway for takeoff. Nathan would need to lift this system by himself and somehow get a bead on the plane. He raised one end over his head and rested it on the roof of the van. At the other end, he sat on the ground and flipped the power switch. The electronic components blinked on. Scooting forward on his butt, he leaned his head in close and peered through a scope. He saw a readout. Target lock, distance, time to detonation. Looking back over his right shoulder, he spotted Nasri's plane rising up over the hill, headed nearly straight for the house. It went over him at a distance of three hundred yards, far too close and too fast to get a bead on it. As the plane gained altitude and moved away toward the east, he suspected that on board, Nasri, Brogan and Dubois were celebrating their success. It was all coming together. The world was theirs. Until it wasn't. The plane passed through Nathan's viewfinder. The engines glowed red through the scope. He lined up of a set of crosshairs until he got a lock. Distance to target, 1,200 meters, 1,400 meters, 1,600 meters. Nathan flipped up a safety switch and pressed the launch button. The missile roared out of the tube in a terrifying display of raw power, hurtling through the air as it honed in on its prey. It was only a few seconds more before impact. The plane exploded into a massive fireball, just like the one he'd seen in Africa six weeks before. The wreckage fell to earth with the ensuing crash reverberating across the island. The Fox and The Mouse and The Senator were dead.

Nathan dragged the missile launcher back into the garage and closed the door. He climbed into the van and headed for town, slowly this time as emergency vehicles raced in the opposite direction toward the crash site. At the harbor, Nathan parked the van, locked the door and walked back out to the waiting cigarette boat. He untied the lines and climbed on board, fired up the engines and headed out onto the dark sea. The fuel tank was nearly full. From here, he could make it to just about anywhere in the Med. He opted to head south, toward the Libyan coast. Nobody would be looking for him there. If all went well, in another few days he'd be back in the good old U.S.A., trying to put this whole affair behind him. For the moment, he allowed himself a deep sigh of satisfaction. Despite the odds, he'd actually done it. With that, Nathan raced off across the dark and turbulent sea, toward the next chapter in his life, whatever it had in store.

Chapter Twenty-Four

Back in Virginia, Nathan agreed to meet with Graham Masterson. He didn't have much choice. He needed the CIA to help smooth things over with some of the other foreign intelligence services, the French in particular. They'd need to be talked down to keep from coming after him. This mission was all about protecting the President of the United States, Masterson explained to them, where their government had clearly failed. Now Masterson wanted a full accounting from Nathan of what exactly had gone on.

The meeting was arranged to take place at Masterson's private home in McLean. That was fine with Nathan. He still didn't want to show his face around CIA headquarters. That was his past, not his future, and he preferred to face forward. Driving over to Masterson's place, Nathan listened to news on the radio.

The President of the United States arrived back at the White House today after a three-day climate summit on the Island of Elba in the Mediterranean Sea, vowing to bring justice to those responsible for the deaths of Senator Jed Brogan of Texas and American businessman and philanthropist Farid Nasri of Detroit, Michigan. This was just the latest in a series of terrorist attacks to rock the global community.

Nathan flipped the radio back off. Pulling up to Masterson's property, he was met by a security guard wearing civilian clothing and sitting in a small guard shack. Nathan presented his identification and was let through the gate, where he continued up the drive and parked in front of a comfortable two-story home with Greek-style columns. He was let through the front door by a member of Masterson's staff and brought into a cozy study, with windows overlooking a snow-covered lawn ringed by bare maple trees, dormant for the winter. A fire snapped and crackled in a stone fireplace.

"The assistant director will be with you shortly," said the staff member.

"Thank you." Nathan took a seat on a plush leather couch and waited. It didn't take long before Masterson strode into the room, carrying a computer tablet.

"Nathan, welcome, thank you for coming."

Nathan stood and shook Masterson's outstretched hand. "Did I really have a choice?"

"Of course, you no longer work for me, you're a private citizen. Not that I wouldn't welcome you back."

"That's not going to happen."

"No, I didn't think so. That episode with Babouche, that was on me. It was a bad call."

"You ought to be more careful before consigning an innocent man to death."

Masterson wasn't used to being dressed down by an operative, and a former one at that. He clearly didn't like it. "Sit down, Nathan, let's talk."

Nathan took his place on the couch and Masterson sat in a facing chair. "How did you figure it all out?"

"I guess you could say it was good old-fashioned detective work."

"Not bad for somebody with no experience as a detective. Let's start from the beginning. I want to know everything you know."

Nathan obliged, talking Masterson through all of it and answering any questions. At the end, it was Nathan's turn to find out some additional details that only Masterson might reveal.

"What do you know about their plans for Elba? How do you think they were going to do it?"

Masterson powered on his tablet and opened a file, then handed the device across to Nathan who saw a photo of the Asian man he'd witnessed boarding the *Renard Rouge*. This picture, however, was a mug shot, with the man scowling as he faced the camera.

"Who is he?" Nathan asked.

"He goes by the name of Hwang Jong chol."

"Let me guess. North Korean?"

"Bingo. Italian authorities picked him up at the airport in Rome on his way back home. In his luggage they found a container with traces of VX nerve agent. We believe he supplied Dubois, who passed it along to Senator Brogan. All Brogan had to do was to put on a glove and squirt a little bit of this stuff on anything the President might touch. A doorknob, a phone, the armrest on a chair. The senator would have been long gone before any symptoms set in. He might have gotten away with it."

"All of that in a mad quest for power."

"One by one, these guys knocked off every contender in the upcoming election that might have posed a challenge."

"What about Ambassador Cartwright? They never got to her."

Masterson shook his head. "The trauma was enough. She'd already pulled out of contention. All they had left was to take out the President himself and Senator Brogan would have waltzed right into office."

"In return, Nasri and Dubois get direct access to the American drug market. They branch out from Europe and put in place a distribution system straight to our shores."

"All while the Pentagon goes to war with the Mexican cartels. With their man in the White House, the world would have been theirs."

"And the North Koreans have an ally in the oval office as well."

"Everyone gets what they wanted. Until Nathan Grant came along. We owe you a debt of gratitude."

"I'm glad I could be of service, one last time."

"What's next for you, Nathan? If you won't come back to work for me?"

"I haven't figured that out yet, sir. Something a little less exciting, I hope."

"You're sure you could handle that?"

"No, sir, I'm not, but I'll give it my best."

"Good luck with that." Masterson stood and then escorted Nathan back through the house. "If you change your mind, there's always a place for you on my team."

"Thank you, sir. Have a good evening."

"You, too, Nathan. Something tells me I should be telling you to have a good life."

Nathan didn't answer this one. Instead, he walked out the front door and down the steps to his Jeep. He climbed in and drove off the grounds, then took the George Washington Parkway along the Potomac and headed back to his condo in Arlington. It was a stark winter scene that confronted him, with chunks of ice floating down the river. Somewhere warm sounded nice. Maybe he could find a little online consulting work if he tapped the right sources. Or maybe he'd pick up another gig as a scuba instructor. That wasn't so bad. The bottom line was, he had nowhere pressing that he needed to be. Nathan Grant was a free man. In every way that mattered, the world was his.